Finch Books by Britt Cooper and Erin Dulin

The Chronicles of Fayble
Queen of Shadows
Mistress of Blades
Daughter of Neverwoode

I0674524

The Chronicles of Fayble

DAUGHTER OF NEVERWOODE

BRITT COOPER & ERIN DULIN

Daughter of Neverwoode
ISBN # 978-1-80250-566-5
©Copyright Britt Cooper & Erin Dulin 2023
Cover Art by Kelly Martin ©Copyright September 2023
Map illustrated by Amanda Jeppson ©Copyright September 2023
Interior text design by Claire Siemaszkiewicz
Finch Books

Published in 2023 by Finch Books, United Kingdom.

Finch Books is an imprint of Totally Entwined Group Limited.

DAUGHTER OF
NEVERWOODE

Dedication

As ever, thank you to our wonderful husbands and families for their steadfast support as we continually throw ourselves into the chaos of outlining and storytelling. Never could it happen without your love and patience! Writing fairytales pales in comparison to living one.

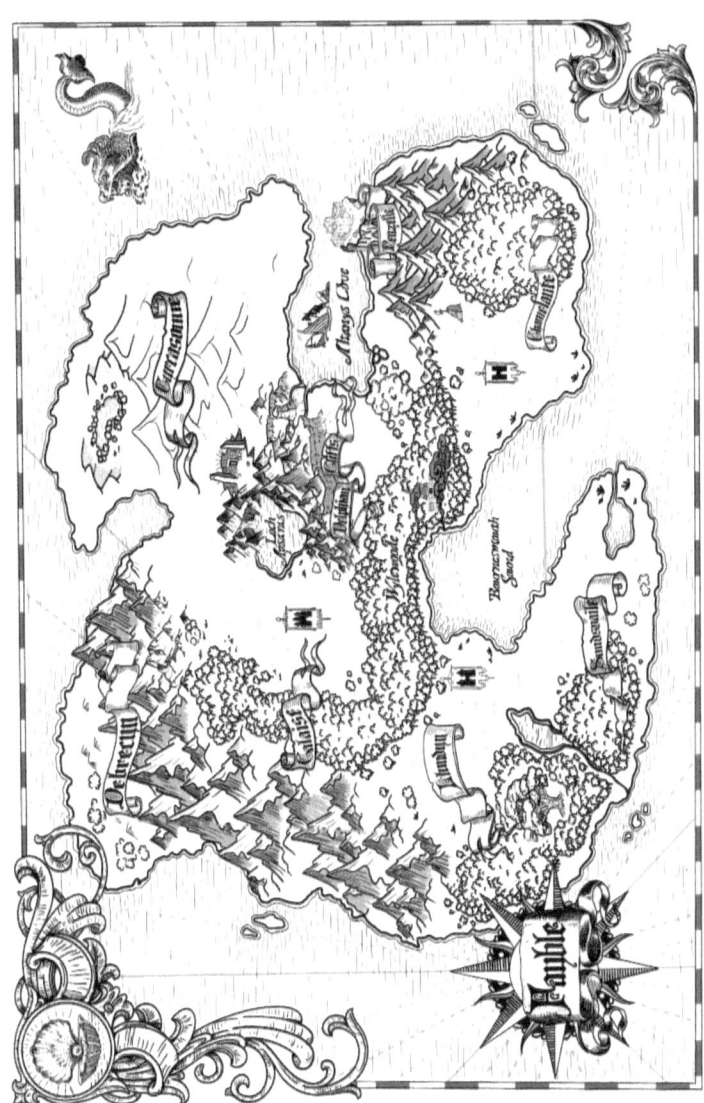

Chapter One

There was something inherently risky about roving the streets of Llundyn in the dead of night, regardless of efforts to bring the town into submission under an honorable reign. Doubtless the queen would have their heads if she knew of their pursuits, though she'd have to find out first.

"You need not accompany me. Stars only know the hell there'll be to pay upon your return to the palace." James Much wasn't wrong, his eagerness to be on his way overriding his unrivaled civility. The pair scuttled past pitch-black alleyways and decaying shanties lining the seafront, the creaky boards beneath their feet making each step an agonizing exercise.

For all their efforts to traverse in silence, they may as well have announced themselves to the waterfront. It was no matter. They were nearly there, and they'd seen nary a soul, the eventide surf crashing ashore all around the harbor providing at least some semblance of cover.

"Ella is nothing if not forgiving," King Riccard muttered, his words carried on the ocean breeze toward his companion. "She'd have to be, given our union. Imagine being married to me."

"Yes...imagine." James smirked, running his only remaining hand through the dark, tousled waves of his hair. The loss of his left had been a hefty blow, with the former sheriff of Llundyn having removed it by force with a saber and a smile, his devilry leaving the young sea captain abruptly bereft of usefulness.

Certainly, James had found his place, readily pillaging from the wealthiest of Llundyniens with Ella and her merry men. It had been the adventure of a lifetime — and a fulfilling endeavor at that. But something more had gone missing alongside his hand.

He'd always found purpose in the workings of them, having performed the duties of a carpenter at Locksley Manor for a large portion of his life. Indeed, they were his livelihood, and while he knew that he would never be on his own, never be left to fend for himself, the last thing he wanted was to be served.

Ella, the newly crowned Queen of Llundyn, had been his most faithful friend, their comradery carrying them through tragedy and triumph. She'd been there on that fateful eve, cared for him, bandaged his wounds. She'd blamed herself for his predicament, though it had had nothing to do with her. His decisions were his and his alone, rendering her guilt pointless where he was concerned.

What followed had been the epitome of success, with the pair having seen the starving citizenry return to prosperity, even as they helped preserve the rightful king through an attempted coup.

But those harrowing months had evaporated into monotony with order restored. King Riccard was just, ruling alongside Ella, who'd easily maintained her humility, despite her lofty new position. His bandmates had found their places within the palace, quickly achieving success in their most unexpected endeavors and readily adapting to their ever-changing roles.

James, however, had sought refuge far away from the confines of the castle walls. He'd been apprenticed to a sea captain and had quickly risen within the ranks, performing each of his tasks in prompt compliance and earning a sterling reputation as he went. It didn't hurt that he'd been raised upon the waters as a boy, having seen much of the continent of Fayble with his late sea-master father as they skirted the coastline.

A figure in the distance brought the pair up short. They'd been largely ignored until then, the slumbering town proving to be an easy companion with which to travel incognito. She was stood upon the wharf facing the ocean, her cloak fluttering in the air. It was almost as if she'd materialized out of nothing, but then again, that was Ella's way.

She turned as they approached, a knowing smile upon her lips. "Two of my favorite boys gallivanting about without guardians. How did you manage to slip away unnoticed?"

Ric took to her side, grinning from ear to ear when he slipped his arm beneath her mantle, pulling her nearer as he encircled her waist. "Perhaps I'd ask the same of you."

Doubtless, their lack of guards was potentially dangerous—perhaps even stupid. But the king and queen of Llundyn had loathed giving up the freedoms of Sherwood Forest for the shackles of courtly responsibility. Even so, *this*—their endless love and adoration for one another — had always seen them through their duties and sustained them in uncertainty.

James shifted his weight from one foot to the other before looking away. The pair never flaunted their affection for one another. It was merely the natural state of things, and he'd be lying if he weren't to admit that it had him mildly jealous.

"We were to celebrate your upcoming voyage this evening, but something told me you wouldn't wait," Ella said, withdrawing from her king enough to look at James.

"You know that's not for me." He gazed at the water, his heart full of conflicted longing as he wished to be on his way, but leaving his friends caused a bitterness he couldn't quite describe. A celebration of his impending departure would simply be too much to bear.

Ella nodded as if that was the response she'd expected. Of course she had, for she was there, awaiting his sneaky escape from Llundyn. She knew him, perhaps better than anybody else in the whole of Fayble. "You two have become quite the conspirators of late." She poked her husband in the ribs. "How will you ever do without him?"

"How will you?" Ric returned.

"You speak as if I'm to meet my end," James added. "I've every intention of returning unscathed."

"We know nothing of these people, these *pirates* of Wylewoode." Ella grimaced, her features pinched with worry.

The threat had revealed itself in only a week past when James and his crew had been targeted by what they'd later found to be a large iron ball, launched from the foreign ship by an explosive charge that had left a sizable hole in the heart of his vessel. The siege had taken them all by surprise, if for no other reason than that Wylewoode was not known to harbor many citizens, let alone seafaring ships.

"I must go, Elle." James' eagerness for a new adventure quickly surpassed his desire to continue on in the familiarity of his Llundynien routine as he strode down the pier to his beloved vessel with Ric and Ella at his heels.

He could feel every ounce of their trepidation as they moved down the length of the dock behind him. Never would they force him to go. Hell, they hadn't even asked him—but somehow it felt right.

Ella paused, eyeing the mammoth ship with wide, bright eyes. "Your crew..."

James could finish her sentence, even as he felt the disquiet churning beneath her polite exterior. His sailors were rough around the edges, with some old and some mere boys. They were surly, bitter, *lost*—some of the last people with which one would expect to endeavor around the continent. "They're a sorry lot, I admit." He grinned, offering a shrug. "But for some reason, they fall in line. We manage to make a way. Maybe we aren't all that different in the end."

The trio fell into silence, with Ella averting her gaze. He hadn't meant for his words to seem spiteful—only that he felt he finally belonged, leading his very own band of misfits on a dubious journey with an outcome that was anybody's guess.

And he would return knowing that he'd given the voyage his all. Putting some arrogant pirates in their place along the way was an added benefit, allowing him to defend his kingdom, to prove himself worthy of the inherent trust from his beloved sovereigns.

"Well," Ella managed, "I'd be remiss in sending you on your way without a little something." She reached beneath her cloak, presenting him with a wide, flat box tied shut with a hunter-green ribbon. Plucking the cords with delicate fingers, she opened the case, offering the contents to James, her expression bashful.

"A hook?"

"I felt silly," Ella continued, pulling the gleaming silver crook from the velvet-padded box before handing it to Ric. She cradled the curved metal appendage, smiling at last. "Still do. But I've seen them used all over, both on ships and around the harbor, and I thought…"

James shook his head, floored by her foresight. "It's perfect. I admit I'd never considered the possibility before now, but to have the use of my hand—or my hook, rather? It's ingenious."

"As ever," Ric beamed. "If there was any doubt about the wisdom behind the Crown, it was laid to rest by this Queen of Shadows."

"Doubtless," James agreed as Ella moved toward him, rolling up his shirtsleeve. She attached the polished hook to the brace covering his forearm, a task simpler than he'd have guessed. He held his arm up, the moonlight bouncing off the contours of the hook as he shifted it. "It's effortless. Shall I test its usefulness on Sheriff Dane?"

Ella furrowed her brows, biting her lip to suppress a smile while Ric laughed openly. It was reassuring to James, their ability to see the humor in his remark, even if it was a little dark.

"Ahoy there, Captain!" came the familiar voice of his quartermaster. Second in command, William Smee was an eccentric sort—a man James had known for the whole of his life as he'd served in the same role for James' father. He made his way down the gangplank, blowing the wild springs of his salt-and-pepper hair from his face with a hearty puff of air.

"Mr. William..." Ella breathed as recognition dawned. Not long ago, he'd been the very man who had prepared her tiny band of heroes for the ball that had been their greatest strike against tyranny.

"Alas, I'm no longer a purveyor of borrowed goods, Your Majesty." Smee bowed deeply, first to Ella then to Ric, his face an unabashed mask of delight as he clapped James on the shoulder. "I always knew we'd set sail again someday! Your father would be proud."

"This feels wrong." Ella glanced from Smee to the ship behind him, her countenance troubled. "We know nothing of the people in Wylewoode, save that it's where *criminal exiles* are frequently sent to live out their days. And goodness knows there can't be many remaining, given the dangers lurking within that savage territory. There's a reason those lands are avoided at all costs, and we don't even know if any of this is real! It feels like you're chasing a ghost, Much!"

James moved toward her, wrapping her in his arms as she angrily wiped her eyes. She always worked to control her emotions, to be the unflappable rock upon which the kingdom could steadily thrive. Her concern for his wellbeing was nearly enough to have him second-guessing himself, but the prospect of leaving his country exposed to the dangers of what did, admittedly, feel somewhat like a phantasm...

Well, he simply couldn't justify it.

"It felt real enough to me," he whispered to her alone. He took her by the shoulders, looking her in the eyes. "The hole in my vessel was no accident, and the enemy ship? It appeared out of nowhere, and —"

"And I can't lose you." She fisted his cloak, choking back her tears. "*We* cannot lose you. Your kingdom and your people need you."

James took a deep breath. Ella was as dear as the closest of sisters, and he knew she meant only to keep him safe. "I must go. This threat to Llundyn cannot stand. Whether it's a figment of our own minds or a legitimate menace remains to be seen, but one way or another, it will be dealt with. I'll return before you've missed me."

He kissed her cheek before backing away from his beloved friends, offering a wave and a smile in parting. Ric saluted him, taking to his wife's side as they watched him make his way up the gangplank behind Smee, whose steps bounced with obvious expectation.

When he reached the deck, James refused to turn around. Moving forward was the only way. "Haul out!" he cried to his crew, and as the ship came alive with the tumult of departure, he finally found peace as he was lost to the chaos of the sea.

Chapter Two

Petra's bones felt heavier somehow. A thick, floral perfume filled her nostrils — so potent she swallowed back the bitterness rising in her throat. Stagnant air suffused her lungs, and she knew in an instant what it meant.

She was awake — truly and wholly awake.

As she opened her eyes, her heart thundered. The subtle shimmer of condensation revealed a large glass panel above her, separating the renegade love child of Neverwoode's esteemed late ruler from the outside world, though nobody had ever seen or acknowledged her as anything more than the unfortunate result of her father's dalliance with a beautiful wanderer.

It was of no consequence to her, for she'd always watched her half-siblings and pitied them. Still, while Petra knew her sister despised her, she never imagined such evil could lurk within Wendolyne's calloused heart until the self-proclaimed Queen of Neverwoode ordered her dead.

In truth, Petra never thought she'd awaken from the induced slumber in which she'd thrived – a curious reality wrought with peril and excitement, wherein the stars shone brighter if only one gave themselves into its otherworldly draw.

As it turned out, waking was nothing more than a prison replete with harsh circumstances and scant odds of survival.

Her belly ached, its groan echoing off the walls of the crystal box she found herself lying within. Hinges shrieked as Petra carefully pushed open the panel above her, straining weakened muscles within her arms and shoulders for the first time in saints only knew how long.

Propped up on her elbows, she took in her surroundings, foreign and dark as they were. Mossy stone stared back as cool, humid air embraced her, and ribbons of golden sunlight stained the earth, peeking through a curtain of tangled vines. Snow-white petals plucked from her father's personal gardens padded her slight form, the aroma assaulting her anew. Petra knew the roses and their silken touch better than her own flesh, for days she'd spent tending the family grounds were her peace, and those chittering creatures among them treasured confidants.

Wendolyne never cared for such things.

Beauty, yes, but the queen never deigned to look beyond any pleasing veneer to question or marvel at the genesis of its splendor. It was an obsession, and Wendolyne's most considerable weakness, her enslavement to elegance and grandeur driving her into the madness of discontentment.

Never satisfied, Wendy was a reflection of their father and his father before him, their sole, unified ambition one of insatiable prosperity.

Petra saw such fixation as a cancer. It grew and spread as Neverwoode's populace increased – a citizenry of exiled, lost souls pursuing shimmering delusions and gilded fantasies.

But if all had gone according to plan, the queen now believed her to be dead. Her half-brother Javan hid their deceptions well, considering Petra awakened at all, the only of her kin who did not abhor her for the indiscretion she represented.

How gracious of Wendy to lay her to rest in a coffin of glass and gold. Their beloved half-brother was undoubtedly tasked with the burial, marking an empty plot in Petra's name and concealing her in a stone hollow out of sight and mind.

Bless Javan for all he'd done to protect and sustain her. Mikhail would never have gone to such lengths. He'd loved her once when they were children, but those memories faded day by day, tainted by the dependencies and hatred Wendolyne nurtured with her serpent's tongue.

Abiding revulsion for Petra had, by all appearances, tormented Wendy after their father unabashedly displayed his preference, gifting his bastard daughter with a cherished family heirloom. He'd loved Petra, despite the reminder that she was of a personal failure on his part. He cared for his children, and Petra treasured him for his stories and ambition.

Patting over her corseted bodice, Petra searched in vain for the angles of the heart-shaped ruby adorning its case. It was the only piece of finery she valued, and she kept the small timepiece chained to her at all times, just as her father had. But the reassuring weight of it was missing, accompanied by a familiar gut-wrenching desperation.

"Queen Wendolyne has taken your heart, and I would not attempt to reclaim it if I were you."

The voice effectively consumed her composure with a few honeyed words. Petra hadn't anticipated anyone would be present when she awakened, much less someone other than her half-brother or, perhaps, her most beloved pest, Ffion. But she couldn't let her thoughts drift to what might've become of the boy after she'd abandoned him. *Not yet.*

"Who are you?" Petra's question rasped past her lips, clawing up her throat like a flame scorching arid earth. The stranger was no more than a hint of a shadow in an already dim cave, a broad male form leaning casually against the mouth of her shelter. Terror seized Petra as echoes of her nightmares surfaced.

Little distance lay between them, but if she moved quickly enough, Petra could likely find a way past him. She cursed herself for leaving the few belongings she'd brought from the castle outside her forsaken lair. At the time, she believed herself clever, hiding her blowpipe and practical clothing far enough away from her resting place that no one might discover them.

It was pure idiocy.

Grasping one of the cold glass panels beside her, Petra rose. Her absurd gown was thin enough that the gentle shift in the air from her movement made her shiver.

The man laughed. It was far too alluring to be real, but what was true after her time in the dreamscape of Otherlande? Her mind was foggy and her legs weaker than they should have been had Petra only been asleep a few days, as she'd hoped. Dreams blended with the present so seamlessly that she could scarcely tell the two apart, which made contemplating how she might gain an advantage over this disquieting visitor a genuine trial.

"You are radiant in gold. I daresay, even more breathtaking than she made you out to be." The darkened figure pushed himself from the stone at his back, cocking his head to one side as he surveyed Petra. She'd never felt so vulnerable but didn't dare move, fearing she might collapse altogether.

"Such beauty *and* a will of iron. You can hardly stand, yet, like a feral beast, you bare your teeth at me. The queen remains exhaustively predictable in her jealousy, however well-founded it may be."

Petra didn't trust herself enough to speak after feeling how her body betrayed her, with knees trembling like a newborn fawn. Yet, it made little difference as the male seemed to prefer listening to himself, prattling on despite her silence.

He already knew too much simply by having discovered her. Still, if permitted to amuse himself further, he might divulge some facet of his designs. Petra had seen careless words uttered by fools fate them cruelly.

So, let it be. *The tongue is a fire.*

"You were difficult to find. I'll credit Javan that much, and that dress – " The figure whistled through his teeth.

Petra's eyes adjusted, and she loosed a bated breath, her tremors steadying when she noted both of his hands fall to his sides. In Otherlande, the fanciful existence she'd lived within while dreaming, a shadow with no owner had stalked her relentlessly, but he'd had a crook for a hand. Relief flooded through her, for doubtless this man, though he was every bit the stranger that her shadow had been, was not the phantom being of her reveries.

The faint light offered her a small kindness, revealing sharp angles of the man's cheeks and jaw. Ink-black hair fell over his thick, dark brows, exposing a face and silhouette as tempting as his voice, at least from what she could tell.

She should have known from the way her skin tingled and the unnatural potency of the petals now underfoot that these thoughts were not of sound mind. Petra knew the seductions of sift, and while the fine, golden dust caused no physical or mental harm, she believed with her entire being that it was dangerous on a more profound level.

And Neverwoode was brimming with defenders of its merits.

She clenched her hands into fists, testing whether she might have regained some semblance of her former vigor. The tips of her fingers had little feeling, and the pads of her feet felt like she stood upon needles rather than a cloud of petals, but panicking over her circumstances would not serve her well. Schooling her features into a mask of apathy, she stepped out of the coffin, her muscles protesting with each movement. With a fortifying breath, Petra willed her voice not to shake. "What is it you want? I have nothing of value."

"I was merely curious."

Petra watched intently as the man turned on his heel, casting a final glance over his shoulder. He pushed aside the tangled vines obscuring them from Wylewoode's whims, filling the cave with warmth and light. The stranger smirked, his face fully visible to her at last. Disarmingly handsome, there was no doubt with whom he was associated. She could nearly scent her sister on him as he studied Petra with self-indulgent, crystalline eyes.

"And what have you concluded from our encounter?" Moving toward him, she considered how her bravado might rouse lamentable repercussions, but Petra was no coward. She felt how her burial gown hugged the gentle curves of her body, knowing Wendolyne's pet had not missed that detail by the way his gaze followed each careful step she took. "Do you think my sister was right to have me hunted by our brothers? Are you here to complete the task they failed?"

"And rob myself of telling her you still breathe? Not a chance." Some part of Petra relaxed at his words, though trust was far from her mind as the stranger adjusted his intricately embroidered tunic, narrowing his gaze. "But if I were you, I'd run as fast and far as you can. The queen has eyes and ears everywhere, mine among them – both in these rejected lands of Wylewoode and that deceptive dominion she calls Neverwoode."

Petra snorted. "I'll do no such thing. How I wish I could see my sister when you tell her about our meeting."

"It would be better for you if you were dead." With that final word, he was gone. The vines fell back into place over the hollow's exit, casting shadows over the pebbled floor. A shudder ran up Petra's spine, not because of the man's prediction but the swaying shapes that had swallowed daytime's glow.

In her dreams, a darkness with no master watched her. Not once in that strange reality had Petra seen another shadow besides the one which had followed her. Even in its absence, the figure haunted her, ever present in her thoughts.

But if she had awakened from that perilous slumber, had the shadow as well? The question crossed her mind when she'd made out her spy's lurking figure, yet they were plainly not the same.

A broad silhouette with a hook for a hand had been the last thing Petra had seen before she'd awakened from Otherlande. Ffion and his friends had tried hopelessly to draw her back to them, but fear had devoured her.

Something had snapped before the trio found her, a vital piece of her ceasing to exist. She had been lost to herself, trapped within her mind, until the scent of her father's roses called to her.

While the stranger may have warned Petra not to pursue what was rightfully hers, she couldn't bear the consequences of heeding those words. And if what he said was true, Wendy had henchmen everywhere doing her bidding—lurking, hiding. *Hunting.* She needed to learn *why.*

Petra parted the rustling vines from before her, the sun warming her chilled flesh. Colors shone brighter, and birds trilled harmoniously, a song so pleasing she was reminded why the world seemed so enchanting.

To her knowledge, the effects of the golden powdered sift were short-term, but when Petra examined herself and any exposed areas of her body, she noted nothing. Instead, she found the grotesque work of sheer mesh—cobalt blue panels embroidered with shimmering gold floral accents, which cascaded into an equally fine gossamer skirt.

The material was smoother than silk and left little to the imagination. Crystals made up the thin straps that dug into her bronzed skin, continuing to her shoulders where the small stones adorned capped sleeves edged with dangling blood-red rubies.

Petra's knees buckled as the revelation struck her. Never had she seen sift wielded in such a manner, but perhaps it explained why she'd been hard to find. Much like the dust was used to shroud Neverwoode, the dust was woven through her burial gown, keeping Petra hidden and under its influence.

It made sift a weapon.

Petra made her way to the foot of an aged pine, the largest of the surrounding trees. She clawed at the dress and dropped it to the earth before sinking to the ground, where she began to dig. In short order, her mind cleared of the fanciful outlook, and she kept digging, even as dirt caked beneath her fingernails.

She'd buried it deeper than she recalled, but there it was. Petra pulled a wooden box into her lap, tossing its lid aside. Her darts were there, along with her pipe, pouch and fitted leather trousers folded neatly on top of a tattered olive-toned tunic. She slipped the top over her head and arms, then tugged on the laces at either side of her hips, cinching the waist of her pants.

Stretching a hand toward the shallow sun, Petra squinted as she judged when eventide would fall. Her sister's theft of her beloved timepiece weighed heavily upon her mind. Doubtless, if Wendolyne was desirous of the heirloom, it was due to more than simple jealousy. Her sister did nothing without calculating the risks, the rewards. Something wasn't right.

Petra would take back her heart. Perhaps it was time to destroy it.

Chapter Three

Some things in life would not be undone, not through raw effort or sheer force of will – not even through wishful thinking.

It was finished. His hair was gone.

Not all of it, but for the grace of God alone. Still, it was far more than James would've liked. Perhaps it was what he should've expected, given the wielder of the sheers was Smee. A quartermaster was he – not a gifted barber.

"Ye've to look the part if your men are to respect ye," Smee chirped, brushing the plentiful clippings from James' neck and shoulders. "Aye, we've a ship full of suspicious intent, we do. These sailors will suffice so long as they stay in line, but Lord knows they're all runnin' from somethin'."

James merely grunted in reply, his skin crawling from all the hair splinters that had slipped down his shirt. He agreed, of course, but Smee's merry chatter was beginning to grate. That, alongside his freshly shorn hair, and he was less than enthused by the musings of his second in command.

The sides of his head were cropped short from temples to ears, leaving behind a mop of dark, unruly waves that Smee had twisted and tied into three separate rows atop his head. It stood in stark contrast with the carefully trimmed stubble upon his upper lip and chin, making him look very much like a damn pirate.

But maybe that had been Smee's plan, the sneaky bastard.

It had been the sly old quartermaster who'd first identified the flag of the enemy ship – an unknown entity to everybody aboard the *Jolly Roger*, save for Smee himself. Since he'd returned nearly a decade ago, the man had taken endless guff for his tales about the supposedly non-existent kingdom.

He'd been the lone survivor of a devastating shipwreck among the turbulent waters of Altanys Cove, the very incident that had cost James' father his life. The gulf was a well-known nautical risk, a part of the seas best left avoided due to its low visibility and the fierce, choppy waves. And, if the environmental concerns weren't enough of a deterrent, there was no shortage of stories. The siren call of the deep drove men to madness, and the passage leading to the Neverwoode Forest was said to be a cursed portal into a realm filled with wild realities best left to the confines of the imagination.

Wylewoode was a land replete with nightmares.

Doubtless, it was absurd – fabrications meant to discourage exploration and hide a kingdom. It was what James' father had believed and what Smee had professed upon his return to Llundyn, but his revelations had fallen upon deaf ears. The citizens had thought him nothing more than a lunatic and had treated him as such, relegating him to a life spent making ends meet through stealing and bartering.

For decades, the criminals of Fayble had been sentenced to lives lived out in the mysterious kingdom of Wylewoode, which was less a nation and more a prison camp. Indeed, it was considered a death sentence by most, but if the hole in the side of his vessel was any indication, it seemed increasingly likely that the country had been severely underestimated.

"That'll do," James said by way of dismissal, rising to his feet as Smee excused himself from the captain's quarters. He wandered about the cabin, straightening his almanacs and sea charts, all startlingly insufficient. That was no surprise, given the lack of travel among the vast waters of Altanys Cove.

With so few willing to venture into the misty bay, his maps would have to suffice. He wasn't worried, at any rate, for he'd always been ready to meet a challenge, regardless of the likelihood of success. It was how he'd become one of Ella's band of merry men – an endeavor that would've seemed destined for failure on paper but had been wildly prosperous in practice.

James left his room, pulling the door shut behind him as he entered the fray. The ship was tightly run, with every man's duty clearly defined. The westerly winds made the voyage highly manageable, sending *Jolly Roger* barreling toward Altanys Cove at a brisk clip.

He was ready. James hadn't been convinced of that notion from the outset of his travels, but as they closed in on the vaunted bay, he became eager to take it in. His father had sailed the same route, at least according to Smee, and some reckless part of James reveled in that knowledge, even in spite of his father's untimely end.

To see what he'd seen, feel what he'd felt – it was, in part, a fool's errand, but the young sea captain couldn't help himself.

Stood upon the quarterdeck, James beheld the chaos of his vessel's daily operations. Like a well-oiled machine, his crew moved above and below deck, with none willing to cross the enigmatic fellow with a hook for a hand.

Contrary to Smee's suggestion, looking the part was unnecessary for compliance after all. The man was, at times, a nuisance, pushy in his opinions and excessively helpful in a way that wasn't always constructive, but James trusted him unequivocally.

Almost.

He watched as Smee excused himself from his order-barking on the main deck, making for the hatch leading to the cargo hold. He'd done as much each day they'd been at sea, always at noontide. James hadn't thought anything of it the first few times, but his curiosity had spiked the day prior as an excess of food had tumbled from his second's pockets.

The men were well-fed, and Smee was no exception. A small part of James was amused by the thought of the burly quartermaster gorging himself upon leftovers in the darkness of the hull, but instinct told him it was something more.

James scuttled down the staircase, narrowly avoiding a flustered cabin boy as he sprinted toward the hatch. He opened the door, squeezing his way through the opening and relying upon Smee's heavy footfalls for direction.

The quartermaster wasn't far off, hopping over cargo and yapping commands at the idle crew as he passed them by, his lantern swinging with each step.

Deeper into the darkness, he wandered, roaming to the farthest end of the ship where he was nearly alone.

It seemed a lot of effort for extra grub.

The captain observed from behind a large store of water casks, only to find that Smee wasn't through with his covert journey. Shoving aside some wooden boxes, he uncovered the hatch leading to the bilge.

"Ye've not to wait any longer, friend," he sputtered, emptying his pockets as he tossed their contents into the bunker below.

What the…?

Displeased by the notion of a stowaway in the underbelly of his vessel, James could wait no longer. He moved from cover, stepping into the flickering light of the lamp and scaring his second half to death.

Smee jumped, his face ghastly pale when he took in James' presence. "Ah, Captain! I was just – "

"A stowaway," James hissed, his temper flaring as he cursed his misplaced trust. His faith was hard won, but his father's reliance upon the old quartermaster had been enough to satisfy him.

No more.

He stepped toward the opening. "Move aside."

"Sir, I – "

"Move *aside*," James commanded, his patience having fled. That Smee would so readily disobey him had him wondering who could be worth the loss of his employment, for surely Smee would have to go.

The older man stepped aside, offering only a sigh of resignation as the captain eased his way around him. The odor hit a moment later, fetid and stifling, as James approached the hatch. He covered his nose with the crook of his elbow, his stomach lurching as he reached for the lantern, looping his hook through the handle.

A deep rumble echoed through the void, startling James as the stowaway came into view, though it was no man. *Not even human.*

"What the hell?" James stumbled backward, colliding with the bulkhead as he caught his breath. "There's a —"

"Please, sir, allow me," Smee cut in, tossing another crust of bread into the bilge. The crocodile snapped, catching the shard and choking it down his gullet before lunging at the portly quartermaster. "Easy, there! I've more for you to gobble down, you pot-bellied brute!"

The creature shifted, his broad mouth angling into a toothy grin as he crept nearer to the short staircase leading to his freedom. Smee approached the croc without reservation, rewarding him with more rations and heedless of his dire proximity to the beast. "'Course he likes you. Will you look at that smile?"

James fought the urge to sprint away, instead cautiously leaning toward the hole in the floor. "I think that's just his face."

Smee cackled, evidently unconcerned with the captain's annoyance. "So said your father, Hayes, yet no fiercer protector had he than Ben. You'd never guess he began as a runt." He gestured toward the croc, who displayed his good graces by again lunging for the hand outstretched toward him. "On many a voyage, your father sought to leave Ben behind, to let him grow in the wild and be the natural predator he was. Hayes felt it was only a matter of time before the creature would turn, but never was it to be. Ben always found his way back to the ship, and your father had not the heart to continue driving him away."

That seemed about right. Hayes had been a collector of misfits — the giver of second chances and the benefit of every doubt. That his goodwill would extend to an orphaned crocodile was no surprise.

"He's got his finer points, at any rate," Smee continued. "Ben's eaten many a man, staving off a mutiny or two in his day." He flashed a yellow smile, his candid admissions nothing shy of alarming.

Yet, with a long-suffering sigh, James made excuses of his own. "You should've told me."

"Aye, sir. And now ye know."

* * * *

The pair emerged from the cargo hold none the worse for wear, and the captain worked to make peace within his soul, finding that his quartermaster's deceptions were much easier to dismiss when he viewed them through the merciful lens so often employed by his father. For now, that meant maintaining a crocodile in the hull. Surely, there were worse prospects.

As if to echo those very sentiments, James found not one of his crewmembers about their work. Instead, they'd all gathered upon the quarterdeck, encircling the main mast where one of his crew was rapidly scaling the ratlines, pausing just out of reach of the raucous shipmen.

"A thief *and* a female! Indeed, she is *no* Thomas," bellowed Crispin, the ship's sailing master. "I searched her bedroll and found this!" He held the offending object aloft – a golden compass he'd presumably lost, while in his other hand was clutched a woolen cap he'd doubtless stripped from atop her head.

Her hair streamed in the mild breeze, auburn and flowing, the afternoon sun revealing its subtle red highlights. Curses flowed from her lips, showering the men below in her righteous indignation as her secret lay exposed for all to see.

The situation was rapidly eroding, with the crew growing more agitated as each second passed. It would never do.

"*Avast!*" James shouted, his fist clutched in anger at his side. Striding toward the ruckus, he found he was teetering on the edge of control. Maintaining authority upon the water was a dubious task under the best of circumstances, with revolt ever a breath away.

Parting for their captain, the men stepped backward, making way for James as he planted himself at the base of the mast. "Down with you," he barked, waving the cornered woman toward the fray.

With an exasperated sigh, the woman once known as Thomas made her way to the ground, her demeanor shifting from irritation to obvious anxiety with each length she dropped until, finally, she stood before her accuser.

"That's not all I found, neither," Crispin continued, his features filled with contempt when he eyed her from head to toe and back. "Chest bindings, a corset – as if we needed any more proof that she's not a man."

"And what of it?" Crossing her arms over her chest, she raised her chin, the defiant tilt reminding James of another woman who readily handled her business. "I've done my job better than any of you!"

Crispin snapped, grabbing her by the collar as he yanked her toward himself. "Oh, that's rich, you little – "

Without a thought, James wrenched the man away with a twist of his hook. "You dare to lay hands on a woman?" He shoved Crispin away, doubling his efforts to recover his temper.

The sailing master stumbled before regaining his footing, squaring his shoulders even as defiance shone in his eyes. "Aye, sir. She's a liar. Surely we can't have this sort of discord here upon the *Jolly Roger*."

"You're right." James smiled, a sense of calm settling over him as a solution dawned. "So, will it be the plank, then, or the crocodile in the bilge?"

Silence fell for but a moment, followed quickly by frantic whispers as the crew worked to make sense of the captain's alternatives. Their fear multiplied as utterances of *crocodile* and *madness* filled the air, their eyes growing wide as they mulled the sanity of their commander.

"Please. *Please*," the woman begged, her pleas nothing more than a breath. Panic lingered in her gaze while, beside her, Crispin wore a satisfied smirk.

"Apologize," James demanded, and the woman fell to her knees, tears streaming over her bright cheeks.

"Sir, I –"

"Oh, no." James waved her off before stepping nearer to help her to her feet. "Not you. *Him*." He indicated Crispin with a nod of his head, all the while suppressing the fury he felt at the sight of the sailing master. The man was too arrogant for his own good – the sort to incite a mutiny.

Crispin scoffed. "You cannot be serious."

"But I am." James waited, his long coat catching the wind as his patience with the stubborn crewmember thinned.

"I won't! She's a liar and a thief! How could you possibly take her side?"

"The only evidence of any wrongdoing I can see, that you have yourself admitted, is your going through her personal items. Now, *if* you *please*."

The man moved toward the captain, bowing up as he looked James in the eye. "I would rather die."

"So be it." James shouldered past the ingrate before turning on his heel and addressing the entirety of the ship's crew. "Crispin has chosen his lot, and so shall he choose his punishment. Will it be the crocodile or the plank, then?"

He turned to find the sailing master suddenly bereft of bravado, trembling where he stood as the gravity of the situation unfolded. "You don't mean – "

"I do. And if you will not choose, I'll do it for you." James paused, collecting his fraying nerves. It was a bold showing of strength, of authority, and there would be no return. Still, he held no doubts over the matter. A man like Crispin was a risk to his command, and inaction would doubtless result in more insubordination. He swallowed hard, determined to see it through. "Might I suggest the plank? There's likely time to make it to shore before nightfall if you swim well enough."

"The Mistress of the Fishes will surely see me dead! She grows angrier by the minute," Crispin cried, gesturing toward the churning surf that was, indeed, more violent than usual as it slapped the ship's sides.

"Doubtless at the thought of your presence within her depths," Smee sniped, shooing Crispin toward his destiny at the end of the wobbling plank, jutting from between the balusters.

"She thrives on the stench of fear," James added. "Buck up if you don't want her to devour you."

Crispin paled, straightening as he prepared to meet his fate. "You'll regret this. Some captain you are." He offered a scornful salute, only to follow it up by spitting on the plank before he stepped backward, dropping like a rock into the deep.

The crew remained still, spellbound by the unexpected turn of events. Unsettled. Wary.

Good.

"There'll be no more harassment aboard *Jolly Roger*, lest you end up in the drink like Crispin," James uttered, his quiet voice carrying over the rapt shipmen. "That is all. Carry on!"

The men dispersed, quickly returning to their tasks with more eagerness than James had seen in some time. It seemed his bold performance had paid its due, leaving behind no questions as to who was rightfully in charge.

"I would've handled myself, but I'm ever grateful for your aid." The woman extended her hand in greeting. "My name is Bellamy."

"A pleasure," James said, taking her hand in his. "Let it be known that I brought you on for your exceptional skill, fully aware of who you are."

A subtle smile split her lips. "Aye, sir. You won't be disappointed."

"You've nothing to prove. You're doing the job well, and that's all I care about. You're accepted as you are."

Bellamy nodded, seemingly at ease despite the revelation of her identity. She moved to continue her work a moment later, leaving James alone with his thoughts.

She'd held her own for weeks, this Bellamy, impressing James with her courage and instincts. He knew women who could move mountains with their determination, who modified kingdoms through sheer force of will.

Would that Bellamy be no exception.

Chapter Four

A light tread rustled in the woods at Petra's back, the grass and lush foliage softly sighing under nimble footsteps. To trained ears, there was no doubt they belonged to a human, and whoever it was seemed to be running straight for the cave mere paces from where Petra stood.

Crouching among the undergrowth, she waited, pipe and darts at the ready. Her aim was true after months of practice, and the bolts were tipped in a rare herbal blend that would incapacitate any foe long enough to elude pursuit. The cardinal feather, packed within the hollow of her pipe, would mark her prey.

Petra's body tensed in anticipation, awaiting her quarry with her heart in her throat. The target's strides slowed just as he came into view, his boyish frame halting before the mouth of the cave.

A silent sob escaped from Petra, her eyes stinging with tears at the sight of Ffion. In her dreams, she'd deserted him when she gave into Otherlande's whims. The guilt of her weakness was enough to swallow her whole. It all felt so real, so unbelievably true, her time with Ffion and his friends – the Penzellian heir, Aurora, and her brute. She'd feared for him there as much as she had in her restored consciousness, somehow the parallels blurring into one.

Ffion turned when he heard Petra moving through the brush, his eyes wide. The boy lifted his hands in surrender as his gaze fell to the pipe in her hands.

A playful grin spread over Ffion's features, lighting his youthful visage. "I'd rather you not shoot me this time."

Petra laughed, hurtling toward him and embracing him with more desperation than she meant to betray. His words settled as she looked him over, inspecting his face and limbs for any signs of harm. "You mean–"

The boy nodded, his smile broadening. "They did it! The kingdom has awakened." He could hardly contain his excitement, gripping Petra's forearms as he gently shook her. "I knew we would see each other again, that you weren't gone. And Artyrus... He will recover. The princess will make sure of it." Ffion's features sobered, his concern evident when his brows knitted together.

It was a ridiculous impossibility, the life they'd lived together in Otherlande. And yet, Ffion knew what Petra had dreamed and had lived it alongside her.

"We could go to them," Ffion added, his voice low. "No one in Chamelaute knows you."

"I won't run, Ffion. Wendolyne cannot win." Petra averted her eyes, unable to bear the disappointment she'd see in his. He was the most faithful friend she had apart from Javan, but how long would the young nuisance endure her indignation and poor temper?

Mikhail had not been much older than Ffion when he'd turned on her. But she was used to being alone, for even Javan did not dare reveal the depth of their bond. It was the very reason Petra had befriended the endless hinterlands of Wylewoode, along with the thriving creatures who lived there.

They were not lost, nor were they alone, and when she sojourned there with them, neither was she.

Ffion sighed as if he'd anticipated Petra's response but didn't object to her sentiments. "That deranged queen has almost killed you twice now." He rifled through the leather satchel hanging loosely over his chest, retrieving a small fold of stained cloth. "She sent your own brothers after you like dogs. Would you have otherwise risked poisoning yourself?"

Petra nodded his way. "What excuse do you claim?"

The boy squinted back at Petra, following her line of sight before rolling his eyes at the berries in his hand. Ffion pinched one of the toxic fruits and flicked it back into the woods, tossing the rest aside. The boy hadn't even the decency to appear shaken by the fatal error he'd narrowly avoided.

Slumping back against a towering cottonwood, he retrieved a few strips of dried meat. Life had never been easy for Ffion, a boy with no family or home that she knew of. His nonchalance over the berries would've troubled Petra, but instead, she envied his neutrality. He lived to the fullest every day, disregarding the consequences. To his credit, he did it well.

Ffion tore off a bite of the meat with his teeth, offering a piece to Petra. She accepted it without a second thought, her belly aching from hunger.

"Once the queen learns her efforts failed, she'll not rest until you're in the ground. If not for Javan finding a way to nourish you these past weeks, she would've had her way."

Petra felt the affirmation of his words in her shaky limbs, in her throat and the pressure thumping against her skull and temples. In truth, it was through sheer will alone that she could stand upright.

"The poison should never have lasted so long. Javan saw to your needs when he knew she wouldn't think anything of his absence, but once the foreigner arrived, he couldn't sneak away so easily. Sustaining you wasn't enough, though. Your breathing was so shallow there was no rise and fall of your chest. I thought you were dead when Javan brought me to you." Ffion swallowed hard, and Petra nearly reached out to him, but something within her wouldn't allow it.

"He did what I asked of him. We knew it was a risk."

"A risk? You heard rumors from Penzellian refugees and held it as gospel!" The boy had never raised his voice at Petra. She knew he considered her family but didn't anticipate the betrayal she sensed in his stare.

Her throat tightened, nearly choking off her words. "You'll not speak to me like I'm some common *ass*. Do you think I wanted to be trapped in that hellscape?"

Ffion gave no response save for a raised brow as he chewed another bite of jerky. Petra groaned, her frustration spiking. "It's not as if you're so much better. You had to have similar sources if you believed you might somehow find and awaken me from within a *dream*."

"Look at you." The boy gestured, indicating her too-slender frame. "I had to do *something*."

What was she doing? Arguing with her most steadfast companion was a fool's errand. Petra felt the shame of her annoyance heating her cheeks. She couldn't be angry with him, not really. He owed her nothing and was everything good, everything kind…

Why Ffion chose her to share his days, she could not understand. Petra had made little effort to know much about him in return. In fact, she took great pains to avoid learning anything. She was deliberately cruel, which only seemed to amuse him, and never permitted his aid in any of her pursuits, not that any of that deterred him.

And she was in grave danger of becoming attached. Hell, she already was.

He was so much like her half-brother, Mikhail, before Wendolyne's web of deceptions had won his obedience. It was the first time she could bring herself to acknowledge their similarities, because to think of Mikhail and who he might've been was enough to break Petra's heart anew.

Even as she attempted to put him from her mind, he was the most compelling reason why she couldn't allow Wendy's machinations to advance.

Petra gathered herself, determined to move beyond her childish attitude. The tit-for-tat with Ffion would be so easy to avoid if only she'd behave like more of an adult – a lamentable consequence of growing up.

"What do you know of this foreigner you mentioned?"

"Aeric," Ffion confirmed, the corners of his mouth tipping into a smirk. "The queen's mirror. He's her insight into the kingdom, and he's kept things interesting since his arrival, provoking your relations as much as he flatters them."

Ffion was everywhere and nowhere at once – a ghost of sorts throughout the whole of Neverwoode. The boy could effortlessly prowl about the shrouded lands unnoticed, which meant his survival for all these years. Petra wasn't surprised to hear of the knowledge he'd gained regarding the foreigner due to his cunning.

"It's a wonder he's not been left at the cove's mercy."

"Not really." Ffion withdrew a small vial of liquid gold sift from a pocket in his trousers. "I crossed paths with him one day long enough to lift this from him. There's more to him, I suspect, or your sister would've sacrificed him to the sirens long before allowing him to set foot near the palace."

He was right, for Wendolyne wasn't one to show leniency or pity to strangers without the assurance of some personal gain.

Petra had only just met this *mirror* of Wendy's, and by Ffion's description, there was no mistake. The man all but told her as much, at any rate. He was called Aeric, then.

"He was here," Petra said. "So near when you came to find me, I thought that you were him, still lurking in the woods. He spoke to me then left."

The boy glanced over his shoulder, straightening a little as he surveyed the trees, doubtless more alert than before.

"I don't care about myself. It's what she took from me." Petra paused, working to make sense of all the chaos in her mind. There was plenty at stake and so much to lose.

She was supposed to be dead.

"Doubtless, my brothers will be under close watch if Wendolyne believes they may have conspired against her, but she'll make no moves if they're sensible enough to stroke her brittle ego. She can't see past the admiration."

Perhaps it was for that reason Wendy deemed Aeric's reflections on her territory necessary. Sift was as vital to her as the breath in her lungs—but not without cost.

When the queen's enigmatic spy had spoken to Petra, he was not addled or rapt like those under sift's pull. Aeric, if relatively sheltered from the dust's effects, could offer invaluable coherence. But that revelation only resulted in more questions.

Twilight beckoned beyond the bowing treetops, moving gracefully to a gentle summer breeze. "We'll soon lose the sun." Tucking her pipe away, Petra clung to the strap crossed over her chest, the small pouch at its end containing her poisoned darts.

It was Ffion who'd given her the idea to arm herself with bane. And while she'd ultimately settled for something slightly less potent, he'd concocted the poison with startling proficiency—a choice he undoubtedly thanked the heavens for when she'd used it against him once before.

There was no use telling the boy to stay behind. He knew his mind and answered to no one. If Petra were honest, she was still not herself, stranded somewhere between parallel existences. Together, she and her friend stood a chance. They made good time, stopping only once before cresting a timbered ridge.

Referred to by many as 'the shrouded kingdom', these lands belonged to exiles from all over Fayble—to the lost, existing in intentional camouflage, but never from Petra. Faint contours of the veiled dominion pierced a thick, ominous fog. Neverwoode didn't materialize for the naked eye, appearing instead as a hostile valley brimming with certain peril. The sinister haze above Wendolyne's kingdom was like a slithering creature, coiled to strike anyone who dared near its lethal den.

"I've never seen it like this," Petra breathed. "It's hardly visible at all."

"You have a purpose." Ffion crouched atop the hillside, extending a brass spyglass in his hands. "The moment you doubt something exists, you cease to be able to see it. Look closer."

The boy's outlook on their world was a treasure, but how he shared his insights made him even more endearing. Though Petra never asked his age, Ffion's knowledge was beyond his years. She thought him somewhere around fourteen or fifteen, but looking at him now with his monocular in hand, it was almost as if she was watching his boyishness fade by the minute.

In the few years she'd known him, he remained ever a child in her heart and mind — a subtle manipulation devised to shield him from the consequences and expectations of adulthood. Convincing a sift-washed mind is easy, as they simply just believe. Ffion carefully crafted his façade of youthfulness, though the boy's mask had recently begun to slip.

The boy peered through his spyglass at the territory below, adjusting the sight with a twist of his hands. With one eye closed, he studied it, from east to west, scouring the scenic panorama as far as Altanys Cove, where something caught his attention. Again, he rotated the brass contraption with dexterous precision before motioning Petra closer.

The boy pointed just beyond the cove. "There."

A ship on the horizon, too large to be one of the queen's small column. Few captains were skilled enough to venture through the skull and survive the seductive call of the deep, and even fewer were stupid enough not to retreat once they had.

Wendolyne's fleet of vessels had not yet set upon the foreign craft, which could only mean she welcomed it. The queen was setting something into motion and doing so under the nose of every neighboring nation.

Pieces of her scheme were already coming to light, but what they meant and how they fit together remained unknown. Sift had been employed in a manner Petra never dared consider when she'd awakened clothed in a glittering skirt of gold with her cherished timepiece lost. Their father had warned Petra never to lose sight of the watch and its many secrets.

Though Aeric had warned her not to pursue it, she couldn't bear the thought of its loss, especially to one such as her sister.

Petra should be dead. Instead, she was about to show her sister that she, too, was their father's daughter and all the parts of him the queen should dread.

Wendy had already failed.

Chapter Five

A thin fog rose off the roiling waters as though the seas were moving in concert with the tumult of James' troubled heart. He'd decided early on to approach the shores of Wylewoode via the easternmost coast of Fayble, resolving to brave the mysterious waters of Altanys Cove despite their supposed dangers.

It was there when on his first tentative explorations of the continent's borders his ship had been set upon by none other than Wylewoodean pirates – a strange predicament, given the penal colony origins of the kingdom.

With that incident, his mind had been made. Leaving the territory to its own secretive devices seemed a grave error indeed, especially when the safety of Llundyn was at stake. The perils lurking within its borders had yet to be observed, at least with his own eyes, thus rendering any reservations baseless. It was time for action.

An eerie quiet settled over the *Jolly Roger* as the shoreline came into distant view. The lands were obscured by a jagged outcropping of rock and spire, forming an ominous passageway leading to a secluded lagoon, further amplifying the peculiar nature of the little-explored territory. Still, the captain would not yield. Legends and fables were just that – fictitious tales meant to entertain, to caution. Far from facts were they – or so he told himself.

Besides, Crispin yet swam, not but a quarter league away. It couldn't be that dire.

"Well, we're properly lost now," Smee said, sidling up beside the captain, the pair leaning over the railing where they took in their quarry. "I can't see it, but I know it's there. I can feel it in my bones." He clasped his hands together, his eagerness to set foot upon the Wylewoode shores evident on his face. He'd waited years for the opportunity, endured scorn over the stories of his experiences, only to finally return.

James did not share his level of conviction. With a monocular in hand, he monitored what little he could see of the shore, searching for signs of life, signs of danger, but to no avail. It seemed nothing more than an empty beach – not the fantastical oceanfront jewel of which Smee had spoken.

Yet a part of him still believed. The old man's stories had been just wild enough that James regarded them as truth, contending that no sane mind could ever conceive of such nonsense.

Then again, perhaps sanity was an issue for both of them.

The crew's silence gave way when they neared the craggy archway leading to the lagoon. Mist clung to the surface of the water, obscuring the briny deep as it grew thicker and more unforgiving, even as the swelling tide settled around them.

James consulted his map, noting no rocky landmark. He knew his charts were lacking, but this seemed a startling oversight, given their prominence.

"It's like a skull," Bellamy uttered, her eyes glued to the stony passage. "And we're passing through the bloody jaws."

She was right, for just above them, two voids beneath the apex of the upper curve left the distinct impression that they were being watched with somber, vacant eyes.

He would name it Skull Rock and add it to his father's charts. Why did it feel so foreboding?

The sense of unease James felt as they sailed into the cove was stifling. Again, he searched for Crispin, who had, oddly enough, been like a touchstone as they'd made their way into the unknown, but he was nowhere to be seen. The captain knew better than to make anything of it, for the sea had its own fickle soul. The man could be hidden by the fog, could've dipped beneath the surface as he stroked his way to shore. His absence off the bow was surely no omen.

"We're in," said Smee, his glee nowhere near contained. "Never again did I believe it would be, and never would it've been without their permission."

James watched his quartermaster, all the while feeling a sudden spike of anger. He felt duped, wondering if his loyalty to his father's memory had somehow tainted his mission. He'd been hellbent on returning and learning of the truth hidden within the confines of Wylewoode, but a sinister little voice within him mocked his gullibility.

A soft melody swirled around them as if carried on the waves from the ocean floor, and rapt sailors dropped their work, wandering to the railing with blank expressions on their faces. The captain's crew was a listless body, spellbound by the haunting voices that melded into one, filling the cove with harmonious splendor.

James fought the urge to succumb. The sirens of the deep were a myth — or so he'd always maintained — chalking it up as nothing more than fiction.

He was apparently so very wrong.

Panic surged through his veins, even as he resisted the impulse to wring Smee's neck. The man had led them on a fool's errand, though James was every bit as much to blame. He hadn't demanded enough answers or done nearly enough research before they'd set sail. He'd trusted in the knowledge of his father's dearest friend, only to drift into certain jeopardy...and for what?

All at once, the refrain melted away, leaving the seafarers suddenly dazed when, at long last, the shrouded kingdom was revealed. Exclamations of awe rang across the decks of the *Jolly Roger* as the realm emerged before them, seemingly out of nothing, for the coastline had been an empty beach not but a moment before.

A gleaming palace set within the hillside beckoned them forward, its solid lines softened by a haze of golden dust. The castle was vast, situated high above a growing town, with more dwellings and shops materializing before them like a mirage. The subtle glow of the modest borough set the cove alight, shrouding the hollow with inviting warmth.

"Just as I recall." Smee sighed, seemingly overwhelmed with relief. He'd returned, at long last vindicated, despite the disbelief of his countrymen.

"Come what may," James said, mustering a smile though his insides were in knots. He squeezed Smee's shoulder, leaving the fellow to his thoughts as he moved to sort his own. The turmoil of the journey and the uncertainty of what lay ahead were wreaking havoc on his mind. Then there was the added emotion, for it was where his father had died. It was a lot to reconcile, but he couldn't afford to break. Not now.

"If I may, sir." Bellamy approached, holding a narrow box. "An invention of mine. I wonder if you wouldn't find it of some use." She opened the box, presenting him with a strange-looking metal tube. "Setting fire to the fuse will send a flash of light into the sky. Perhaps we could announce ourselves so as not to catch our hosts off guard?"

"How clever," James agreed, though he didn't yet understand how she would pull off her claim. He gestured toward the deck below. "Please, do your worst."

Bellamy smiled, moving to the quarterdeck where she set flame to the braided fuse, and when she pointed the open end skyward, her invention didn't disappoint. Streaks of brilliance blew into the twilight like shooting stars, bursting into a blaze above the ship.

James followed her down to the quarterdeck. "How did you manage such a thing?"

"I like to tinker," said Bellamy. "It's a favorite pastime. I'm only glad it worked."

"Like a charm." James grinned, happily diverted if only for a moment.

Smee came running, folding at the waist to catch his breath. "We're not alone." He handed the monocular to the captain, waving his hand toward the bow. "Both starboard and port. Look."

Sure enough, they were being flanked, with a vessel quickly pacing them to either side of *Jolly Roger*. And much like the time before, they flew the flags of Wylewoode.

"*Bollocks*," James hissed, dashing toward the helm as he began barking orders. "Do *not* engage! Raise the white flag!"

Smee balked, his face a mask of disbelief. "Sir, you can't – "

"Do it! They must know that we're prepared to negotiate." James took control of the wheel, working to steer the ship as it barreled toward shore. The journey into the cove had been surprisingly serene, but no more, as the wind worked in tandem with the pair of convoys. It was almost as if the gale was forcing his hand.

They were well within the harbor in a matter of moments, dropping anchor. "You, and you." James indicated Smee and Bellamy with a flick of his wrist. "To the launch boat. We'll make our way to ground."

The remainder of his crew watched on as the captain prepared to disembark, climbing into the launch where it hung overboard. A sense of dismay seemingly consumed the sailors, wholly unprepared to be without their captain in a foreign land.

"They'll be fine," Smee uttered to Bellamy, though it sounded as much to assure himself as it was for her benefit.

"I care not," Bellamy spat, climbing into the launch behind Smee. Doubtless, she was eager to be free of all the riffraff on board, and James couldn't blame her. Never would he leave her behind.

The three rowed to shore, tying the boat to the dock that hadn't been visible until they were nearly upon it. The experience had James on edge. He silently prayed that he'd not lead his entire crew to ruin.

James reached for Bellamy, hauling her from the launch as Smee scrambled his way onto the landing. For all his recent bravado and excitement, he looked to have withered under the fallout, doubling the captain's fear that he'd severely miscalculated the necessity of this adventure.

In sober resignation, James wandered up the pier with Bellamy and Smee at his heels, working to focus his attention. The beauty of the kingdom that lay before them was breathtaking, yet somehow felt...false. *Tainted.*

"Wylewoode welcomes you," came a voice from before him. Two men stood not but a dozen yards ahead, their arms crossed over their broad chests. They were as tall as he was, one dark of feature where the other was fair.

"Hands in the air," the darker one continued, his umber hair falling over his forehead in a curly wave. Donning a broad smile, he scoffed as the trio raised their hands, eyeing the silver crook at the end of James' arm. "A proper pirate, I see. Very scary, you."

The fairer one jabbed him in the ribs with a winged elbow. "Shut up. My apologies," he said, directing his attention toward the captain. He was the older of the two, bespectacled and proper in his manner. "My name is Javan, and this is my brother Mikhail. Our sister Wendolyne will see you now."

* * * *

It was appalling.

How the opulence of such a place could go ignored for so long was unfathomable. The golden haze enveloping this shrouded kingdom was only the beginning, as the wealth within the palace walls seemingly knew no bounds.

James followed behind his captors, though he was as yet unbound, taking in the ridiculous splendor of his new surroundings. He'd left Smee and Bellamy on the beach, bidding them farewell in the hopes that they'd be safer on their own.

Inwardly, he cursed his audacity. His sovereigns had entrusted him with a ship and a crew. They'd taken him at his word, sending him on a mission of his choosing. Forcing a deep breath, he collected himself, unwilling to allow his circumstances to dictate his future, even as his thoughts grew more clouded with each passing second.

Their footsteps sounded through the hall, echoing from the high ceilings as they entered the candlelit throne room. The soft light of flickering flames bounced off countless precious stones set within the archways stretching from the easternmost wall to the west. A plush, emerald-green runner spanned the length of the marble floor, leading to a mahogany throne inlaid with gold. Both imposing and grotesque in grandeur, it was an architectural wonder.

Sat between two pillars was a woman James could only surmise to be Queen Wendolyne, though he'd never before heard of a Wylewoodean ruler. She rose to her feet, her movements fluid and lithe as she made her way toward him. The brothers parted, making way for the exceptional beauty, her white-blonde hair unbound, falling about her bare shoulders.

In truth, *she* was nearly bare, adorned in the sheerest fabrics James had ever seen. Shades of gold and cream crisscrossed her torso, gathering at the waist where they fell into an airy gossamer skirt. She strolled toward him, her wide green eyes trained upon him in a way that made him twitchy. James averted his gaze, determined to regain his composure.

It was then that he saw it. Clutched within her slender fingers was a timepiece he'd long wondered after. Known to him only by artistic rendering, he'd seen its likeness among his father's charts – a singular piece of parchment with a drawing he could never make sense of alongside a simple phrase.

At time's end. Its presence among his maps and logs had confounded James for years, but he was sure.

A casing of green gold trimmed in precious jade gemstones formed the lid, while a series of shallow etchings created a delicate network of veins originating from the heart-shaped ruby inset within the center of the shell. It was jarring to see the watch firsthand and further perplexing that this creature possessed it.

She slipped it into her pocket when she reached him, gazing up at him with a broad white smile. Much too close for propriety, James took a step back, only to be set upon again by the beguiling woman.

"My sister, Queen Wendolyne," said Javan, his tone one of dutiful annoyance.

"Leave us." Wendolyne prowled nearer, appraising the captain, her fingertips tracing the lines of his chest and shoulders as she moved around him.

The two men disappeared without another word, seemingly eager to be free of their charge or, perhaps, their sister. It didn't matter. Either way, they were alone, which somehow felt worse.

"Your presence here in Wylewoode is a surprise," she lilted, a dangerous gleam in her eyes. "And a sea captain at that. We're unaccustomed to men of your caliber in our humble kingdom. I shall consider myself honored by your presence, Captain Hook."

"I'm nobody." James was already growing tired of her overt attempts at seduction. Indeed, he wished to be anywhere else. "A gross oversight, I'm afraid, led us to your lands, and we were powerless to fix it."

She continued her inane perusal, moving around him once again as she trailed her fingers down his arm, tracing his hooked hand before making her way back to his chest. Without another thought, he made his move, reaching for the watch as her hip brushed against his, drawing the prize from her pocket with the tip of his hook before quickly slipping it into his own. Thieving was second nature after his glory days in Llundyn, but this? This was stupid.

"A shame," Wendolyne uttered, and for a moment, he feared he'd been caught. Yet she'd only paused in her appraisal, reaching for the crook that served as his hand and drawing it toward herself. Caressing the polished steel, she continued. "We do not permit visitors here. How is it, then, that you've come to stand in my presence?"

"I allowed it," came a feminine voice from behind them. James turned to find a woman, slight of build with rich, dark skin, her raven hair arranged in a low bun set beneath her tricorn hat. Clad in a knee-length jacket in the same emerald tones dotting the palace's interior, it seemed that she, too, was a sea captain.

"Who made you queen, Lillia?" Wendolyne turned her attention to the wayward woman, offering James a moment of relief after his reckless plundering. He tapped his pocket, ensuring the timepiece was well tucked within his coat.

Lillia was undeterred, apparently confident in her decision, despite the anger of her supposed queen. "I believe him to be an asset, Your Majesty. Never before has a ship evaded our measures, surviving even the full charge of our cannon."

James observed the exchange, fascinated by all the information he was suddenly privy to. He'd never before laid eyes upon a *cannon*. Indeed, he'd never heard of such a thing, but the hole in the side of his vessel was proof enough of its utility.

"I'd like him in my employ," Lillia continued. "There's much to be gained—and with his expertise, we could—"

"Perhaps this is only a futile attempt to correct your own significant failures where he's concerned, for never should he have entered the cove!" Wendolyne's face was a mask of scarcely contained anger as she moved around James to object. "Who gave you the authority?"

"You did when you hired me to do what I do." Lillia put her hands on her hips, evidently unwilling to back down. "That I may choose my crew as I please…and I choose him."

"I'm not working for anybody." James backed up, eager to be on his way. "I work for myself alone."

"Funny. Those look like Llundynien colors," Wendolyne purred. "You work for the newly minted king of Llundyn. Still, perhaps I could make you a deal."

"Imagine the things we could do," Lillia agreed.

"Not a chance. My apologies for any inconvenience our presence has caused you. For the sake of all future relations between our kingdoms, we shall be on our way. I'll see myself out." James bowed, a stilted, shallow effort completely lacking in deference.

The queen scoffed but made no move to stop him. The captain left with no difficulty, leaving him wondering what was off. Nothing about the situation made sense, but he was not about to waste any time.

It was high time for this misadventure to be over.

Chapter Six

With trembling hands and arms, Petra descended deep into the belly of a vessel called the *Jolly Roger*.

The foreign ship was, by all appearances, entirely abandoned. Save for a few quiet squeaks from a rodent or two and creaking timbers, the silence was deafening.

She was a fool to be there, but what other option was there? Her fingers were numb from climbing the anchor line, even as she flexed them, balling her fists to regain circulation and function.

The ship rocked gently atop placid waters, its groans and flapping sails an ever-present reminder of Petra's mindless pursuit. But there was no mistaking what she'd seen. She couldn't have stopped herself if she'd tried – driven by her father's plea and morbid curiosity.

The visit to her former home yielded more than she'd anticipated – a nightmare given flesh.

Petra had kept hidden at the palace, quietly padding through its empty corridors to the queen's quarters. Wendolyne's private wing of their grandfather's castle smelled sweeter than memory served, though it was no surprise, with every surface lightly dusted in gold. And after carefully searching every inch of Wendy's chambers, she knew where her watch would be.

The timepiece was attached to the queen when Petra discovered her, though it seemed the least of her worries when she saw with whom Wendolyne spoke. He stood before her sister, broad and tall, as Wendy moved around him with feline fluidity. The queen walked her fingers up the man's chest to his shoulder, carefully running her hand down the length of his arm, tracing the curve of his hook with her fingertips.

Her shadow had, indeed, awakened.

Petra hadn't been able to look away—like some force, some compulsion held her captive, trapped in a moment observing the two creatures who haunted her every thought. But as she'd watched, light refracted between their figures. At first glance, it appeared only to be the shadow's hooked limb, but when Petra narrowed her focus, she saw the silver of his hook and her father's watch glinting with firelight. He'd slipped it into his pocket without Wendolyne's notice as she'd teased him.

Captain Hook, the queen had called him.

Try as she might, Petra had hardly heard a word between them or the others – Lillia and her brothers. Her head throbbed too fiercely, and her entire body protested every step she took. It was why she'd sent Ffion to steal food from the kitchens. Yet when the captain made his exit, she knew she couldn't miss her chance.

She'd beaten him to his ship, but to what end? Petra had no plan, no leverage against this *shadow*—the tormentor of her wearied soul. She shivered, surveying the hull to the best of her ability, with a scant stream of golden candlelight illuminating the captain's immaculate vessel.

Soaked and chilled to the bone from the short swim, she wrung as much moisture from her tunic as she could, not that it helped prevent the ice from stiffening her veins.

Petra's mind raced, and she staggered forward into a wooden post and away from the light. Steadying herself, she took hold of it, pushing herself upward into the dark rafters above. Her muscles strained with the effort, but she threw her leg over one of the upper beams, straddling the joist as her heart thrummed in her ears.

A handful of times, Petra caught herself dozing, her whole being too exhausted to remain conscious. Though she hated herself for it, she thirsted for the freedom it offered.

In that parallel reality, not once had she felt weak. She didn't fatigue in Otherlande, nor did she hunger. It was there that Petra had learned how vastly different anxiety and frailty were, for it had been the former that crippled her. And while a shadow seemed to stalk her like prey in sleep, it was not the silhouette itself she feared but what it represented.

Though Otherlande beckoned, it wasn't long before a distinctive tread sounded overhead with long, languid strides. A door slammed, and glass shattered. Petra's skull pounded, blurring her vision as every inch of her body tensed. The footsteps grew faint, and she exhaled sharply, willing herself to relax.

Resting her head on the post at her back, she took a moment to simply *breathe*, and when she nearly fell after her meditations lured her into blessed oblivion, Petra determined it was time to act.

Dropping silently to the floor, she was reminded anew of her discomfort, but exertion would keep her blood pumping. The warmth of the light increased, shifting into a deep amber glow, but it was already too late when she turned. A lantern flickering with flame hung from her shadow's hook.

He set it atop a nearby barrel, and Petra raised an eyebrow, meeting his eyes, dark as coal. With a dagger palmed in his good hand, the captain's gaze was bitter and raw as he took her in.

"What will you do, Captain?" She indicated her material form before retrieving the blowpipe and a pair of spare darts from the pouch at her hip. Flipping it end over end between her slender fingers, she stepped nearer, appearing far bolder than she felt. "Has my sister convinced you of the risk I pose to her wicked reign?" Petra feigned indifference at the present company, though tremors of trepidation coursed through her hands. "She's a gifted storyteller, the queen, but I assure you, she trades only in delusions. I assume you've been privy to her deranged fictions."

The captain's dusky gaze never wavered. His eyes followed her every move as if he were waiting for her to crumble. She watched intently in return, noting the subtle shift of his focus when at last, he spoke. His voice was low and harsh. "Don't. Move."

Above them, on the main deck, more footsteps sounded. The distraction was a godsend, and when the captain glanced over his shoulder, Petra rushed him. He reacted quickly, twisting her in his powerful hold, but not before she plunged one of Ffion's darts into his muscular shoulder.

The tip of his hook hovered over her throat. She didn't dare move, feeling the rise and fall of his chest against her spine, his heart hammering in time with her own.

The captain's grip faltered, and he stumbled backward. Petra thrashed, scratching and clawing at the exposed flesh of his forearm across her collarbone. She bit into it, clenching her jaw, and something feral escaped from his lips as he pushed her to the side. He swayed where he stood, plucking her dart from his arm and tossing it to the ground.

A flash of red from the dart's cardinal feather disappeared behind a stubby clawed foot. Petra fumbled, falling into the captain, who took hold of her once more. The creature drew nearer, his footsteps obscured by the shouts of men bellowing for the captain from above.

Petra made out a massive, scaled body with a hide that appeared more like armor than skin, slowly inching closer in the dim glow of the hull. She managed to squirm from her shadow's arms before the crocodile reached them, but the beast stilled as figures descended into the hull.

"*Climb,*" growled the captain. Turning from Petra, he staggered into the darkness toward approaching steps and voices. She considered his words and chose instead to run. Soon, he would succumb to Ffion's paralytic, and what became of him then was left to fate.

She made for the exit, shoving past one man before colliding with another. He grunted and pushed her aside just as recognition dawned between them — a stooge of Wendolyne's guard. The man sneered, and Petra used his moment of shock to throw her elbow into his jaw. Pain surged through her arm as he spewed curses in her direction, but she evaded his fist and ran.

Neither knew what awaited the other.

Petra ascended the steps to the main deck, greeted by a pitch-dark sky sprinkled with stars. Others were lumbering about the platform, though none had yet seen her. From behind, the brute she'd struck pursued her, issuing threats through his decaying teeth, only to fall with a sudden thud on the wooden stairs. His head bounced, and he shrieked in agony, hitting each step on his way back down.

Petra watched in horror as the crocodile tore through the man's arm, ripping it from his body with ease. Like a dog with a bone, the creature gnawed on his limb as he writhed on the floor below.

His screams drew the attention of the others on board as they searched for the origin of his distress. With a sickening crunch, the croc ended his wailing, but not before Petra was spotted. Still soaked from her swim out, she braced herself for the shock and impact of the sea as she hoisted herself onto the ship's external railing and jumped.

Breaking through the water's surface, she swam as far as she could in a single breath. No one followed, but then again, few would risk disturbing the Goddess of the Deep.

Foamy tongues of yawning tides lapped at the shore, where Ffion began to run for Petra. She turned to her back, allowing the waters to drag her to land, her eyes stinging from the salt. The boy waded out to her, thrashing and cursing until he reached her when the world rippled into blackness.

* * * *

The queen preened, dipping a finely tipped brush into her jar of ground kohl.

Her hands trembled. Whether with need or tension, she knew not, for the evening thus far had been fraught with…*surprises*. Wendolyne considered for the dozenth time that hour what she'd seen in her periphery earlier as her brothers presented her with the handsome captain.

Petra still haunted her memories. The queen's paranoia always seemed to best her, but then there was sift to calm her anxious nerves. It was Petra's form she'd noted observing her in the hall – a ghost. How very like her to torment Wendy, even in death. She had yet to ask if Javan or Mikhail had also seen her, but could a spirit survive without acknowledgment?

Mikhail had wept the night he'd found his half-sister dead somewhere in the heart of Wylewoode. It was the brothers' sworn duty to end her, but since then, Wendy assigned an attendant to Mikhail, ensuring his wellbeing. He adored Petra, always trailing her as a boy, so blinded by his affection that he was incapable of seeing the dishonor she'd brought on the family.

Wendy did for him all she could to help him understand, but he was as willful as Petra. With the gilded orchard's aid, with the sift it wrought, Mikhail finally understood the danger she posed to Neverwoode and their family's esteemed name – even if, at times, that understanding faltered.

Despite the bond he shared with their bastard sister, Javan never required any intercession, bless him. His soft spot for her had soured when she abandoned him months before. Still, even before Petra showed indifference toward him, Javan was indisputably committed to the kingdom's prosperity.

But what chaos would she wreak upon her ghostly return?

The queen took in her reflection, seated at the vanity in her private chambers. She hadn't heard him enter, but then again, she rarely did. Aeric stood several paces behind her, staring back at her through the mirror.

Wendolyne rolled her eyes. "Do come in." Leaning closer to her likeness, she lined above and underneath her black lashes with the brush in her hand in precise, dexterous motions, winging the outer corner of her eyelids.

He donned an arrogant smirk, at once as beautiful as he was irritating. "You look exquisite, my queen."

A gift to Wendy from the Undersea, Aeric was a pleasing distraction for such trying times. He had been sent to her unexpectedly a fortnight past, his inky curls hanging over crystalline eyes, still soaked from the waters' mercurial conduct.

With a legion of crabs serving as escorts, they surrounded him in waves of oranges and reds like a bright, drifting sunset. His wrists were bound in a tangle of weeds, and he wore a note pinned with an eel's tooth upon his salt-spoiled vest, reading…

For your enjoyment.

Another exile in a kingdom brimming with them, Aeric's face was far more appealing than most. Fortunately, his striking countenance offset his tiresome candor and irreverence. He was tolerable enough – useful for some of her more inane taskings. Her alliance with the Undersea was tenuous at best, just like her ongoing negotiations with Chamelaute, each forged over recent months. Better to accept the lady's offering than risk offense.

"You missed a new arrival earlier." Fingering through her pale, silky tresses, Wendolyne recalled the cold steel of the foreign captain's hook as Aeric watched intently through the mirror, drawing closer behind her.

"This newcomer has improved your mood since last we spoke. Should I be jealous?" A featherlight sweep of Aeric's hand over the curve of her neck stole her breath. He twisted an errant strand of hair between his fingers, gently brushing her bare skin, and she leaned her head to the side, savoring his touch.

"As if you ever would be. Your heart clearly belongs elsewhere. But I do love possessing something someone else cherishes." Wendolyne's mouth twitched at the corners, forming a slight smile. "Perhaps *I* might be jealous if not for..." Her sentence trailed as Aeric leaned in, his lips nearly skimming the curve of her ear. "What was it you called me? The fairest of them all?"

He chuckled quietly. "If only."

The queen pulled away, every muscle in her body seizing before he could utter another word. "There's only ever been one who could reasonably be considered fairer than I—and she's dead."

Wendy's stomach twisted alongside Aeric's silence, and the faint glimmer sparkling in his eyes confirmed what she'd already refused to accept as possible.

No.

Fury clouded her vision. She'd *known*. Wendolyne had seen Petra and had not trusted her own eyes, unable to grasp how such a devastating oversight could've occurred. Panic swelled as she stood suddenly, causing her seat to clatter to the marble floor behind her.

Aeric retreated unhurriedly with a lazy grin lighting his flawless features and, to her dismay, watched on as she fell to pieces.

"Where is it?" the queen hissed, searching the long panels of her gown for Petra's heart. Running her hands over her hips and chest, she searched in vain.

"She's come for you already, then...your sister?"

Wendy reached for the kohl jar on her vanity, hurling it at Aeric. Glass shattered against the wall inches from his face as black dust wafted through the air around him. "Get *out!*"

Wendolyne's madness consumed her entirely, with the revelation of Petra living and well too much to bear. She clutched the stemmed glass from atop her desk, filled with fermented apple cider. Chilled and soothing to her palette and essential being, she drank it down to the last drop, desperate for something to ground her before mania further muddled the soundness of her mind.

The queen steadied herself, squaring her shoulders. "Bring her to me," she ordered.

But Aeric was already gone.

Chapter Seven

It was the same thing every night.

For more weeks than he could remember, James' dreams had progressed in the same standard fashion, with he himself nothing more than a specter. Before long, he would see the shadow – a silhouette of a woman with no defining characteristics beyond her petite form and wild hair.

Yet, in the back of his mind, he knew it to be more, that *she* was more, given the striking resemblance between the shadow of his nights and the untamed creature who had invaded his ship.

He wandered a short distance, pausing just outside a grove of trees. Not far from where he stood was a sharp drop-off – a cliff bordered by the roaring waters of the deep no fewer than a hundred yards below. And while the scenery always seemed to vary, the company never did.

Almost as though he'd conjured her with a thought, his shadow appeared, and much as he'd expected, she was no longer a colorless, depthless being. She was the woman who'd assaulted him upon the Jolly Roger.

Materializing before James, her back faced him as she stood on the precipice, seemingly in deep concentration. It was jarring to make the connection, to realize that the girl from his vessel had been his constant companion in his dreams, though he'd never before had the misfortune of meeting her in reality until that very day.

James watched for a moment, working to reconcile the past few weeks with the current state of affairs. She hadn't seemed to register his presence on most occasions as he'd maintained a respectful distance, watching her from afar out of simple curiosity. Then there were other instances, times that she'd seemed gripped by paranoia, running and flying as though her very life were at stake.

He hadn't cared at first, for a shadow was nothing more than the absence of light. Yet her repetitive presence, coupled with the utter lack of shadows in every other facet of his dreams, had left him confounded and unexpectedly intrigued.

His first instinct was to leave her to her thoughts, but something kept him rooted in observation. She'd been nothing shy of hostile, perhaps as paranoid in daylight as she was in dreaming.

Why he cared was another matter altogether, though he wasn't about to waste any time considering such things. Slowly, he moved her way, his footsteps concealed by the sounds of the choppy surf.

The girl turned abruptly, her sun-gold eyes piercing him to his core. "I wondered if I'd see you again." She pursed her lips at the sight of him, and her indignation was plain when she drew nearer.

His breath quickened. Something about her madness called to him. "I never knew it was you. Why could I not see you before?"

"You lie. You hunted me." She clenched her fingers into fists, but not before he saw her hands tremble. *"I went nowhere without seeing you, following me like a phantom. Say what you want. I know she sent you."*

If her aim was to provoke him, it worked. She was small, the top of her head just clearing his shoulders, but she was a force for the reckoning.

She stepped closer, rising on tiptoe to whisper a warning. "Leave me. I won't spare you next time."

He woke in a panic, his heart racing as he started where he lay. His dreams had taken on an entirely new significance, with the manic woman leaving him both fascinated and furious.

Turning to his side, he groaned, for he was not in the familiar surroundings of the great cabin upon the *Jolly Roger*. Fluffy white linens covered the overlarge bed, complete with so many downy pillows that it was almost as if he were lying on a cloud. The bedposts reached to the high ceilings, burnished in gleaming gold leafing while a cord of emeralds spun down the length of each post.

A fur rug covered the floor, laid before a smoldering fire within a white marble hearth. Tools made of iron and gold stood beside the hearthstone alongside a tidy wood pile, and a pair of sleek armchairs sat before the mild blaze.

The opulence of his chamber was much like that of the throne room, leaving him with a sense of irritation when he realized where he was at last. James rubbed his temple with the heel of his hand, as much to soothe away the memory of his dream encounter as it was to calm his rising temper.

The palace was the last place he wished to be. Even now, his mind felt hazy, just as it had the evening before when he'd met the supposed High Queen herself. A strange calm seemed to pervade his senses – a sentiment he'd not sincerely felt for some time.

That alone was enough to put him on notice. Something about Wylewoode was dubious...*false*. He couldn't put his finger on what it was that rang so hollow other than an overwhelming sense of peace.

With a long-suffering sigh, he fell to his back, only to discover that his chest was bare. He flung the covers from his legs, finding that he, too, was clad in white, in a pair of soft pants he'd never seen before.

The whole of his body had been scrubbed from head to toe, leaving him smelling too...*good*, with skin that was far too clean for one accustomed to long stints free of fresh water with which to bathe. Even his face had been newly shaven, leaving behind only his standard stubble.

Damn, if he didn't feel violated.

He rolled from the over-fluffed bed, moving to his feet only to sit back down once more to gather himself. His head swam, and he nearly blacked out, gripping the bed's frame for support. Whatever the girl had stabbed him with had been potent. That, or he'd been out for far longer than he'd imagined.

James tried again, this time rising more slowly. He swayed slightly but found his balance, ignoring the dull headache developing in the back of his skull. He was eager to go – to be on his way to Llundyn with the intelligence he'd gathered, along with the strange pocket watch. Whether either of those things had anything to do with the other made no difference to him. There'd be plenty of time to make sense of all that later.

He staggered toward the door, his steps becoming more sure as he moved, only to find it was locked. *No surprise there.* A minor inconvenience.

The rest of the room was unremarkable in its contents, though each element appeared to be of the finest quality. It was difficult for him to reconcile how all of it – the palace, the luxury, the kingdom itself – had been hiding in plain sight and yet remained such an enigma to the whole of Fayble.

A table tucked beneath a small window drew his attention then. Laid with a crystal bowl, it held the most pristine blood-red apples James had ever seen, standing in stark contrast with the bright white room. He picked one up, holding it toward the dim light cast from a nearby sconce, noting a subtle sheen.

Unnatural.

The skin was glossy, polished so beautifully he could see his reflection. The scent of it, too, was almost sickly sweet. His stomach twisted, registering his hunger for the first time, but he couldn't bring himself to taste it.

"They're the best in all of Fayble." Wendolyne stepped into James' quarters, catching him off guard, though he managed not to show it.

"Indeed. Perhaps a little too tempting, like everything I've come across in your kingdom." James smiled in what he hoped to be convincing fashion, even as he cringed inwardly. Flirtation had never been a strong suit for the young captain, and even less so when he was bereft of any feelings.

She moved before him, seemingly satisfied with his efforts as she stood much too close. "I don't so much mind your presence here in Wylewoode. We may even be of some use to one another." Gazing up at him, she ran her fingers through his dark hair before tracing the line of his jaw.

James watched her in silence, consumed by her uncanny resemblance to his shadow. "There's another who looks much like you." Her eyes narrowed, and he covered her hand with his own, eager to pacify her. "Only she doesn't treat me nearly as well."

"You've met my sister then." Wendolyne stepped away, the train of her silken skirt trailing behind her. She kept her back to him, her petulance shining through in a way that grated his nerves.

He doubled down, attempting to regain the ground he'd lost. Rubbing his shoulder, he continued. "The little hellcat stabbed me with a poisoned dart. I daresay there's no comparison when it comes to the two of you."

That got her attention. She turned, donning a victorious smile as she strode toward James once more. "That's why you're here. We found you soon after she struck and brought you here for safety."

"What does any of this have to do with me?"

"It's not so much you as it is your nation. I believe my sister means to make us known to Llundyn and other countries like yours, that she hopes to strike a blow that will provoke a war." Wendolyne's wide eyes were slick with tears, drawing an unexpected sliver of empathy from the captain.

He held no regard for either of the sisters but understood how tenuous the grasp on any kingdom's reins could be. Still, the last thing he wanted was to be in the middle of a turf battle between siblings. He'd seen enough of such conflicts to last a lifetime already.

The fuzzy sensation returned, and James suddenly found Wendolyne's vague confessions utterly compelling. Not coherent quite, but...

The spotless apples beneath the window filled his periphery – a stark reminder of the oddities so pervasive within the realm.

He needed to get out of there.

"What was it you wished for me to do?" James moved nearer to the queen, close enough to note that she smelled much the same as the sickly sweet fruit within the crystal bowl.

Her demeanor shifted in an instant. Trailing her finger down the length of his chest, she smiled broadly as if she finally had him where she wanted him. "Join me for dinner this evening so that we may discuss this development. It seems we've a lot in common. My sister is trying to steal my kingdom, much as she stole your crew."

"It was her?" The absence of his sailors had frustrated him, though he hadn't had time to consider their fate. In truth, he'd forgotten they'd gone missing amid his poisonous slumber.

"Who else?" Wendolyne made to go, glancing over her shoulder as she reached the door. "I'll send someone to tend to you."

James offered a bow. "I thank you, Your Grace."

He sighed in relief upon her exit, grateful to have a moment to collect himself, only to be set upon by another one of Wendolyne's minions.

The man had entered in silence, quietly observing James from the doorway. "I'd have thought someone like you would've taken longer to crack." He crossed the room, entering a small closet before returning with a crisp white linen shirt. Piercing blue eyes set beneath a mop of wavy raven hair, appraising the captain with a narrowed gaze. "She must really like you. Perhaps she's growing tired of me, God willing," he added under his breath.

The man continued his efforts, wandering around James and slipping the garment over his arms before stepping in front of him again, where he buttoned the plackets and straightened the collar with efficiency. "The delicacies of this place are not nearly as satisfying as they look. But it seems you may have figured that out."

He moved toward the exit, pausing briefly. James followed his line of sight, landing upon the crystalline bowl once more. "Remember why you're here, or you'll become as lost as the rest of them." Ducking out of the door, the man disappeared without another word, leaving James in confusion.

What just happened?

Chapter Eight

A table large enough for fifty men sat at the center of the dining hall. Boards of assorted cheeses and bread were arranged atop it, too elegant to eat, alongside place settings laid before each chair made with stacks of gold-gilded plates and flatware. The opulence might've once been jarring were it not for the many hours James had already spent in the godforsaken stronghold.

The excess of Wylewoode had, oddly enough, readily become an expectation, with more riches and splendor around every turn. That perplexing development would've been the last thing the captain would've anticipated, given what was known of the shrouded kingdom, but it seemed there was yet much to be learned.

One of the queen's countless minions escorted James to his chair, where Wendolyne and the two oafs who'd delivered him to her the day prior were already waiting. He offered a slight bow before sitting, smiling in response to a hateful stare from the younger brother, who slouched lazily in his seat with a flute of bubbling drink in his hand. Sparkling vapor fizzed from his glass as he drew it to his mouth, downing large gulps of liquid until none was left.

"Why is he here?"

The queen shot a warning glance at her brother. He answered her scowl with a raised brow, scarcely acknowledging her rebuke as he raked his fingers through his hair.

Perhaps her authority was not as esteemed as that of traditional royalty.

"Please excuse Mikhail, Captain." Wendolyne's eyes remained fixed on the young man beside her, though he didn't indicate whether he noticed or cared. "A wolf raised him, but we've accepted his boorishness. It's not his fault, you see. He was young, his mind malleable in the hands of our sister, and the effects of her manipulations are long withstanding."

"I'm not a child, Wendy." Mikhail raised his glass, signaling for more drink. He shifted in his chair, leveling his gaze at the queen in challenge. "I *would* like to know how your guest survived Lillia's attack, and why you thought it wise to let him into our home."

Wendolyne clenched her jaw, doubtless biting back her desire to reprimand the brute, and James didn't blame her, for her brother was nothing shy of insolent.

In blessed distraction, Aeric strode into the room, inclining his head toward Wendy, who merely sighed in response. A broad, gleaming smile spread over his face as he moved past the vast table, and though there were numerous place settings, he didn't bother to seat himself, instead leaning against the doorframe like he'd joined them solely to observe.

Servants entered with trays of mouthwatering duck, roasted vegetables, caramelized fruit and filled pastry rolls. Mercifully, James would not be expected to endure multiple courses with the present company.

As the palace staff plated their dinners, Aeric coughed. Wendolyne and her brothers paid him no attention, but the captain glanced his way – an impeccably dressed man cast aside like some overindulged house pet meant to be seen but not heard. James didn't miss the subtle shake of Aeric's head while a servant portioned his plate with the fruit and pastry.

The aroma was nothing if not utterly consuming, sweet and sinful in its allure. A lustrous sheen dusted all but the vegetables, with each of the tempting delicacies glazed and powdered in finely ground gold, just as the apples left within the captain's chambers.

"You're correct, Mikhail." The queen poked at the food in front of her before turning her attention to James. "Captain Hook is exceptionally adept at his job. I can think of only one other who has survived our cove, and even so, it's been years. Lillia was wise not to challenge you a second time."

"She would've won," said the elder brother, though James hardly registered the words before his thoughts began to fog. He was hungry and tired, but something about this place, this food, seemed *off*.

The sensation reminded him of valerian root and how it had muddled his mind after losing his hand. Then, it kept the captain from descending into darkness. It gave him freedom, quieting his grief and enhancing his triumphs, but it was nothing more than a fabrication of contentment. He hated himself for relishing the escape it offered, choosing instead to endure — and *feel*, even when desolation sought to bury him alive. Feeling was still better.

Feeling was real.

Aeric stifled a yawn, raising a fist to his mouth. "I would've stayed in your chambers had I known the conversation would be so dreadfully dull." He moved to join the servants, all silent and stoic, peeking under the domes covering the array of trays. Plucking a stem of the vegetable from a brass plate, he took a bite. "I do love asparagus, don't you?"

Not a soul present acknowledged Aeric's commentary, though James was reluctantly amused by his nerve and grateful for his boldness. In truth, it didn't matter why Aeric saw fit to help him, so long as he could fill his belly. It was an empty pit.

Wendolyne watched as the captain cut into his steamed greens, and he considered how he might make it through the remainder of their gathering without offending her. He devoured the vegetables, appreciative of the generous quantity. It would have to be enough to tide him over at any rate, till he could flee this forsaken territory or forage something on his own.

"You may have noticed the golden sheen of our surfaces and some of our food." Wendolyne took a sip of her bubbling drink. "It's called sift, and it protects the very existence of this kingdom, concealing Neverwoode from the tedium of Fayble's continental politics."

James chided himself for being so obvious with his hesitation, though the queen seemed relatively unfazed. Still, her assertion got him thinking.

"I mean no insult, but your shores were not difficult to identify. Rumors of a shrouded kingdom have swarmed the continent for decades. Yet, it's unmistakably existent and tangible." The captain's puzzlement was genuine, and Wendolyne's scarlet lips twitched with delight.

"Then you're lost," said Javan, turning to James.

"You mustn't be so brash with our guest, Javan. One doesn't have to be lost to discover our sanctuary of exiles." Wendolyne folded her hands upon the tabletop, seemingly enjoying the opportunity to enlighten her guest. "They need only believe this paradise exists and must yearn for more from this world. Any fool who thinks they know their own mind will never see this veiled dominion, nor will one who's convinced of a loftier purpose for themselves. Fulfillment of that sort is farcical – a lie taught by those who've abandoned the *impossible* dreams of their youth." Wendolyne's eyes held a faraway gleam, matching the haze overtaking the captain's mind.

Beside her, Mikhail licked his thumb, leaving its print on the table where the soft, glittering dust had settled. He drew it to his nostrils and inhaled the rich redolence before swiping it over his tongue. Javan muttered in disgust, low enough that only James must've heard, mirroring his sentiments.

He had to get out.

"Enough of this dismal chat. Did you tell them the news, Wendy, darling?" Aeric sauntered toward the table, seating himself in an empty chair where he kicked up his feet.

The queen's focus turned to her pet, though no tender regard warmed her features. Wendy closed her eyes, rolling her head shoulder to shoulder as if the strain of what she had to share physically pained her. "Aeric made an interesting discovery."

Javan watched her, his demeanor wary, while Mikhail seemed unaffected as he polished off another glass of cider. *How much does this sift inspire the younger's aloof bearing?*

Wendy turned to Mikhail, slamming her fork down on the table, sending all the tableware teetering. "It would seem our sister is alive and well. Tell me, *brothers*, how this is possible." The queen practically spat each syllable, her every word bleeding disdain for the enigmatic creature who'd caused James to question the soundness of his mind.

"Do not toy with us." Javan shook his head, disbelief warring with irritation in his features. Pushing his specs up the bridge of his nose, he issued a haughty sniff. "She was dead before we found her – pale and chilled to her bones. You cannot convince me she lives unless I see her with my own eyes."

Across from him, Mikhail remained silent, his stare glazed and distant, and James idly wondered if he was registering anything that was happening.

Wendolyne stood from her seat, her face flushed with anger. "Do you think I believed the impossible so readily? I *did* see her. She was here, in *my* quarters and *my* court, only yesterday! Tell me. Why would I make this up? Do you think it doesn't grieve me to know one of my own might have betrayed me so severely?"

"You believe either of us capable of such deception and treachery? I didn't hesitate when you ordered Petra hunted for the good of Neverwoode, but I'll not claim I didn't mourn her." Javan's voice was low, but there was no mistaking the rising fury boiling beneath the surface. "You were right about the threat she posed, so we did as you asked. We all saw her. Mikhail wept as he carried her limp, breathless body back to you – the proof of your demand met."

The queen's gaze narrowed on Mikhail. "And you. What have you to say for yourself? Do not think I didn't recognize your love for her. Tell me now that you aided her in her artifice, and you'll be forgiven."

His lower lip trembled at Wendy's words, but his eyes never found hers. A harsh sob escaped from him, and Mikhail buried his head in his hands, gripping fists of dark, tousled hair. "I don't know."

Wendolyne patted his back with what appeared to be perfect indifference, ignoring his torment with an obligatory gesture of consolation. "Don't blame yourself," she crooned, his body quivering under her touch. "You'll not be punished for your waywardness, brother. It will take time to heal your mind from her sordid manipulations." She pivoted, facing the help and snapping her fingers toward a slender figure cloaked in white. "See my brother to his room."

Mikhail didn't argue, wiping the moisture from his cheeks as he lumbered from the room, leaving behind stale silence. He was hardly more than a boy, judging by the youthfulness of his face. So profoundly broken, he was staggering down a path of self-destruction. In him, James saw a more hopeless, numbed version of himself.

"She took it," uttered the queen, her voice just above a whisper, and when nobody responded, she stiffened. "Did you *hear* me? That viper stole our father's watch!"

Aeric smirked to himself before catching James' gaze, offering a wink.

Questions whirled through the captain's consciousness. He thought of the parchment belonging to his father and the significance of the timepiece. It could be a mistake to keep it, but the queen's sister had allegedly risked her life in search of it, making it, perhaps, more valuable than he'd realized. He needed to leave and never return, but without his crew, he was stranded.

Leaving on foot was an option, of course, but it would mean leaving his shipmates and his vessel behind, not to mention a sketchy trek through the ills of the Neverwoode Forest. It seemed he had options, though none were any good.

"Let me help you," he said, surprised at hearing his own voice.

Wendy's gaze fell upon James, her eyes full of curiosity over his offer. A part of him wailed in protest, knowing there was a strong likelihood he was making a mistake, but he refused to forgo a challenge out of uncertainty. Some of the greatest triumphs of his life had originated in times of doubt.

"If I find her and bring her to you, you will help me locate my crew or provide me with a new one," he continued, prepared as he was to up the stakes.

"Interesting," the queen purred, walking her fingers along the tall backs of each chair as she made her way over to where the captain sat. To his great relief, he'd stowed the watch upon his ship before encountering Wendolyne's sister.

So far, so good. At least she hadn't sent for anyone to remove his head or stow him in the dungeon...yet. "What would you have me do?" he pressed. "Is it the watch alone you seek?"

Wendolyne laughed, a cold, bitter sound—ice cracking like thunder. "No, no." Her fingertips trailed down James' arm to his hook. "If you find her, I've no use for her alive. I want her still, lifeless heart."

Aeric whistled through his teeth, and not a moment too soon, for the captain's musings ran dark as he considered the same fate for Wendolyne as he'd contemplated for Sheriff Dane when first he'd received his hook. The sound brought him around, but sift clouded his judgment, devouring his sensibilities with each breath.

"You will do this for me," the queen continued, her black-hearted desire forged by a petulant temper. Her eyes met his, as if to will him into compliance.

"It seems a shame to waste such beauty." Aeric sprawled in his chair, mindlessly playing with a tassel dangling from the table linens and inadvertently rescuing the captain from his rapture with a few witty words.

Wendolyne snapped, turning her furious gaze upon her minion. "I won't hesitate in feeding you to the Lady of the Deep if you dare speak of my sister again. Do you understand?"

A lazy grin lit the man's countenance, too unblemished to be low-born. He sighed contentedly, evidently unimpressed by Wendolyne's fit.

"When I bring her to you, you'll do as you wish. I work for myself and my kingdom alone. No one else," James cut in, unwilling to suffer another minute. The queen was mayhem incarnate, shrill and unreasonable, yet somehow a ruler in her own right, with nobody to rein in her reckless whims. One wrong word would have him executed on the spot.

"*Soon.*" She brushed her knuckles over the sharp line of the captain's jaw before turning from him, her sheer gown flowing behind her as she made for the exit. Nearly every inch of her willowy figure was visible through the fine fabric, with a thin slip underneath, more like a night shift, fitted flawlessly to her gentle curves.

James loosed a breath upon her departure. With no attendant waiting to escort him back to his prison, he was free to return to his vessel.

And while the remaining trio shared some level of twisted camaraderie, James doubted it would serve him well. Though the two remaining men seemed to think the queen mad, neither appeared willing to make any moves to subvert her authority. It was weak...pathetic.

"You'd do well to flee while you still have at least some of your wits." Javan rose, snatching a stalk of broccoli from his uneaten meal. He bit the head before turning on his heel to leave.

Aeric simply scoffed. "An overlord, a bondsman and a pirate. We do make for wicked bedfellows, do we not, Captain Hook?"

* * * *

James made quickly for his ship, his thoughts murky from the substance Wendolyne boasted as a treasure. It wasn't far, but his limbs were still heavy, weighted by whatever had laced her wretched sister's dart.

It was nearly midnight if the captain was to believe what the clocktower claimed, yet the streets were full of people. Restless and watchful, they moved about artfully bricked sidewalks, their faces beaming under flickering lights.

A final tick of the massive clock caused the ground underfoot to shudder as if the continent itself was shifting, and a reverberation not unlike the canons that had blown a hole in the side of *Jolly Roger* echoed through Neverwoode.

Streaks of shining, luminous gold shot through the sky, lighting it up as brightly as the sun. Glittering plumes rained down over the city while people shouted with pleasure, the dust painting their garments and flesh.

Sift.

James covered his face with the neck of his tunic, breaking into a sprint for the cove, passing locals ambling about, staring into the gilded sky with awestruck wonder, breathing in its sickly candied aroma.

Neverwoode, it seemed, was not a promised land for the lost but a dominion of acolytes beholden to an utter fallacy.

Chapter Nine

Petra wondered how it was that she would so often awaken to find that she was irritated with her half-brother Javan. Moving to the other side of the tiny apartment, she ignored her rising anxiety.

There were no windows and only one exit. It was stifling, given her propensity for the freedoms offered by a life lived in the vast open forest of Neverwoode.

"How is it that you so casually go about your days here in Wendy's presence?" Petra paced, forcing her shaking hands to still, though whether they trembled out of anger or panic was up for debate.

"She's sift-washed out of her mind most days," Javan answered. "Mostly, she blamed Mikhail, and I didn't bother to correct her. Even Aeric didn't contradict me."

Petra was confident then that it was anger. "How could you blame Mikhail?"

"I didn't. She did." Javan took another bite of his cheese, seated at the tiny table in the center of the room.

His mild manner was frustrating Petra's sensibilities, much as his callous attitude toward their brother did.

She'd come to in the shanty some moments ago after an unfortunate bout with exhaustion – the result of little energy and no food from the time she'd awakened within the glass coffin. Inwardly, she cursed her weakness, the susceptibility to all the whims and necessities of life.

Ffion had dragged her, somehow navigating the darkened paths of the Neverwoode, to deliver her to her brother in the cursed little hovel. The boy merely observed as she resumed her pacing, his face troubled as he pretended to be preoccupied with his rations. He deserved a better companion than she was.

"This Aeric…" she began again. "He knew where I was. He was there when I awakened. He must've followed you and knows you're involved in covering up my demise. How can you possibly continue your duties at the palace under such dangerous circumstances?"

Javan shrugged, kicking his feet up on the table. "He didn't rat me out. What else am I to do?"

Petra groaned, rapidly reaching the end of her patience. He was so…*indifferent,* and it was driving her to distraction. Would that he might maintain at least some semblance of self-preservation.

Yet, perhaps it was to be expected, given his constant presence within the castle walls. Maintaining any sense of self, of motivation, was a dubious task in a sift-filled environment. It was the best excuse for him that she could offer, at any rate.

"Aeric's nothing more than Wendy's eyes." Javan moved onto a piece of jerky as he continued. "He reveals the kingdom's activity, though it's coming through his own tainted vision. I don't think she fully trusts him, but she doesn't see him as a threat, either. I think she's wrong."

Petra shook her head. "Why him at all? Who is he?"

"He was a gift to her from the Lady of the Deep." Javan raised his eyebrows as he watched his sister for a reaction.

She didn't disappoint. Petra scoffed, meeting Javan's gaze as she waited for him to crack, for his words had to be in jest, but there was no correction. "Come on. So nobody wants to be on the water in the dark, and people can be afraid of the turbulent surf. Isn't that only natural?"

"Is it?" Javan rose to his feet, moving toward Petra. "You can excuse every extraordinary occurrence as natural, but sometimes there's more to the story."

His assertion was preposterous to Petra, but he wasn't backing down, causing some latent part of her mind to wonder if his words were valid. Further complicating her ability to deny his declarations was the matter of her recent emergence from a unified dreamscape that she'd entered through the aid of poison.

Unbelief and truth were not always mutually exclusive.

"The enchantress of the sea is indebted to Wendolyne more than you can imagine," Javan added, his dark eyes earnest. "For our beloved queen has been supplying her with her very own stockpile of sift, extracted from a mine I've not yet managed to track down. Now eat." He shoved a wedge of cheese into her hand before retreating, leaving that startling revelation in his wake.

"*What?* What do you mean a mine?" Petra's mind raced to catch up. "I knew the orchard at the edge of the Altanys coast to be her only supply."

"I'm afraid not. I hope you know what you're doing, sister." Javan sighed, tossing Petra a nervous smile before patting her shoulder.

"Better than you do, says I," Ffion spat, his anger palpable. "She's relied only upon herself for the whole of her life. Goodness knows you aren't much help. She nearly died in her slumber!"

Javan's face filled with anger. "What more was I to do?"

"Well, *I* found a way!" Ffion's outburst caught Petra off guard, his righteous indignation refreshing to her soul, as she'd never had anybody fight on her behalf. In truth, he was every bit as much a brother to her as Javan was.

"I've returned, darling. Oh – " The pirate captain, Lillia, entered the apartment, tossing her cape over a nearby chair before settling next to Javan. "I see she's awakened. Bringing her here was probably unwise."

The woman leaned toward Javan, kissing him in a way that suggested great familiarity. Petra stared unabashedly at the pair, unsure how to make sense of the scene unfolding before her.

"Nowhere here is safe," Ffion said. "You, of all people, should know that."

"Obviously. Why do you think I hide in this poor excuse for a dwelling with my wife?" Javan took Lillia's hand in his, planting a kiss on her knuckles. "Some day, we'll have better."

So.

It didn't quite make sense, but it was enough for Petra. She was overwhelmed – weary on a soul-deep level.

She needed some space.

"If you'll excuse me for a moment... I need some air," Petra said as she made for the door, but not before she managed to swipe the wicked little paring knife Javan had been using for his supper from the table.

Petra exited the apartment to a chorus of blame-throwing and complaints between the trio of Wylewoodean misfits, grateful that none attempted to stop her.

* * * *

It was, perhaps, not the smartest plan of Petra's life, but never would she have a better opportunity.

Sneaking away from Javan and Lillia's love nest proved as simple as running down a flight of stairs into the awaiting woods. Their place was set above a small apothecary and was nothing more than an attic converted into living quarters.

That her brother was not only involved with the pirate captain Lillia but was also married to her was a genuine shock. Knowing that Javan maintained a secret life was off-putting in a way that surprised her, causing a seed of doubt within the back of her mind to grow.

All the more reason to execute the plan at hand.

A part of Petra believed herself mad as she rowed toward the ship called *Jolly Roger*. The waters were tranquil, no more ominous than usual, but the conversation from only moments ago yet rang in her ears.

The Lady of the Deep.

It was too preposterous for words. Still, it made her warier of Aeric. The man was not to be trusted and had to have an agenda all his own. Indeed, she couldn't believe her sister could be so naive.

She reached the main deck with greater ease than her previous journey, silently making her way toward the captain's quarters, though she was hopeful he remained detained within the palace walls. With any luck, she'd leave with her pocket watch, and the scoundrel would never know she'd been there, dashing through his domain like a shadow in her own right.

Cracking the door, Petra began to step through the doorway when she saw him. There, the captain lay on the bed at the center of the tidy cabin. A sliver of moonlight cut across the room, illuminating the planes of his angular face before landing upon the crook at the end of his arm, winking off the silvery curve as the ship swayed with the mild waves.

It was as if the universe were taunting her.

For a moment, she considered turning back, but never again would she have so great an opportunity. Slinking about the room, she quietly searched through drawers and beneath furnishings. There were few hiding places to speak of, as the cabin was nearly as spartan as the apartment from which she'd run.

Petra glanced over her shoulder, eyeing the dozing captain. The pocket watch was innocuous enough on its face, but there was no telling what damage might be done in the wrong hands. In truth, even she didn't understand the full scope of its potential dangers.

Inching toward the brigand, she gritted her teeth, determined to see her mission through. The captain stirred as if he sensed her presence, shifting to his back.

It was now or never, it seemed, and she would not yield.

Petra gripped the handle of the stubby knife, willing herself forward. The man was young – not much older than she – and not nearly as intimidating in slumber. So why was her heart racing a mile a minute?

She crept onto the bed, straddling his narrow hips and praying she wouldn't lose her nerve as she hovered above him. She pressed the tip of her knife into the soft flesh beneath his stubbled chin and took a deep breath. *"Wake up."*

For the second time in as many days, James woke in a panic, only now, his reality felt more like his dreams. The same sun-gold eyes from the night before stared back at him, the woman's face so close they were breathing the same air.

The point of her blade nicked his skin, irritating him more than it hurt. The intensity on her face threw him off. What in the world could he have done to earn such ire?

He flipped, rolling the feral woman to her back as he thrust the knife away from his gullet with his free hand. "You hesitated," he growled. "Doubt could mean your demise."

She scowled, her chest rising and falling so quickly beneath him he was amazed she hadn't yet fainted. He watched her for a moment, oddly enamored by the depth within her gaze. She was a secret, gilded and fierce, her white-blonde hair splayed about her head like a halo spun of starlight.

The woman bucked her hips, twisting as she threw him from on top of her. "You were snoring. At least I don't allow sift to knock me silly."

Her words were baffling, but then again, very little about the strange kingdom of Wylewoode had made sense to James. The last thing he wanted was to seem ignorant. He rose to his feet, reaching for his tunic. "Our run-ins are always a delight. To what do I owe the pleasure?"

"You stole something that belongs to me. Give it back, and you'll never see me again." Challenge filled her features as if she dared him to defy her demands.

"You did the same. Where is my crew?"

Her familiar glare returned. "How am I to know? As you're well aware, I've scarcely been awake these past few days."

A strange sense of understanding passed between them, though neither acknowledged the oddity of that truth. "She said you're to blame," James admitted after a moment. He didn't bother to elaborate upon the *she* of which he spoke, instead folding his arms across his chest, awaiting her response.

The woman sneered. "If you believe her, you're a fool. The queen is nothing more than a skillful liar." She pushed herself to her knees, waving a dismissive hand. "Still, I might have an idea of where they are. But I won't help you unless you help me first. Where is my pocket watch?"

"That was yours?"

"Why did you take it?" she demanded, her desperation becoming more evident with each word.

"I've seen it before." James moved toward his desk, shuffling through a handful of charts before he found it. "Here." He held the parchment out for her appraisal—a complex illustration with strange colors for a chart. She joined him by the desk, examining the uncanny rendering of the timepiece with an eagerness that made him suspicious.

"I recognized it immediately," he continued. "It was easy to snag from your sister, given my life of thieving in Llundyn."

"A strange background, to be sure." A ghost of a smile formed on her face as she held out her hand. "Now, the watch, if you please."

"It's not as simple as all that," James said, ignoring her proximity, for her nearness was rather distracting. "I've hidden it aboard my ship, and your interest in it is reason enough for it to remain such."

The woman huffed, her anger spiking. "You can't – "

A loud crack sounded from behind them, cutting off her words. James turned to find the crocodile Ben in the doorway, tearing up the floorboards of *Jolly Roger* with his mouthful of jagged teeth. His tail whacked the bulkhead as he plowed through the planks, rattling the sconces and knocking a framed map to the floor.

"Hades!" James shouted, moving toward the creature, who showed no signs of slowing his destruction. He watched in helplessness as the small chest he'd kept hidden beneath some false flooring disappeared down Ben's gullet, cursing his damned affinity for the sweets his former bandmate Alan a Dale had sent along for the journey.

He'd kept them there, hidden from his crew, from Smee, alongside the pocket watch.

Hell.

James dragged his hand over his face, suppressing his rising temper. He had to keep his head about him, but *blazes*, it felt like the world was against him.

The woman had fled, leaping to the bed where she clung to one of the four wooden bedposts. "Save yourself!" she shouted, eyeing the captain as though he were insane.

Perhaps she was right. What had possessed him to keep the monster on board? To feed and care for it like some stray dog?

He knew the answer, of course, with the memory of his father bedeviling his every decision.

"Well," James said as Ben slowed in his havoc. "It seems you'll be waiting a bit longer for that watch of yours." He approached the croc, noticing the subtle smile the creature wore. As stupid as it was, he didn't feel threatened, remembering that Smee had mentioned the same grim expression when first he'd met Ben.

"Not a chance," said the nymph. She climbed from her post, setting a tentative foot on the floor before gathering the courage to join James at his side. Wielding her knife in one hand, madness and fury shone in her golden eyes. "You hold him down. I won't hesitate this time."

James laughed, though there was no humor in it. Her audacity was breathtaking. He had to give her that. "We'll wait for nature to take its course, I think. He's done nothing to warrant his death."

"Speak for yourself," she spat, standing rigidly at his side. "What, then? We just sit here and wait for him to take a dump?"

"Not here. We go somewhere safe." He held his arms wide. "I'm crewless and at your mercy. Where can we hole up?"

The woman sighed, seemingly resigned to a bit more time with the captain and his frightening pet. "I might know somewhere. Follow me." She skittered past the beast and his master, leaving the cabin for fresh air and freedom on deck.

James followed, surprisingly unbothered by the croc, who tailed him at his heels. Moving about the deck, he gathered a handful of supplies in his satchel while Ben waited patiently alongside the wary girl. Making his way up the stairs, he reached for the helm, opening a small compartment to retrieve his spyglass.

"Oh, it's you!"

James started, turning to find Bellamy staring down at him from her perch atop one of the lower gaffs. She made her way toward him, climbing nimbly down.

He offered his hand, helping her down onto the deck. "You came back aboard?"

"The crew began to leave, whether compelled by the sirens of the deep or the queer kingdom on the hill, I couldn't say. But either way, I didn't want to stay ashore." Bellamy straightened, stretching alongside a massive yawn. "I heard people come and go, but I didn't bother them, so they left me to my own devices. In truth, I don't know what I was waiting for."

"You'll be safe with us," James said, determined to will his words into truth as he gestured toward the woman. "This is... Who are you exactly?"

"Petra." She anchored her hands on her hips, her stance suggesting annoyance. "And you are?"

"This is Bellamy. And I'm James Much, though your sister seems to prefer Captain Hook."

"Ah. My sister was always lamentably juvenile in her observations." Petra sighed, evidently at a loss over her circumstances. "So we're going to shore with this *thing* at our backs?" She gestured to Ben, who appeared unbothered by her venomous outburst.

James nodded. "Indeed, for I see no other way."

After loading Ben into one of the remaining launch boats, the trio seated themselves into another, having lowered him to the surf below. It was an absurd sight as they rowed to shore, towing the beast behind them like some royal prince in his own special vessel.

Moonlight guided them to shore, but not before illuminating a figure upon the sands. Petra groaned, evidently familiar with the young lad standing stock still in the ebbing tide.

"You have to stop doing this," he called, his voice carried on the light breeze as they came to a crushing halt upon the shore.

"Who's that?" James asked as the boy moved for their beached crafts.

"Only my fiercest protector," Petra uttered.

Chapter Ten

Ben...

The damned crocodile's name was Ben, and Petra had never hated a creature more. It was the captain's fault, she supposed. If he'd fed his pet, perhaps she wouldn't be probing through a mound of excrement.

"Care to help?" Petra blew a strand of errant hair from her face, pieces of the tangled knot she'd bound falling free as she searched Ben's feces. Swallowing priceless family heirlooms didn't sit well with his bowels, as it was the third pile of droppings she'd found in as many hours.

Ffion sat at the base of a nearby tree with an irksome grin while he snacked on a handful of nuts. "You've been managing well enough. I'd hate to get in the way."

The odor permeating their surroundings made Petra's stomach turn. She'd wretched several times already but was nowhere near surrendering to a reptile, even if she had watched it tear a man apart.

He popped another nut into the air, catching it in his mouth. "What does the captain want with you, anyway?"

"He wouldn't permit me to slice his beast open, so here we are."

"I saw him, too," Ffion said, dropping his voice. "I know it was him, there in Otherlande. He was only a shadow, and you were terrified. So scared you..."

Petra remembered, and if the way Ffion's thought trailed was any indication, what he saw had frightened him as well. But she didn't need him to recount her failings or any reminders of her cowardice. It was never for herself she'd feared, anyway...but for her friend and brothers. If the captain had ended her, there'd be no hope for any of them.

She'd never forgive herself for what Wendolyne had done to Mikhail when she went into hiding. For years, her sister spun deceptions, whispering wretched lies about her to their younger siblings. Javan was old enough to see through the queen's stories, but Mikhail was just a boy, torn between deeply rooted affection and a lack of understanding of how far Wendy was willing to go to win his loyalty.

Much like Petra, Mikhail hadn't been easily influenced by sift, but that didn't matter once their sister began heavily dosing him into compliance and dependency. Javan reported Mikhail's washing to Petra as she'd hidden in Wylewoode. It was Wendolyne's cleansing of his dedication to the bastard-born disgrace — or so the queen described it.

Petra's younger brother was drowning in a lambent pool, lost to himself, though Javan readily claimed Mikhail fought it and outwardly detested Wendy. Still, what difference did that make when he was bound to her through utter mania and desperation?

Petra couldn't bear it.

Ffion pushed off the tree behind him. "Not all shadows are bad."

"I know. For I've got a shadow, not my own, that follows me everywhere I go. I suppose it's not so bad if not for his wagging tongue and aversion to dirtying his hands." Petra was always grateful for the unique way the boy could remind her there was still good in a world plagued by debauchery, but to admit it felt dangerous – like acknowledging how much she treasured his friendship would only result in losing it.

Ffion grinned as she rose from her search, her fingers and nails foul with waste. She tried futilely not to let his joy affect her, but it tugged at her defenses, reminding her of the brother she'd unwittingly betrayed in the name of self-preservation.

"You smell like shit."

It was not Ffion who spoke but the captain with his underling, Bellamy, at his heels. Petra turned to challenge his depthless stare, his eyes dark as a moonless night. Amusement flickered in his gaze, and her insides boiled when she beheld her father's watch dangling at the end of his hook. She trembled with fury when his lips tipped into a wily smirk.

"You could have used a stick. Anything, really."

How she somehow missed it was the least of her concerns now that, once again, James possessed her timepiece. Petra seethed. "Give it to me."

The captain cocked his head slightly, with his careful gaze fixed upon her, but something in it was curious...unexpected. He said nothing and made no move to return the heirloom to her. She'd anticipated as much, that he might toy with her, but Petra was in no mood for games.

Petra made for him where he stood mere feet away. She was quick but came up short when he evaded her charge, snatching the watch out of reach. Bellamy reached for the small blade sheathed at her hip, but James held out his hand, a silent order passing between them. His subordinate's posture stiffened in response, flexing her fingers like they craved the authority the steel offered.

"My friends and I reshaped an entire kingdom through thievery. Will you so easily best me?" Petra swiped for him again, and James' smirk grew when he shook off her attempt.

Ffion's steps were quiet as he approached from behind Petra. "Which kingdom?"

"Llundyn," said James, and Petra didn't miss the note of accomplishment in his voice.

"You were one of them, then." Recognition rang in Ffion's speech. "You know the princess and her guardian. She told me about you and all you did for your lady's people."

Intrigue colored James' features. "What princess?"

"The lost heir of Penzelle, Princess Aurora. I met her in the Otherlande." Ffion beamed to speak of her, and Petra couldn't fault him, though she'd never become overly close with the raven-haired scion.

The captain shook his head, pinching the bridge of his nose. "Rory. It seems I've only begun reconciling the connection between consciousness and slumber."

Ffion's expression shifted with pensive consideration. "You'll never sleep quietly again, now that you see one realm is as natural as the next. We all have noses but only notice them once we close one eye or take in our reflections. If we can't trust our minds to show us what's right before our eyes, how can we not question whether there's more than just what we see?"

Adept and clever, Ffion thrived in a world that wanted him to fail. The façade of adolescence he'd assumed while Petra had known him served him well, but more and more, she saw the man he was becoming as he allowed the mask to slip. It pained her as much as it filled her with pride.

James furrowed his brow, slipping the watch into the small pocket of his fitted leather vest, evidently through with small talk. "Show me to my crew, and I'll give it back."

"The word of a pirate is undoubtedly trustworthy." Petra glowered, searching for her pipe as she reached for the pouch at her waist.

It was gone.

James winked. "What choice do you have, love?" He stepped closer to Petra, the earth crunching beneath his boots, where he towered over her. Behind him, the crocodile wended toward them, working in tandem with his master to unnerve her.

Ben's long, leathery tail whipped back and forth across the earth like a dog awaiting praise. Petra didn't dare move, didn't so much as breathe as the captain leaned in so close his nose grazed the curve of her ear.

"Next time you hold a knife to someone's throat, finish the job."

Her hair rustled against a whispering breeze. James indulged in the warmth of her scent like the sun itself somehow formed her, the unbroken sister of an unknown kingdom's queen standing utterly still in front of him. Petra's eyes were fixated on his vest pocket as she wiped her fetid hands with a rag she'd kept tucked in the waist of her leather pants. Before she could move for him again, the captain retreated a step.

"This watch..." James began. "Is it truly worth more than your life?"

"More than yours, mine and all of Neverwoode combined." The woman shifted then, sparing a glance at her companion, who only smirked knowingly at James.

The captain remembered a silhouette of one like him from his dreams – perhaps not quite as tall but of the same manner and air. Maybe the young man was not so far-fetched in his assessment of blurred states of being. He'd made no move against James, at any rate. If Rory saw fit to trust him, he was no enemy to James – and neither was Petra.

For her part, Petra must have arrived at a similar conclusion to divulge what she did. Still, her demeanor suggested anything but camaraderie. "Your crew will not be hard to find, but you'll likely discover them altered. They'll only be useful to you if you help me first."

Lovely.

It was a complication James had already considered. The effects of Queen Wendolyne's compulsion over the dominion would have seized his ship's complement by now if they were anywhere within her territory.

"Seeing only one member of your company remains with you, I assume the rest have been absorbed into my sister's depravity. The reason this shrouded kingdom is ignored is all around you. Surely you feel it." Petra's eyes were ablaze with revulsion, but something more behind the disgust resembled a similar melancholy that afflicted James to his very core.

"The queen explained the phenomenon to me, and while I find it disturbing, I want no piece in your strife." In truth, that was an understatement, as Queen Wendolyne's use of sift was, in a word, vile. The woman before him was right not to back down, but her genuine motives were still unknown.

"You're wrong if you believe this is merely some battle for dominance or a spat between siblings," Petra continued. "Every word out of Wendolyne's mouth drips with deceit."

No part of the captain questioned Petra's declaration, but whatever was brewing between the sisters of Neverwoode would not end well. Entering their quarrel was a surefire way to get stuck. He wanted out of their communal hell before it was too late to avoid being burned.

His mind was made.

"Did you not hold a knife to my throat just last night? And today, you expect me to trust you. If you'll excuse me, I'll be on my way to drag my addled crew home now." With a curt bow, James turned from Petra and Ffion. Wylewoode and its shrouded kingdom were a curse upon the continent, and the sooner he could relay his discoveries to Llundyn, the better for all of Fayble.

"You're a coward and a fool."

The words struck him like an ax to his spine. James pivoted to meet Petra's wild, brilliant stare. He worked in vain to avoid further confrontation, gritting his teeth as if to cage all the valiant reasons he was in the right. He had nothing to prove to her, no reason to convince her of his righteousness.

He failed.

"Was I a coward when I watched as a crooked lawman severed my hand from my body? Did I not do all within my power to prevent my friend's heart from crumbling when she had to choose my fate? And was I a fool when I risked everything to keep the people of Llundyn from starving?"

Petra's gaze shifted to the captain's hook, her delicate features unchanged by his temper, and loath as he was to admit it, James couldn't look away. Her eyes narrowed, finding his once more before Ffion approached them.

"You may convince your king and queen this place exists, but you'll likely not survive the cove again if that's your aim. It's possible to endure Wylewoode on foot, but you'll find it difficult to track the kingdom upon your return when your resolve is firm." Petra's friend didn't waver in his reasoning, and he appeared earnest enough. The pairing seemed unnatural, Ffion's ardor entirely at odds with his counterpart's odious disposition.

The young man's words aligned with those spoken at the palace by Javan, who suggested James was a lost soul to have discovered Neverwoode so easily. If they were correct, departing this tormented region would be a grievous error resulting in an inability to return. If that were the case, there would be no resolution, no counter to the evil being perpetrated by the wicked queen.

"What is it you seek to accomplish?" It hurt nothing to ask, but his curiosity felt like a betrayal of himself, nonetheless, especially after the feral nymph's needling.

Petra glanced toward Ffion, the two of them sharing a nonverbal understanding to which the boy nodded.

"I'm planning to destroy her distribution points," said Petra, her countenance grave. "Sift is a weapon that will change the art of war as we know it. My sister has discovered a new source, the location of which was known by our father and grandfather alone. In the fortnight I was away, she vastly increased the utilization and shaped a violent dependency among her subjects. What once inspired serenity, albeit falsely, now rouses aggression if the need goes unmet. To Wendy, subservience is a victory."

James told himself he should walk away. Neverwoode was not his homeland, nor were these people surrounding him friends. Hell, they were hardly acquaintances, but no matter his inclination to abandon these lands, something kept him rooted to the ground before the wildling.

"And what, then?" James asked, drawing a scoff from Bellamy, who moved nearer to the trio as Ben snapped a fallen branch at their feet. The whole scenario was absurd. He would've laughed with his fellow mariner over the preposterous circumstances if they didn't feel so dire.

To share the tales of his journey with his sovereigns would be a triumph, for Ric and Ella had surely never heard their equal.

He looked toward his shadow – a bewitching woman whose confidence in herself seemingly never wavered.

Lightning flashed through Petra's golden eyes like a star's final encore. "Then we destroy her supply."

Chapter Eleven

They'd formed a quartet of doom.

For longer than she could remember, Petra had struggled to let anybody in, to work in concert with anyone beyond herself. Ffion had changed all that with a spirit of loyalty that had shattered her walls, and somewhere along the way, she'd made peace with it.

But this? This would never do.

She wandered along the roadway with James and his minion at the fore with the captain's beast between them. Ffion walked beside her, his chipper outlook doing nothing for her sullen mood.

And if the company weren't enough to sour her day, the errand they were set upon was sure to do it. There was no way they'd find James' men in any state of mind for leaving, for operating a ship and escaping the clutches of Wylewoode. They'd be lucky if one of them could manage so much as a coherent thought.

Those newly exposed to sift were likely to be useless for many days, given to flights of fancy and attempts at the most foolish of fantasies as they worked to acclimate to the hold of the toxin on their minds and bodies.

The thought of it all made Petra burn with renewed urgency. To relieve her kingdom and the people within it of their dependency upon the golden dust was her heart's greatest desire, and to elevate the realm to a known state within Fayble, even better.

But for that blessed dream to become a reality, her current associates would have to go.

She eyed the crocodile lumbering along before her and sighed, wondering how she'd made such a shambles of her situation. James tossed Ben another crust of bread, and she cringed as the creature snapped, catching the grub between pointy, yellowed teeth.

His breath was foul, and his razor-sharp claws were even worse.

"We'll pinch my watch, then we'll split," Petra hissed, her voice low so only Ffion would hear.

He nodded idly, and she knew she'd soon be too late, for he was already growing attached to their new companions. She'd seen it before in Otherlande, where the boy had readily latched on to the princess and her brute.

They had to act quickly.

"You'll need this," James said, pulling a dark cloak from the satchel at his back. "Your likeness is pinned up all over town. I daresay your resemblance to the queen does you no favors."

"Thank you, no." Petra reached into her hip pouch, retrieving a pointy green cap, and placing it on her crown. "This will do. If you believe it well enough, so will they."

James shook his head, and Petra didn't miss the way his eyes met Bellamy's, a look of disbelief passing swiftly between them. Their silent communication annoyed her deeply, perhaps even more so than his apparent doubt over her words.

It was she who knew the inner workings of Neverwoode and doubtless far better than the recently landed captain. Would that he might find it within himself to trust her. But then again, she had just been conspiring with Ffion to make off with her watch.

James was too wise for his own good.

"Midnight and noon?" The captain pulled her beloved timepiece from his pocket, and it took Petra a minute to understand what he was getting at. "We've only a quarter of an hour before we'll be sift-washed."

"Why not head for higher ground?" asked Bellamy. "Would we not stand a better chance of avoiding a torrent of that blasted dust?"

"I would like to see how it works," James added.

It was just as well. And while Petra didn't believe it would make much difference in the aftermath, it would at least delay their trek into the heart of Wylewoode — a task she'd much rather avoid altogether.

They diverted to a ridge at the edge of the woods that overlooked the kingdom's interior, taking up post upon the precipice. "There's a sift silo to the east, just there. It exits through the roof, blanketing the countryside in poison." Petra indicated a distant tree with an otherworldly shimmer that could only be the result of its unfortunate proximity to the golden dust. "Another sits parallel to it, off to the west."

James shielded his eyes, reaching for his monocular to take a better look, while Bellamy was decidedly less interested in the silos. "Why haven't you destroyed them already?" She cast an accusatory glance Petra's way. "You say you want them gone. What have you been doing all this time?"

"It's not as easy as all that," Ffion said by way of defense, his even tone conveying a maturity that Petra's would not have had if she'd answered first.

"I once went straight for the source." Her mind darkened with the memory — a well-laid plan that had gone sideways. "I set fire to the orchard at the edge of Neverwoode, the very trees that produce Wendolyne's precious sift-filled apples. "I burned a significant portion of the grove and threw the kingdom into chaos. Only then did I fully understand the dire situation of our citizenry. Our intrepid queen poisons the people, all in the name of *peace*." Petra paced, suppressing her rising anxiety. "I was nearly caught, and I've been hiding ever since. She'd love nothing more than to display my heart upon the end of a pike — a warning to the realm, a declaration of her sovereignty."

She turned from Bellamy and Ffion to stand beside the silent captain, facing the rolling hills and woodlands below, forcing her stilted breaths into a more natural rhythm. Recalling her misadventures, all in the name of freedom, was painful. Working against the vast resources of her deceitful sister felt like an endless nightmare with little progress to speak of.

Despite its failings and its less than exemplary populace, Petra loved Wylewoode. She hoped to see it to prosperity — real and true — with a seat at the Fayblean table, no longer shrouded in secrecy and surviving on the fortunes of lawlessness.

An errant tear slipped over her cheek, and she wiped it away, determined to regain her composure.

She refused to give up. Her sister would *not* be victorious.

"You're devastatingly brave," James uttered from beside her, a hint of admiration in his words. He didn't look at her, only backed away with a slight bow as he excused himself, leaving her to her thoughts.

Sift-washing was an experience with which James wished not to become any further familiar. He'd endured it many times now, and while it hadn't worsened, neither had it improved. Ffion and Petra had seen the captain and his boatswain through the golden haze, helping them recover their minds from their lapse into delusion, and he found himself grateful that they'd managed to develop their tolerance to the peculiar dust.

Perhaps the sensations would be more welcome if he didn't understand how false they were. It gave him a newfound sympathy for the people of Wylewoode, at any rate, knowing that they'd lived with it all for so long that they could no longer consider a life without it.

"Is that not your quartermaster Smee?" Bellamy nodded toward the heavyset seaman as he made his way toward the cliffs not far from where they recuperated.

James furrowed his brow, curious as to what may have drawn his second up so high. Further perplexing were his vacant features, causing the captain great alarm as Smee reached the brink, with nothing more than several dozen feet separating the man from the edge of the bluff.

"Whoa there!" James called as he leapt to his feet. He was off and running before his mind could catch up with his body, his head swimming as he raced toward the muddled sailor.

The captain reached for Smee not a moment too late, hooking the man by the collar when he raised his arms as if he wished to take flight. With all the strength James could muster, he pulled, leaning his full weight back toward solid earth, drawing the daft fellow to safety.

Smee staggered, landing with a hefty thud atop James, who cursed under his breath. "What in the blazes were you doing, old man? You'll die!"

"It's my merriest thought," said Smee, rising from his prone position, only to head for the cliff's edge once more. "I've always dreamed of flying like them." He picked up speed, only to drop like a stone before reaching the brink.

It was then that James noted the scarlet feather jutting from his quartermaster's rump. He turned to find Petra tucking her returned blowpipe away in her hip pouch. "This is only the beginning of the turmoil the sift-washed wreak. They don't know their own minds. Or, perhaps they know them all too well." She pressed her lips together, and it was clear she didn't find their circumstances the least bit amusing.

It was a gut punch to acknowledge the reality of her assertions, for he knew he had more than his fair share of darkness lurking within his heart. And if all his men were similarly affected by the damned stuff, there was no use in attempting to restore order to his crew or his ship.

James heaved a resigned breath. "What's to be done about these silos?"

"I've never been on the inside," said Petra. "And I would've burned them as well, but they're made of stone. I didn't see much point in taking a risk like that when it wouldn't ultimately destroy the supply—not while the whole of Wylewoode is on the lookout for me."

"We just need a key." Ffion delivered the words as if they were the most logical conclusion, but that was easier said than done.

The crew fell into silence, each contemplating the best way forward. Nothing about what they wanted to do was straightforward, but James had faced daunting odds before.

"We could… Never mind." Petra shook her head. "It would be next to impossible."

"What is it?" Bellamy demanded, her patience thinning. "We can do nothing until the stupid dust has settled, and to be quite frank, I'm prepared to do whatever it takes to get out of here."

Doubtless, they were of a similar mind, though James would never have been so brusque. He couldn't imagine leading the lives they led here in perpetuity, forging a strange sense of empathy.

"The queen. She jaunts through the center of town each day in the late afternoon after she checks the silos, the better for *her people* to see her majesty." Petra spat the words as though they tasted vile in her mouth. "She's the only one I know who maintains a key to the silos around her neck. If we got our hands on it, we would have to act quickly."

"I'll do it," James said without hesitation. "She believes me to be for her cause, so an audience with her wouldn't be out of the question."

"You are quite the thief." Petra eyed the captain, and though she sounded a bit spiteful, a part of him believed her to be reluctantly impressed. "A word of warning, however," she continued. "Looking as if you belong will go a long way toward your preservation. If she believes you to be thoroughly sift-washed, you just might walk away alive."

Well. If that was all...

They made their way into town, depositing the woozy quartermaster at an inn. Petra's paralytic would wear off before long, but it always took a bit longer after exposure to sift. She wouldn't have minded leaving him where he lay, but the captain had insisted.

At James' behest, Petra wore the dreadful cloak, slinking into town like some shrouded cleric. The man was mighty emphatic, an irritating quality given his lack of understanding of the kingdom's inner workings, but it was easier than arguing.

"She'll likely come from the easternmost roadway after inspecting the silo nearest the cliffs." Ffion donned a similar cloak, though he wore his with far less attitude. Something like excitement rang in his tone. "I've tracked her routine for weeks. She switches it up daily, but always in the same pattern."

Petra suppressed a sense of pride, welling within her without permission. The boy was nothing if not thorough and savvy beyond his years. Doubtless, her level of attachment had far surpassed the boundaries she'd framed.

"We'll climb and watch you from the rooftops." Bellamy didn't wait for agreement, making for one of the nearby merchants, where she scaled the wall to the top.

"Best of luck." Ffion scampered away, following after Bellamy and leaving Petra and James alone.

"I watched you before," Petra uttered, stepping nearer to James. She met his eyes, holding his gaze.

"Wendolyne is shrewd, but her mind is tainted, ever polluted by that vile poison. She's drawn to you. Given your propensity for piracy and the like…" She smiled a little, drawing a wily smirk from the captain. "Take care," she added, touching his forearm.

He offered her a half-bow before backing away, and she ignored the flutter of butterflies swelling in her chest. Doubtless, he was beautiful, but that was where her intrigue ended.

Petra made her way to the opposite side of the road, taking to the structure across from Bellamy and Ffion, perching upon the berm where she watched James from above.

He hadn't wasted any time, quickly making for the imposter queen, happily chatting with some of her foolish subjects. They lapped up her musings, gathered around her as if she were some sort of luminary. In some twisted way, she was — the provider of their livelihoods.

If only they could understand the truth behind her never-ending deceptions.

James approached, adopting a slightly wayward gait as he neared the queen. His playacting was convincing and somewhat unexpected, inspiring a sense of distrust while Petra observed. How was it that she'd come to accept that her fortunes must be tied to this buccaneer?

Watching him work had her decidedly less confident in their alliance, but there was naught to be done. Her options were severely limited. Besides all that, he had volunteered to take on a risk that was not his own. Perhaps she was being too harsh.

Wendolyne smiled as he closed the distance between them, cupping his face when she rose on tiptoe to kiss his cheek. James swayed, his broad shoulders bumping into hers, and with lightning-quick reflexes, he reached for the chain hanging at her neck, cleanly pulling it away in one smooth motion.

As swiftly as he'd nabbed the necklace, it was gone, tucked away in his pocket before he reached for the queen as if to steady her from the calculated collision.

The audacity was jaw-dropping, confirming in Petra's mind that James was nothing more than a scoundrel of the highest order. He remained there, sharing what appeared to be some witty banter along with a few laughs, their genuine enjoyment of one another causing Petra to burn.

The peril he'd put himself through on her behalf was real, and while his commitment to her plan should've had her trusting him unequivocally, she found she couldn't possibly trust him less.

Chapter Twelve

The Undersea was agitated that afternoon, its waters surging toward their small craft. White caps foamed atop choppy waves only a few meters in the distance, with the surf growing more violent by the minute.

As surprised as she was to admit it, Petra was grateful once they'd boarded the *Jolly Roger*. It wasn't safe from Wendolyne or her whims, but few would risk provoking the Lady of the Deep any further. Even now, a soft, haunting melody floated through the salty air around them, so quiet she wondered if her ears deceived her. Stars only knew what lurked beneath the surface, and surely she didn't want to find out.

It was overcast outside—dreary, with tiny rain droplets falling from dark, silvery clouds above. But beyond the haze to the west lay a glowing promise of warmth. Would that the sun might reach them before the mythical sirens of Altanys.

"Don't ever answer them." Bellamy watched Petra, shrewd and severe in her counsel. The captain's quarters where they gathered was cold, but that wasn't what sent a shiver chasing down Petra's spine.

Despite its size and relative prominence, Neverwoode had remained a secret all these years, at least for much of Fayble. How much more might be hidden in plain sight all across the continent if that were so? Could there be places and creatures so dreadful their existences might only be acknowledged through whispers and screams?

"They can be no worse than the monsters ashore," Petra decided, and as she said the words, she knew she was right. "There's a reason my sister scarcely leaves home."

Across the table from Petra, Ffion laughed without humor, rolling his eyes. "Though she is, perhaps, the most wicked of them all."

Beside him, James sniffed in agreement before offering Ben a piece of dried meat with his hook. The reptile swallowed it whole, his teeth gleaming like ivory daggers, and Petra thought with some amusement of the irony in it all, for they traveled with a creature all their own.

The captain turned his attention to Petra, his dark eyes holding her gaze. "How is it your family came to rule such a place?"

She didn't miss the hint of a smile playing on his lips—a subtle implication that she, too, could be a monster—and she didn't hide her answering smirk. He had every right to think her nothing shy of savage after their previous encounters. Yet, even in spite of her behavior, there was an ease to the captain's manner she'd not anticipated, something tranquil and constant she never dared hope existed.

"The shrouded kingdom is a land of exiles," she began, idly twisting her tangled hair into a mussed knot at the nape of her neck, preparing to recount the critical bits of history she'd kept close to her chest. "Forced to survive or succumb to Wylewoode's perils, the punishment was once considered crueler than death, even if some territories now discard thieves and scoundrels like rancid food.

"My grandfather was one of them, banished from Sundsvaile for courting a maiden of noble birth against her father's wishes. A low-born mariner's son, he was cast out and left to the mercy of an unknown land. But the beautiful maiden followed him, and together they formed a community of lost souls.

"The war between good and evil was, at first, wholly imbalanced. These strays were often violent, rowdy, mutinous — a rejected people abandoned to lawlessness. Sift offered peace among the wayward."

James listened intently, his eyes fixed on her as if he could see her hurt and understood she would never yield to her pain. He was right. These people were her family, her home and all she'd ever known, but her heart broke anew each time she remembered she was unwelcome, even among the rejects of Fayble.

"The passage of time meant many things for the growing realm," she continued. "Not only did the golden dust bring contentment but also prosperity. Contentment bred productivity and, with it, staggering wealth. Families were built, partnerships forged and independent businesses sprouted throughout the kingdom. While the land was cursed with individuals deemed ungovernable, my grandparents helped them thrive. In those early days, before their earthly departure, the gilded orchard of Adym Grove was utilized minimally and only as a means of subduing nefarious impulses through the well water. It was enough, though it never should've been used at all."

"Not everyone who sets foot in Neverwoode is an exile or a descendant of one," the captain corrected. Still, there was no condemnation when he spoke, only confusion. "Your brother, Javan, suggested one must be lost to discover this secret refuge."

"A person doesn't need to be lost so much as seeking, whether purpose or standing. It makes no difference," said Ffion, and Petra couldn't help but notice as James' features hollowed. Perhaps he knew the same emptiness that nagged at her.

James rose from his seat, pouring himself a glass of wine from an ornate decanter that he set at the center of the table between them. Ruby-red liquid swirled within the crystal as he reclined in his chair, manipulating his drink in mindful, elegant movements. It was the only reminder Petra needed to know she required his help far more than he did hers. His manner and decorum were effortless — a testament to his station.

Bellamy pushed off the wall behind her, swiping the bottle and taking a deep swig. James merely ignored her, lifting his gaze to Petra. He nodded once, inviting her to continue.

"I loved my father, but above all else, he was selfish and ambitious — broken, after he lost his beloved wife, Queen Hilde." She rarely spoke of him. To do so served only to embitter her further, with his many failings the origin of all Petra sought to end. "It was he who first encouraged the dependency afflicting Neverwoode and who thought to build the sift towers, orchestrating the acquisition of potash from Chamelaute to operate them. I should've set Adym Grove ablaze sooner, but…"

"He was your father." The captain leaned into the table, narrowing the distance between them, his countenance partially shadowed. "There's no shame in loving him." James' voice was rough, and she hated how her pulse quickened at the sound.

Petra studied the strong line of his jaw, illuminated by soft flames and the whiskers shading his imposing detail, wondering over his reserved manner. He didn't speak much, but when he did, she found she was eager to listen. Shaking her head, she cleared her thoughts, grateful when Ffion broke his silence.

"Wendolyne is worse." The boy glanced at Bellamy, clenching his teeth as he watched her. Without warning, he snatched the wine decanter from her hands, placing it back on the table. He pointed a finger her way, nearly jabbing her sternum. "You remind me of her."

Bellamy cocked her head, her lips tipping up at one end. "Maybe I should alert her to your plans. I'd be willing to bet she'd pay handsomely in exchange." She crossed her arms over her chest, smirking at Ffion before her expression grew serious. "I'll warn you once not to point your finger at me again."

"Children, please." James dismissed their discord with a wave of his palm. "Bellamy, you can go if you wish, but leave the wine. Don't be so dull as to think the queen will reward you as you might hope. And if you two are quite finished, I'd like to learn how we'll achieve our goal so we can all go home. Razing the silos to the ground, are we?"

"Uh-uh." Petra glanced at Ffion, who smiled back. "We're going to blow the stores to bits. But we're going to need some supplies."

"Well, then. You're in luck," said James, his obsidian eyes shining with expectation. "I think I know where to find them."

* * * *

Stealing from Lillia was, in a word, stupid. Petra's stomach was in knots as they approached her newly minted sister-in-law's ship. She didn't believe her brother would've married one loyal to Wendolyne, but regardless of the woman's allegiance, it was best not to trifle.

Despite her nerves, Petra held her head high, issuing orders with as much confidence as she could muster. "Demand every bit of potash they have, and don't let your authority waver. It should be simple enough to convince anyone aboard of our purpose, but we mustn't be here when Lillia returns."

Voices could be heard from the upper decks of Lillia's impressive vessel, but Ffion and James had confirmed the beautiful captain to be away. Still, there was no telling as to how long.

The weather cleared as eventide drew near, a fresh, sea-kissed breeze rustling Petra's white-blonde waves. There'd been little to work with on James' ship, but she made do, smoothing out the tangles in her hair with dexterous fingers and lining her eyes with kohl, winging the edges as she'd seen Wendolyne do. By a stroke of luck, he kept a supply of the deep green powder, claiming that his quartermaster required it. The substance allegedly aided *regularity* for his withering bowels, though that was far more information than Petra required.

She felt James' eyes upon her as she preened. The captain didn't conceal his interest as he watched her, though she resisted the urge to meet his confounding gaze. He cleared his throat, bending nearer. "The queen is right to fear you."

His words were a welcome secret, rumbling through her ear. Petra's heart stuttered as the cool steel of his hook brushed the back of her hand, and she cursed the heat in her cheeks.

They were as ready as they could be.

Behind Petra and James, Ffion guided a pair of brindled horses he and the captain had procured, along with a sizable cart—all to haul their spoils into Wylewoode. She knew she'd underestimated them when they returned just over an hour after departing the *Jolly Roger*.

For Bellamy's part, she licked her wounds and kept to herself while James and Ffion were gone, which pleased Petra enough. The girl walked alongside the wagon, her haughty air a blessing in disguise for her role as one of the pretend queen Wendolyne's hirelings.

Petra and the captain boarded the ship as planned, leaving Bellamy and Ffion at the opposite end of the gangway to receive their goods, if all went according to plan.

Once on deck, James propped himself casually against the gunwale, surveying Lillia's crew as if it were his own. The captain polished his hook with a handkerchief he retrieved from his crimson vest while curious sea hands gathered near.

He examined their work like he had all the time in the world. "First thing's first," he said at last, his words authoritative. "You will not disturb your queen, nor will you so much as look upon her while we conduct our inspection. As is routine, we'll confirm this vessel and all its accompaniment meet Her Majesty's expectations. For your part, you are to off-load every drum of potash onboard onto the cart provided."

Only a few of Lillia's company dared mumble complaints, but even so, not a soul refused to comply. James glanced toward Petra with a wicked grin, and she bit back one of her own. She couldn't have done it without him, and he knew it.

"Move!" the captain bellowed, scattering the crew to do his bidding. They didn't hesitate, bustling about the deck and moving below to retrieve everything Petra needed and more—all to destroy not only Wendolyne's stores of sift but her source. They could only hope what they were stealing would be enough to bring her sister's latest discovery in the mine to ruins.

They were already testing fate by being there, and posing as the queen only increased the stakes, but the opportunity would not present itself again. While it was unlikely there was much beyond a stash of potash to commandeer, Petra had to be sure. The crew was nervous about her presence, believing she was Wendy, making it easy enough to wander about the deck.

"Make haste! Your queen will not hesitate to make an example of your unit," James shouted. He'd remained close to Petra since they boarded, but for the moment, his back was turned.

Petra made her move, taking to the captain's quarters where she pushed the door open. Tidy and surprisingly grand, the room was more luxurious than any officer's chambers she knew. Atop Lillia's desk was a well-worn map, its corners weighted with raw crystals. Petra examined the tattered parchment, taking in the marked water inlets and smudges of ink blemishing the page. But it was what lay beside the map that caught Petra's attention. An odd combination of metal and wood, the object was unlike anything she'd ever seen.

The door slammed suddenly a few paces away where a tall man stood, his eyes darting between Petra and the foreign item in front of her. He lunged for it, but she took hold of its slender silver barrel before he managed to grab it. Her adversary struggled against her tenuous grip when something clicked. Petra shoved into him with her shoulder, using the force of her weight, attempting at once to wrest control.

Without warning, the man kicked her, the heel of his boot connecting with her stomach and knocking the wind from her as she staggered backward, falling to the floor. A deafening crack like ear-splitting thunder reverberated through the air, causing her ears to ring, accompanied by a flash of brilliant orange light as glass shattered across the ground beside her.

Potash. She hadn't known it to be used this way but recognized the residual odor and burst of flames that escaped from the short steel pipe. Petra attempted to scramble to her feet when the man grabbed a fist full of her hair, aiding her effort with a painful tug. He jammed the end of the barrel into the soft flesh underneath her jaw, pinning her to a wall at her back.

"If I'm wrong, I've made a grievous error." His face was so near to hers that they almost touched, saliva sputtering from the stranger's mouth as he spoke. "But if I'm not, the true queen will doubtless give me anything I desire in exchange for you. You might've convinced me, too, had you not arrived with my former captain. Tell me, beautiful, what do you wish to do with all that explosive material?"

Steel burned against Petra's skin, pushed so firmly to her jaw that a bruise would already be forming. His forearm pressed into her windpipe, helping to hold her in place, but she still had some use of her arms, despite the crushing pressure of his body against hers. Petra gasped for air, and the man sneered.

"*Please*," she croaked as he narrowed the distance between them, breathing in the scent of her hair. Without hesitation, she raised her arm and brought it between them with every ounce of force she could manage, thrusting her elbow into his chin.

Her attacker's head snapped back from the impact, and Petra dove out of his reach as he attempted to recover, dropping the strange weapon in front of her. The man was on her again the second she crawled for it, only this time he successfully trapped her under his weight.

Petra clawed at his exposed flesh with her nails, straining against his heavy body. Her foe hissed with frustration, slamming her shoulders to the floor so hard that something crunched. She had to find a way to free herself but rapidly lost the strength to fight with her weakened muscles.

With no leverage or purchase to overcome his advantage, Petra drove her thumb into the inner corner of his eye. She didn't relent, even as he howled in agony, moving a hand to her throat. He tightened his fingers around her neck, and the world began to spin, but still, she plunged her thumb deeper into the socket.

In her blurred periphery, a door panel splintered, then another.

The man's grip faltered, and he roared as James came into view, heaving his leaden form off Petra. Relief flooded her, her vision clearing when the airflow to her lungs was restored. Just past her fingertips, she stretched for the unfamiliar weapon, tucking it into the waist of her trousers.

Petra spared a glance at her adversary, writhing in a heap across the small room with a knife buried in his back. He was nearly double her weight, maybe more, his features twisted in pain.

Good.

James offered Petra his hand, and she took it, thankful to have him there to stabilize her trembling form. Every part of her ached, but the captain anchored her, his strong arm steadying her throbbing shoulders.

"Whatever that sound was, it will have been heard miles from here. We need to leave *now*." James moved toward the broken door, its hinges protesting when it rocked pathetically from side to side. "We have most of the potash." He urged her forward, but she paused, crouching to yank the blade from her adversary's back, tossing it to James.

"One more thing." Petra retreated to Lillia's desk, remembering a small box that sat next to the now-concealed weapon at her hip. She took it without searching through its contents, following after the captain, who shook his head and scoffed.

"You make one hell of a pirate."

Chapter Thirteen

James was nothing shy of uneasy. Looking up toward the top of the silo, he couldn't help but feel that they'd bitten off more than they could chew. The peak of the repository was much higher than he'd realized and the base broader. To blow it to pieces seemed like a severe lapse of judgment.

What were they thinking?

"*This. This* is what you want to demolish?" James folded his arms, preparing himself for the ensuing battle of wills. Petra didn't seem one to bend — more likely to abandon their motley crew than the mission at hand.

"It's a bit of a risk, I'll give you that." Petra examined the base of the stone façade, moving for the singular door located at its rear. "But I'm convinced it's the best option. It's not so unlike dropping a beehive — the initial burst of bees is frightening and dangerous, but before long, the chaos clears, and you're left with restored order."

Bellamy scoffed. "Is that all? You're blasting them with the very thing that makes them crazy. Imagine what the people will be like."

Her skepticism was well-founded, but James didn't want to rock the boat any further. The two women had butted heads more than once, each certain of their righteousness. He knew better than to get involved in that.

Petra shrugged. "It's temporary. And, unless I'm missing something, the citizenry should be even more oblivious than before with the excess released by the explosion."

"Until they aren't," Ffion said quietly, his words carried away on the mild breeze.

"Consequences I'm willing to deal with." Petra waved a flippant hand. She was nothing if not sure of her course, and they were all along for the ride, come what may.

The truth of the matter was, James didn't *have* another option. For as long as his sailors were preoccupied in their sift-fueled revelry, there would be no leaving Wylewoode.

"Well, then, it's now or never, I suppose." James pulled the stolen key from his pocket, relieved that its acquisition had gone so smoothly. The woman, Wendolyne, was plainly out of her right mind, easily deceived, despite her canny ability to mislead others.

James slipped the key into the lock, turning it easily to gain access, and the interior was entirely unexpected. Thin light from a nearby sconce was the only illumination within the confined space—surprisingly tight, given the massive exterior of the silo. To their left, a narrow staircase led to another door, while a strange network of interlocking gears lay before them, with one not unlike a paddle wheel adjoining a series of pipes ran up from the cogs and into the wall.

"What is this place?" Ffion glanced around the tiny room in awe, his eyes shining with curiosity.

"Nothing good comes of it, and that's all I really care about," Bellamy replied, cracking her fingers. "Now, how's about we get to work? It won't be long before our efforts are rendered pointless."

James checked the pocket watch. It was true, already after nine p.m.

"We've got it," she added, shooing James and Petra on their way. "The other storehouse is miles from here. We'll be lucky to pull off this scheme of yours before the midnight eruption."

Petra ignored the dig, instead casting a meaningful look toward Ffion, who nodded his assent. Whatever silent conversation had passed between them seemed satisfactory enough as Petra disappeared, making for the horse they'd stolen earlier.

Bellamy pulled James aside, her countenance grave. "Make sure you're well clear of the silo when you light the fuse. If you're too close, you'll never leave this place because you'll be dead." She backed away, offering a tight smile before heading for the work awaiting her within.

Blazes. If that was all...

James climbed atop one of their two pilfered steeds, realizing for the first time how awkward their ride would be as they had to leave one behind. He didn't know this woman, not really, yet their close quarters were unavoidable. Seating himself before Petra, he thought to make polite conversation. But all pretense was lost when she wrapped her arms around him.

He'd gone to great lengths to avoid physical contact since the loss of his hand. It was stupid, unnecessary, but somehow he felt undeserving. With a piece of himself severed, he'd lost more than dexterity. His self-assurance had filtered away, replaced by a mere shadow of its original design. He'd learned to cope and could readily fake it, yet some part of him had simply gone dark.

Damn.

It was going to be a long ride.

Petra tried not to breathe. Seated behind the pirate captain, she did her best to ignore his presence—the taut muscles of his back, his pleasing scent, all distractions.

But the worst part was that she *liked* it.

She didn't feel like a nuisance with him, nor did she fear for her safety. Quite the opposite was true, in fact, and that was something to which she was unaccustomed. The whole of her life had been spent protecting herself, if not from others' opinions, then from their intent to harm. She didn't work well with others, and James seemed to be one of the few exceptions to her hard and fast rule of going it alone.

Still, none of that mattered—not when there was such urgent work to be done.

"I feel like an idiot," said James, his deep voice reverberating through her as she clung tightly to his rigid frame. "This community eagerly makes use of the explosive powder that Llundyn knew nothing of until a few short months ago. I do wonder what else we're missing."

"Wonder not," she replied. "I believe it's better not to know."

He chuckled, bringing a shy smile to her face. She'd dreaded the ride to the westernmost silo in vain.

"What is that there in the distance?" James indicated a dark figure on the horizon with the curve of his hook. The scene before her roused a peculiar memory — one in which she was running from the very person she now held fast.

Yet as they drew nearer, she recognized the silhouette as Javan, walking away from the silo for which they were headed. What he was doing out that way was anybody's guess, though Petra had no doubt he was on an errand from her demanding sister.

As they closed the distance, she got her answer in the form of a key laced around his neck.

Though as she willed herself to believe better of him, Petra's throat tightened. "What are you doing out here?"

"Our new supply of potash arrived from Chamelaute, and I was securing the stores for another week of sift-washing. It's a delicate process, but I'm guessing you already know that." Javan's expression was neutral, even as his words struck a nerve.

Petra smothered her rising temper. She knew her brother walked a fine line, testing the upper limits of each of his sisters' patience as he attempted to appease them both. She fought her surging sense of betrayal, knowing in the depths of her soul that Javan wanted to be free — the kind of independence that could only be obtained in a siftless world.

She *wanted* to trust him.

"Wendolyne knows you aren't remotely under her influence. How does she trust you with such things?" She nodded toward the key upon his chest while James endured silently before her.

"What about you? Let's not pretend I don't know why you're here." Javan wandered closer, observing the cunning pair. "And with him, of all people. Do you so readily unite with a man who's made a deal with the she-devil? He's playing both sides!"

"Not so unlike you, dear brother," Petra grumbled, issuing a long-suffering sigh. "Look. I'm only doing what needs to be done. Undue risk is part of the deal."

James glanced over his shoulder with a fiendish grin, and Petra ignored the scuttling beat of her heart. Javan, too, seemed to relax, shaking his head with an incredulous laugh.

"Be careful, then. I'll put Wendolyne off your trail for as long as I can. And you," he added, looking toward James, "mind my sister. If anything happens to her, consider yourself done for. I'll hunt you down."

"Noted." James dismounted, offering a halfhearted salute to Javan as he casually led the horse toward the silo.

Petra shrugged, amused by her brother's machismo. It was unnecessary, yet somehow made her feel appreciated. "Protect yourself," she called as she rode by. "You won't want to be nearby when we settle into our work."

He eyed the gunnysack strapped to the horse with a suspicious mien, a hint of a smirk on his face. "Doubtless. Please, don't be reckless."

No promises. Petra wasn't sure what she was getting herself into or if their plan of attack had any merit, though it was better than doing nothing. It couldn't be that dire if they remained clear of the fallout.

Javan disappeared into the tree line, leaving James and Petra to do their worst. The captain pulled the key, allowing them access to the vast storehouse. Again, they entered the space, taking in the strange network of gears and pipes. It wasn't a flawless system, but it seemed pretty close.

The intricate mechanism marched onward, aligned in time with the passage of each minute and hour, with the dainty measure of potash making its way ever nearer to the funnel leading into the fire. The charge generated by their fusion was enough to send the awaiting sift sky-high, blanketing the kingdom in controlled chaos.

It was an impressive feat of engineering that had to be disabled.

Petra studied the room while James went for the sack of talc. While she waited, she decided to have a look at what was behind the other door, just up the short flight of stairs, but nothing could've prepared her for what awaited her.

Light from the main room flooded into the tiny space, illuminating a solid powder supply, contained behind a glass plate window. Doubtless, it went to the roof, with the observance deck upon which she stood only about a quarter of the height of the whole silo.

For some inexplicable reason, she hadn't imagined the entire silo to be stocked to the gills, but it seemed she was wrong. "Up here," she called to James. "We'll fill this inner room with the potash."

The pair worked in silence, lining the base with the explosive material while adding extra portions in the small observance chamber. The fuse was another trick, made of woven fibers and thin wire, split into long fingers that reached in varying directions toward the carefully dispersed potash — a brainchild of the tinkering Bellamy that she'd produced in very little time throughout the day unbeknownst to the rest of the crew.

James and Petra exited the silo, closing the door and making their way into the tree line, where they awaited the appointed time. Propped against a nearby trunk, they sat together, quietly contemplating the potential fallout.

"Here," said James after a time, reaching into his pocket. He withdrew a small paper bag, offering it to Petra. "Try some — Sweets made by a friend of mine in Llundyn. Turns out Alan is quite the baker."

Petra furrowed her brow, amused by the offer as well as the casual conversation. "It must be nice," she said. "Having friends, I mean."

"What do you mean? You've Ffion, and —"

"And that's about it." She pursed her lips, mulling the state of her affairs. "I've never had friends, never had confidants — not the way that some people seem to, anyway. I've always kind of been on my own, for better or for worse, though Ffion and I have managed to take care of one another."

It was a bit unexpected, this rather personal conversation. Petra didn't open up to people, with a life too precarious to foster close relations with anybody. And yet...

James cocked his head, glancing at the lost soul beside him. "You shouldn't have been left alone."

It was a simple sentiment that struck to her core. Somehow he made her feel seen and important within the same breath.

He smiled a little, pulling the watch from his other pocket and flipping the lid up to observe the time. "Well. Shall we? It's nearly midnight."

She nodded, and they covered their faces with thick, fleecy masks, hoping the coverings would preserve them from the worst of the sift-washing. It was the best they could do in such short order, each ignoring the nagging sense of trepidation deep inside. What they were about to do was an unknown. Had they used enough potash? Too much?

How far would the blast extend? Petra hoped they wouldn't be in danger, given how far out they were, but it was impossible to know for sure.

The captain rose to his feet, creeping through the woods toward the fuse they'd lain some hundred paces away, only to return a few moments later. "Get low and plug your ears."

They tucked themselves close to the tree trunk, crouching side by side. Petra cupped her hands over her ears, whispering a hushed prayer while James wrapped a protective arm across her back. The last thing she noticed was lambent moonlight glinting off the polished steel of his hooked hand.

Chapter Fourteen

It was Wendolyne's nightly routine, standing overlooking the streets of her kingdom from a balcony connecting to the great hall. One day had bled into the next since she'd received news that her sister remained alive, and sleep became a luxury for the queen, her mind restless, despite her efforts.

She worried she was like her father, slowly losing her ability to escape the burdens of governance. For years before his death, Wendy had observed his responsibilities surging as tranquility deserted him, unaffected by every remedy at his fingertips.

Perhaps no one was meant to possess both power and peace at once.

Neverwoode was always awake at this hour, prepared to receive its nightly cleanse. The clock tower would strike midnight soon, sending sift like rain over the land.

Wendolyne watched the clock hands from where she stood in her nightshift and gossamer house coat.

Feathers lined the edges of her robe, caressing her skin, softly stirred by a light summer breeze.

She'd never known until she held it that the face of her father's pocket watch matched the large clock exactly. But Petra knew, and each second marked by the tower was a reminder of her sister's beating heart.

Tick tock. On and on, it went like a pulsing taunt echoing through her soul. Morning, noon, and night, the metronome persisted whether she was near the tower or not, and no amount of sift could halt it.

Wendolyne hated this spot as much as she hated her father. He'd given Petra the watch in her stead, even as he knew her sister wanted nothing more than to dismantle everything he'd built. She hated that he was a coward, betraying his vision for this place and all the ways it would change the whole of Fayble for the better.

The fates must have agreed when they saw him to an early grave.

Indeed, they must've understood Wendolyne was destined to bring forth the future her late father was too weak to demand. She'd forged alliances with unlikely allies, from the Undersea to Chamelaute, though they were yet tenuous. In time they would stabilize and pay dividends her father never would've dreamed. Her sister was merely an unfortunate diversion…while she lasted.

Underfoot, the balcony began to quake, and Wendy fixed her gaze upon the clocktower as midnight struck. It provided the largest of the five bursts over Neverwoode, the combustion of which required exponentially more potash to operate than its partner units. The blast never ceased to fill her with awe as the sky shimmered like stars above, illuminating her realm. It was pure, glorious magic…but something was off.

In the distance, a great plume of sift shone brighter and higher than usual. The system was not infallible by any means, and potash was a finicky aid in its distribution. Doubtless, her people would be grateful for the overabundance, but the flaw would need correcting. She would speak to her tinkerer, Marin, the man responsible for so many of the fine inventions that kept her rule orderly.

The sound of metal grinding against itself resounded from the estate's border wall, where Wendolyne's brothers were both granted entry. Javan covered his face with the neck of his tunic as he walked next to Mikhail, who strode toward the palace with irksome impassivity.

More often than not, even under sift's pull, the queen's youngest brother was not to be trusted. It pained her to know he was as fragile as their father, unable to grasp all they could achieve if only they believed. She would never forgive Petra for influencing them as she had, nor could she excuse them for so easily falling prey to her charms.

Javan, at least, recognized the importance of meeting Neverwoode's potential. Assertive and arrogant though he was, he knew his place when it mattered. Yet, if he thought Wendolyne ignorant of his devotion to a particular seafarer, he severely underestimated her sources. Fortunately for him, the queen was benevolent enough to overlook his infatuation with the pirate captain, Lillia.

Let him love a woman beneath his station. What difference did it make to her?

With his tunic still shielding his nose and mouth, Javan entered the throne room. Wendy's brother was never one to appreciate the pleasures sift inspired, but he didn't condemn her use of it, either. The spare was blissfully neutral in most things apart from Neverwoode's shaky relations with the Undersea.

Wendy acknowledged Javan with a sigh. "I take it, by your dramatics, that the northern silo has malfunctioned."

Offering a clipped bow, he shook his head, brows knit with concern. "All was well for inspection, but a discharge of that size will have depleted the north quarter's supply until we can remedy the issue."

Indeed, it was worse than she thought. Javan, however, maintained his calm, quelling the queen's growing distress. "As you know, potash is temperamental, but your people will not suffer for it. They'll be positively delighted by your generosity. I'll evaluate the damage come morning and devise a plan for Your Majesty's review."

Wendolyne considered her brother's assessment and agreed. She swept past him with a wave of dismissal, taking a seat upon her throne. "Off with you, then. I expect a full report tomorrow."

* * * *

The queen startled awake as Aeric shuffled through the great hall, his countenance disheveled and bleary-eyed. Inky curls hung over her new henchman's brow, his bare skin exposed from the waist revealing the staggering excellence of his build. It was evident then why the masters of Altanys considered him a gift befitting Wendolyne.

From outside, a man shouted, insisting on an audience with her. Aeric mumbled curses as he stepped barefoot onto the open overlook. "You dare cry out to your sovereign at this hour? Begone, and let us sleep, or I'll remove your tongue!"

The sky was still blanketed in the darkness of night as Neverwoode yet slept, but Wendy knew her slumber would not come quickly after such a stir. She rose from her throne to see who might be so bold as to rouse her before sunrise. "Bring him to me."

Aeric's narrow gaze met hers for an instant, his vexation plain.

"*Now.*"

He was a looking glass, reflecting the intricacies of the dominion to Wendy, but never once did he pretend to care whether she flourished or faltered. The queen felt nothing for him apart from a carnal draw, thus justifying his insolence a while longer.

Aeric returned with the foreigner in tow, handsome apart from the sickly pallor of his face and deeply bruised eye, the vessels of which were broken, spilling into one another. His waist was wrapped with a strip of linen, crimson-stained toward his back.

Wendolyne's robe flowed behind her as she strode toward the wounded man, unconcerned by how much of her lithe figure could be seen underneath. "You're bleeding on my floor. Tell me what you want before I make you lap it up for creating such a disturbance."

"Your Majesty, forgive my intrusion." Beads of sweat dotted the foreigner's forehead. Wincing, he dipped into a bow. "I'm Crispin, a low-born gypsy's son. I want nothing from you and seek only to inform you of the treachery afoot." Crispin swayed, staggering forward a step to prevent himself from falling.

"Who did...*this*, and why?" Wendolyne nodded toward his hunched form, bloodied and injured as it was.

The man hissed as he attempted to straighten his posture before her. "You did, or so she claimed. A woman with your hair and eyes like the sun alongside a man – a sea captain with a hook for a hand."

Inside Wendolyne's head, she heard it again, each second of every hour throbbing against her skull. She would hear it until she held Petra's cold, dead heart. And James – Captain Hook, as she had called him – had much to answer for. He'd vowed to find the wretch, and apparently so he had. But only time would tell what he intended to do with her.

"I – " Crispin shuddered with pain, and the queen wondered how her sister had so brutally marred his face. "I was under the captain's employ on the journey to Altanys. He abandoned me, casting me out into the Undersea. Your commander, the tigress, Lillia, granted me shelter on the *Gloriana*. Together with two others, the fair-haired woman claiming to be queen and the captain convinced her complement they were under inspection and stole away with a vast supply of potash. I was the only one to challenge them, and when I did, they attacked me."

Wendolyne searched for the key she wore daily around her neck, only to find it gone, just like her father's timepiece. She'd not noticed its absence when she dressed for bed.

Her interaction with James had been diverting, ideal for a thief to lift something valuable from an unsuspecting party. Not once, but *twice*, she realized. Wendolyne had met the enigmatic captain the day her watch went missing, their exchange intimate and distracting just as it was mere hours earlier when she'd happened upon him.

At the time, she'd considered it serendipitous to find James wandering the kingdom, but it would seem Petra had already sunk her claws into him.

Would she take everything? The captain would be vulnerable to her sister's whims after his exposure to sift, leaving Wendolyne undecided over how to discipline his indiscretion. After all, he was a pirate, as evidenced by his aptitude for slipping away with her most precious treasures.

"Did they indicate what they might do with the potash?" While Petra's audacity galled Wendy, she assessed the events with startling poise, like calm before a storm.

"Observers say they went north."

Aeric bristled as the man, Crispin, gripped his shoulder, steadying himself. Her sister's escapades were of no grave concern if all he said were true. To have fled north meant Petra tampered with the northernmost silo, likely with James' help, using Wendolyne's key to get inside. Even if the damage was beyond simple repair, Javan was right. The kingdom would be under an excess for several days with a blast like that, giving the queen sufficient time to recover.

As for the potash, it was of no consequence, for Wendy's cache was more likely to expire alongside the continent than it was to be discovered.

Petra's efforts were commendable, but at the end of the day, they amounted to nothing more than mere inconvenience.

Wendolyne glided toward the two men in her company, cupping Crispin's cheek. "You've done well to bring this to my attention." She examined the strength of his jaw and hazel eyes – anything but ordinary. What her sister had done to the one eye was a shame, for the gypsy man would've made for an exciting diversion. Perhaps she'd save him for later and give him time to mend. Maybe then they might have some fun.

"Send for a healer. Once he's tended to, clean this up," she snapped at Aeric, whose gaze was disinterested. He followed her line of sight to the scarlet-spattered white marble upon which Crispin stood, his face draining of color.

"When you've finished, intercept the sevensome miners and redirect their delivery to the clocktower."

Aeric took a steadying breath, closing his eyes as he inhaled deeply. "Consider it done."

The foreigner inclined his head toward Wendolyne, his gratitude evident, even through his suffering. Indeed, all leaders were met with trials, but tenderness and charity afforded loyalty. It set rulers apart and won the admiration of kingdoms.

"Thank you, my queen." Crispin knelt on shaking knees, a fist resting over his chest.

This. This was the deference Wendolyne expected but lacked from her brothers and her gift from the Deep. The same was equally true among her beholden dominion. They were devout, at least, while sift's influence flowed through their veins, and that was better than nothing.

For a moment, the queen considered how her sister's subversion might, in fact, be a blessing. Unable to keep the smile from her face, Wendolyne returned to her throne. Petra may've succeeded, razing Wendolyne's stores to the ground, but such maneuvers would spark desperation throughout Neverwoode, and the community would hate her for it.

Indeed, she could not fathom the volume of sift at Wendy's disposal. The kingdom would doubtless seek Wendolyne's favor, and she would answer them in the only language that mattered to a community plummeting into withdrawals.

Abundance.

Beyond the balconette outside, the clocktower thrummed in time with Aeric's steps as he retreated into the palace, with Crispin lurching close at his back.

So...let Petra think she'd won.

Tick tock.

It was a countdown to her last breath.

Chapter Fifteen

It had been a long night, but not nearly as trying as James expected. Their plan had gone off without a hitch, with each of the duos dismantling the storehouses in spectacular fashion, blasting the sift into the starlit night, where it fell like snow upon the citizenry.

Their escapades hadn't been without cost, for the captain's ears still rang from the explosion, his mind struggling to catch up with reality as he worked through his memories before they'd lit the sky on fire.

They'd done their best to safeguard themselves from the effects of the poison dust, but some exposure was an inevitability. Yet one recollection remained true through all the haze and doubt fostered by the damned sift.

Somehow, despite their less than cordial introduction, he'd managed to work with the forsaken daughter of Neverwoode.

Her dedication to her cause was beyond reproach, methodically moving through each obstacle and awing him with her quick thinking. Though she'd effectively been abandoned, her resilience had shone in her leadership, in her preparation.

He was duly impressed.

They set about their work at the fourth silo, having parted ways with Ffion and Bellamy once again after they'd opened up the third for its hour of reckoning. They were set to blow the repositories in unison, but that would require some quick effort from Petra and James if they wanted to be on time.

Everything about the previous night's escapades had taken much longer than James had hoped, requiring some time to recover his senses following the detonation.

He'd lain in the dirt on his back, disoriented and confused, only to find his partner in crime had crawled to his side, stroking his face with light fingertips as she murmured...*something*. Petra's words had been lost to the woods around them, with his ears having become utterly useless.

The memory felt like a dream, almost as if it had never occurred at all.

Maybe it hadn't.

"We make quite the team, you and me," said James, all random musings aside. "I don't believe there's anything you couldn't accomplish if you've set your mind to it, and I'm honored to be a party to it."

Petra hid her smile, shaking her head. "I hate to acknowledge I could never do it without you, but soon, I'll have no choice."

That brought him up short. Before long, he'd be on his way back to Llundyn with a treasure trove of information. The thought of it stung, for he was inexplicably drawn to the kingdom and endlessly intrigued by the girl.

Besides all that, he couldn't justify his departure before adequately eliminating the threat sift posed, for as long as it was wielded as a weapon, Llundyn was at risk. James turned to find her sun-gold eyes trained upon him as though she were reading his mind. Something between them had thawed. He wouldn't go so far as to call it trust, but whatever it was seemed a good start.

"You don't need me," he said by way of dismissal. She was imminently capable, and he, in many ways, nothing more than a nuisance as he attempted to make sense of her world there in Neverwoode. He unlocked the only door, tucking the key away beneath his linen shirt, before moving for their stolen horse to unload the potash tied to his back.

"Listen," Petra hissed. "Someone's coming."

They darted from the scene, sending their steed into the brush and diving into some nearby cover. The unfortunate circumstances at the other repositories had kept them off their feet for far too long, leading to the remainder of their work being done near sunrise rather than under cover of darkness.

The forest was awakening all around them. They'd waited too long, though there hadn't been much choice involved in the matter. Buried beneath the pokey brambles and bright green leaves and berries of the underbrush, they observed the storehouse from afar, waiting in silence.

It was several minutes before anybody materialized, their manic whistling preceding them to the silo. Into the clearing marched a crew of seven, what looked to be a gaggle of boys. Varying in stature, they appeared to be of minor age, perhaps thirteen or fourteen years.

They'd traveled with a sift-laden cart, the powder heaped in a glittering gold mound in the high-sided barrow. Each young man carried a satchel full of tools — pickaxes and shovels, ropes and pails. So much of what they did seemed of a single mind as each of them moved through the motions without a word, the soft trill of their chipper tune varying along with their duties.

The sight might've been impressive if it weren't also a bit creepy.

Before long, they set about unloading their precious cargo, loading their quarry into sizable pails. One of the more intrepid fellows set off, scaling the wall of the silo with ease, trailing a length of rope behind him as he climbed.

"I left the door open," Petra breathed, casting a sidelong glance at James. "There was no time."

He gripped her hand, giving it a squeeze. "They don't seem to notice."

Indeed, they were so busy about their work that nothing seemed to divert their focus. The one at the top of the silo wrangled a pulley system into place, feeding the rope he'd trailed around the wheel and back down to the boys below.

The rig served as a delivery system, with each pail attached to the line and hauled to the precipice, where the lad somehow managed to maneuver bucket after bucket into the hatch within the roof. The entire operation was running along smoothly, with the seven youngsters making quick work of the sift.

James had wondered after their first encounter with the inner workings of the silo how the supply was managed, how it was distributed. He didn't want to make too much of the ingenuity involved in the process, but it was altogether fascinating. The queen of Neverwoode ran a tight ship, complete with an eager workforce.

But then again, it didn't hurt that all the participants were unnaturally obliged.

"You are too efficient," came a voice from the woods. Aeric emerged from the receding shadows, stepping into the early morning sunlight. "I commend you and would sing your praises to Her Royal Highness, but we all know how she is."

"Wonderful," called one.

"A fair beauty...or so I've heard," said another.

Aeric sighed, pinching the bridge of his nose as he moved closer to the fray, and if James hadn't thought the chaps were out of their minds before, there was no question of it now. Aeric, on the other hand, was a mystery. The captain hadn't forgotten his subtle directives at the hellish supper in the palace. In truth, the queen's right-hand man seemed as if he despised her.

"Why are you here?" asked the shortest of the seven. "We're nearly finished."

Aeric wandered toward the entryway, pausing at the slightly opened door. He glanced over his shoulders, his eyes narrowed as he appraised the woods beyond. Petra's breath caught, while James resisted the urge to sink lower into the bracken.

A faint smile crossed the henchman's lips. "I was sent to check on the silos. Some have been vandalized, and there is much concern regarding our ability to continue nurturing the citizenry."

"Damn," Petra uttered, the word less than a whisper. Her frustration was understandable, but it was hardly the time for dissension.

"A shame," one of the young men murmured, shaking his head. "Who would want to deprive the kingdom of our peace?"

"Quite so." Aeric moved from the door, making no mention of it and leaving it ajar. "Now, if you'll head to the clock tower in town, that's where the remainder of your efforts are to be spent. I know you aren't finished," he added, waving away their emerging protests. "Just go and get it done. I'm headed back."

He spared the brush another glance before setting off in the opposite direction, mumbling something about the poor lost lads as he sauntered away. The remaining boys merely shrugged, packing it in as they were advised to do, with the one at the top of the silo gliding down the taut rope as several others bore his weight on the other end.

After gathering their tools, they loaded up their satchels and tidied their surroundings before whistling their way away. The only remnant of their presence left behind was a handful of footprints leading to the trail that spanned the woods.

James reached for Petra, helping her to her feet as they emerged from the thicket. They kept quiet for a few moments more, treading lightly through the clearing surrounding the storehouse. The interruption had been unexpected, especially so early in the morning, but it was as good of a reminder as any to remain vigilant.

"That was perhaps one of the single oddest things I've witnessed since I arrived," said James.

"Then you haven't been here long." Petra eyed the door warily. "I do wonder…"

"It was strange," James agreed, picking up her thought where she had left off. He reached for the handle, swinging the door aside as he stepped into the small space. "Aeric left it open – didn't even question why it was."

He examined the room, searching for a reason. Something wasn't right, either with the silo or the man. James hadn't yet decided. Still, nothing within the little room seemed out of place, at least not given what he remembered from the previous night. Winding gears and copper pipes awaited their duty, with the clockwork potash slowly ticking its way toward the flames beneath the funnel.

"Let's make quick work. We won't have much time before the other silo goes up in smoke." Petra set about laying the fusing down around the perimeter of the stone walls, and James didn't miss the way her hands were shaking – something he'd noticed before.

She was surprisingly high-strung, though he supposed with good reason. Even so, it troubled him on her behalf, knowing she'd been going it alone for a long time. Of course, she had Ffion, but that only recently. There was no real family connection to speak of, with her relationship with her sister and half-brothers tenuous at best.

A life lived in the badlands of the Wylewoode Forest seemed a harsh sentence for one with such noble ambitions. James ached at the thought of her loneliness, fighting for justice on her own in a never-ending game of cat and mouse.

It was no way for one so lovely and pure to live.

James cleared his throat, moved to action as he realized he'd been standing idly by for several moments, his thoughts lost to the feral beauty before him. He had to get a grip.

"I'll go find the horse," he muttered, backing away with a half-bow. Silently, he cursed himself over the idiotic move, for she was no royal and likely thought him daft. Yet somewhere in the back of his mind, she was every bit the queen her sister was and far, far more.

He made for the trees, following a trail of broken branches and trampled weeds. It wasn't but a few dozen yards before he came across the creature munching on a bushel of berries. The potash remained fixed to his back, and James was grateful it hadn't fallen away as they'd left it half-tied when they heard the seven lost lads arrive.

James took the reins, leading the horse toward the silo when his world was rocked. From a distance, a massive explosion sent glittering gold dust like a geyser into the sky, visible even above the treetops where the captain remained rapt. Seeing the aftermath in daylight was a sight to behold, but even worse, it meant they were too late.

He picked up speed, barreling toward his own silo, only to pull up short. Petra was no longer alone, stood before her brother Mikhail, who appeared to be out of sorts.

His face was a mess, flushed and tear-streaked, and his massive frame trembled as he pulled a length of rope from the pouch at his back, even as he seemed to be at war with himself. "Why would you let me find you? This isn't what I wanted."

"You aren't her minion," Petra reasoned. She stepped nearer to him, looking him in the face. "You don't have to do this."

"I do. And what you're doing right here, right now, is reason enough." He indicated the fuse running from the entry of the storehouse as evidence, his mouth a firm line of frustration. His resolve was wavering, or so it seemed, as he shifted uncomfortably from foot to foot.

"This isn't right, Mikhail, and I think somewhere deep down you know that." She was fearless in the face of an unknown threat, her brother too far removed from reality to be trusted. Squaring her shoulders, she persisted. "Join me. Please have faith. I'm doing this for you."

The muscles in his jaw ticked as he clenched his teeth, evidently weighing his options or perhaps his loyalties. It was a heartbreaking scene to witness and doubtless worse for the participants. James couldn't imagine their helplessness in that moment, torn between family and duty.

Mikhail's features hardened, his mind made as he scooped his sister into his arms, making for his steed. Petra fought every step of the way, kicking and bucking in his arms.

"Wait!" James ran from the trees, heedless of any fallout. "Take me instead. The queen will be wholly satisfied if it's me you bring."

Mikhail paused mid-step, nearly dropping his sister in his surprise. "*You*. Why would she want you?"

"Let Petra go," James continued, slowly prowling toward the queen's punchy emissary. "I'm enough, I assure you. In truth, she may be more pleased that you've shown up with me."

That last part was enough to make him feel sick, but he cared not a whit about himself. If he could save Petra the grief of being dragged to Wendolyne, it was worth every annoyance.

He approached Mikhail as though he were a frightened hare, determined to keep him from fleeing with his woodland prize. To his great relief, Mikhail relented, gesturing James forward.

Making his way toward Petra, he retrieved the timepiece and parchment from his pocket in one quick motion, holding it before himself against his chest to shield the objects from Mikhail.

"You're a descendant of these Neverwoodes, a daughter of Pan," James uttered, his lips brushing her ear as he thrust the two items into her hands. "Don't allow these hardships to distract you from your honorable mission. Surely a goddess of the woods can defeat a cavalier queen. *At time's end…*"

Petra's eyes flashed to his as he pulled away, shock evident in her features. "You can't do this, James. *Please.*"

He lingered for a moment, his gaze locked with hers. There was so much he wished to know — an unexpected attraction, an unexplored kinship, an unusual riddle. Would he ever see her again?

Now that she had everything she needed from him, he didn't think so. "I've a much better chance of surviving your sister than you do," he said, offering himself to Mikhail with outstretched arms.

If only he believed it.

Chapter Sixteen

Thanks to James and his selflessness, Petra was safe and possessed everything she needed to complete her mission. She couldn't comprehend why he'd done it. They hardly knew each other, but something ran deeper. He'd been a mere shadow when first she'd seen him and had been terrified, believing the captain's menacing silhouette some sort of reaper bound to Otherlande.

She couldn't have been more wrong.

Even there, he was unshakable, like somehow he knew Petra needed an ally.

Only the rhythmic gait of her steed's hooves against the gravel underfoot could be heard. She was grateful for the horse's docile bearing, but the solitude was deafening as Petra recalled Mikhail's words.

Javan had revealed how their brother continued to fight the effects sift wrought on his senses, but to see the struggle in his pleading stare was crushing, like the truths his heart cherished weren't altogether buried.

There was yet hope that their warm, carefree younger brother would return, but Petra would never stop blaming herself for what became of him.

She wondered if her father was not much different from Mikhail in his youth, before sift distorted his thinking. He was a kind man, though rarely accessible to his family.

Petra's memories of him were few, but among the most treasured was the night he passed his father's pocket watch down to her. It was the last thing she'd expected as a child born from infidelity. Only when Petra awakened to find it missing did she know that her father's ramblings were not just sift-addled musings and that Wendolyne wanted it badly enough to have her hunted and killed.

The timepiece was heavier than she remembered, crafted of solid gold with a flawless, heart-shaped ruby at its center, but beauty and precious metal or stones were not what made it extraordinary. Petra was told that only someone pure of heart was meant to possess it.

James should never have returned the timepiece to her if that were true, as he'd proven far more selfless and patient than she was, grieving her all the more over his sacrifice.

All Petra dreamed of achieving was within her grasp now that she'd obtained the pocket watch and James' crumpled parchment. While she never explained its significance to the captain, the document shed new light on fragmented details she'd gathered regarding Wendolyne's new mine.

Their father and grandfather had hinted at its existence, and while Petra prayed no one ever discovered such a sight, Wendy had managed to seize control of it. It seemed Petra's concerns over the missing watch were well-founded after all. It was why she hadn't let James out of her sight when she learned he had taken it.

Likewise, the parchment his father stole during his time in Neverwoode was a map. Though it appeared to chart the stars, Petra had come to realize the image of her father's watch depicted upon it was a compass, with the artistry of his timepiece an exact duplicate of the clocktower and that of the guide represented upon James' chart.

They were all connected, one leading to another, but none of that mattered until the captain was freed.

Ffion would not be far off after realizing Petra and the captain had failed to ignite their potash. She kept to the main road, still vacant during the early morning hour—a narrow, well-trodden path connecting small hamlets of Neverwoode—but the journey was disturbingly quiet without the captain to keep her company. His presence was settling, and she craved the calm James breathed into her spirit.

The stillness of the surrounding woods was unnerving, a harbinger of impending chaos. Once she and Ffion found one another, they'd form a plan to release the captain, come what may.

"She'll be angry if we're not there soon," said a young, boyish voice drifting toward Petra from around the bend. Tugging at her mount's reins, she carefully steered into the trees, patting the horse's mane in praise of his cooperation.

"It's your pig-headed beast's fault. He's as lazy as Almos," another boy answered tersely.

The miners from the silo soon came into view, their carts still loaded with mountainous heaps of sift.

Indeed, Petra had never seen so much at once. She dismounted and dropped to the ground without a sound, observing while the boys struggled to coerce one of their mules into motion.

Petra crawled nearer, creeping along the ground to distance herself from her mount, should one of them spot him through the towering pines.

Another of the seven, barely more than a child, glanced toward Petra. Surely he couldn't have seen her there, camouflaged among the undergrowth, but the knowing light in his eyes suggested otherwise. Wariness colored his youthful countenance. "They're back."

One of the others wiped his nose with his tunic sleeve, sniffling as he followed the small lad's line of sight to where Petra lay hidden. His eyes went wide. "I thought there was something, but I didn't—" He scrunched his nose, shaking his head before he sneezed. Once, then twice, and a third time before he was finished, earning him an elbow to the ribs from one of the older miners.

"They're not coming back, Hatsch. They told us they would never return. Now help me get this stupid creature on his feet." It was the tallest of the seven who spoke—the same one who'd snapped at the first boy Petra heard. Hatsch obeyed, turning his back to the woods, though he couldn't help looking over his shoulder.

She realized three were missing, panic rippling through her core as she shifted to find another less than a meter from her. He'd unmistakably spotted her but said not a word. He was wiry—looked around thirteen years or so—and refused to meet her gaze. Behind him stood one more, broader, maybe fifteen or sixteen. He approached, extending a hand to help Petra rise.

"I knew it." He was cautious, eyes searching hers. "I'm Lason, and this is my younger brother, Gailen. Don't mind him. He's always nervous around pixies, even halflings like yourself."

Petra ignored Lason's outstretched hand and the inanity of his assertion, brushing the needles and dirt from her aching body. The miner watched her wince as she touched her ribs, not yet fully recovered from the battering she'd received the evening prior aboard Lillia's ship.

"I have a root blend in my satchel that might help." Lason raised a brow, indicating her tender midsection.

She shook her head, eager to be anywhere else. "I'm fine. I'll be on my —"

"Whoa, there!" His shout rang through the thicket, and Petra made ready to flee when Ffion emerged out of the bracken with Ben meandering at his back.

Ffion made no effort to greet the two miners standing near her as he quickly looked her over. Ben was at ease close behind him, gradually wending between the arbitrary foursome. Apart from the scaled monster at his heels, he was alone, leaving Petra wondering if Ffion and Bellamy had faced off at last, for neither offered any pretense of amicability toward the other.

She wouldn't blame him.

He was not like these boys. At least, not anymore. He was no boy but a young man closer to Mikhail's age in appearance and manner. Petra had known it in her heart but never dwelled on how he'd convinced Neverwoode to see him. Doubtless, it protected him, but without the illusory mask, seeing him reminded her of the strange way dreams distort likenesses without diminishing the familiarity of one's essence.

Did he even recognize the difference?

"These hewers work for the queen. We mustn't keep them from their work." Ffion feigned exasperation, nodding for her to join him as though she'd gone astray.

Beyond them, the others watched from the road, while the tall one grew more impatient by the second. "If we sacrifice Nesh's ass to their pet, might it draw our carriage to the tower instead?"

"*You're* the ass! Shut up and pull it yourself!" Lason bellowed over his shoulder, quickly returning his focus to Petra. "Cole's just afraid of Queen Wendolyne, but you could help if you're willing. I hate to ask it of you, but even crossbreeds can sway all kinds of creatures." The boy gestured to Ben as though it was the only explanation needed.

At least the miners were friendly enough. Many believed in pixies throughout Neverwoode, just as the sift-washed accepted sirens among other monsters as true. To Petra, however, those were horrors best left undiscovered and undisturbed if, by some chance, the addled were right.

Still, it was certainly new to be mistaken for one.

The youths' occupation alone suggested a profound influence afoot—far more so than any recent silo blasts if they sourced and transported sift for a living. To employ these innocents was despicable, even for Wendy.

"Very well then." Petra inclined her head toward Lason and the shy one he'd introduced as his brother. "What would you have me do?"

Ffion watched on, mild amusement etched across his angular face as she attempted to mimic the behavior of a being she wasn't sure existed. But if pretending she was part pixie would satisfy them, she'd do it to rid herself of the spellbound boys. Each second spent pacifying these children meant more risk for James, who would arrive at the palace with Mikhail in short order.

"Talk to our beast. He only moves if we permit him frequent rests...*long* rests. But Nesh is not wrong that the queen will lose patience." Lason was already moving for the narrow roadway, urging Petra to follow. "I'll share a vial of my root blend with you, free of charge for your benevolence, crossbreed."

"You're fortunate she shows compassion for those in need, unlike many of her kind." With Ffion's flippant mention of the pixies, all that were gathered recoiled, a strange reaction when they purportedly revered them.

Petra shook their peculiar reaction off, moving before the obstinate creature. She placed her palms on either side of its long face, unable to suppress her smile. He leaned into her touch, and she felt the same affinity for the mangy beast she did for all the wildlife that kept her from descending into irreparable despair following her father's death.

"We all must do what is required of us, for the queen is unforgiving." Petra stroked the animal's coarse fur, murmuring sweetly in his ear. His ears fluttered, and he nuzzled her neck. Sometimes a gentle touch was enchanting in itself. He stamped his hooves in place, puffs of sift-tainted air shooting from his nostrils.

"Wake up, Almos. It's time to go." Cole swatted at his workmate, unseen inside the cart. "Out with you!"

Almos grumbled, heaved from the cart by two of his brethren, his boots skidding atop the gravel road as he righted himself. He stretched and yawned, waving off the other six with a scowl when he noticed Petra.

Stumbling backward, he gaped. "I thought they were all gone. Does this mean they've returned?" He shook his head, covering his mouth with the palm of his hand. "No. No, she's too tall, isn't she? But I daresay even more bewitching than they are."

"For your kindness." Lason ignored Almos' musings, lifting the strap of his satchel over his head before letting the time-worn bag fall to his side. He raised its flap, rifling through the contents as they clinked inside. He extended a small glass container to Petra. "For your trouble."

"Thank you, but please save it. I'd be much obliged if you could spare a cloak, though."

Without hesitation, Hatsch presented Petra with a tattered garment, frayed at the edges, and precisely what she'd wanted. Confusion shone on Ffion's face as she accepted it, partnered with an unspoken promise to pepper her with questions later.

In some ways, he was becoming like a stranger to her. His sinewy stature and confident bearing were all she knew he'd one day be. She just hadn't expected it so quickly. And his ironic humor hadn't changed, nor had the glint within his cunning eyes.

Still, somehow it felt like the beginnings of an inevitable end, as she considered why he may have abandoned the mindfully curated façade or if he could even help it. He'd always insisted that purpose was a leading factor in an individual's susceptibility to sift. Perhaps as he evolved, pursuing what he regarded as right and honorable, his ability to exploit the substance ebbed.

Regardless of the reason, Petra's apprehension surrounding all they had to accomplish soared. But she refused to endanger James further by getting herself caught before she could reach him. Wrapping herself in Hatsch's weathered mantle, she indicated the road ahead with a sweeping gesture. "Best of luck to you all."

* * * *

They traveled on foot at a brisk pace, with Ffion leading their remaining horse and Ben moving fluidly over the pebbled earth close by. He'd wandered off for a time, only to return with blood-stained incisors – a stark reminder that he was no pet but a wildling at heart.

The ground they'd covered might have been satisfactory if not for Petra's increasing distress over the captain. The seven shadows trailing after Petra and Ffion made it worse, their zeal so very reminiscent of who Ffion had been to her when her life was only beginning to fall to pieces.

"I hardly knew it was you back there." Petra spoke in a hushed tone meant for Ffion's hearing alone. "And what of Bellamy?" They'd had no opportunity to talk since he'd come for her but discussing anything openly in the present company seemed risky at best.

"We saw James with Mikhail on our way to find you when your silo never blew. Bellamy insisted upon going after him, and she didn't believe we'd want to help. But I wasn't willing to follow until I knew you were all right." Ffion fixed his gaze on the road ahead without acknowledging her initial question.

It didn't matter. She was a fool to wish he'd never grow up.

"You walk really fast." The smallest of the youths was by far the most talkative, seemingly speaking every thought that entered his mind. Petra wanted to be irritated by the interruption, but it was a strange relief to hear him prattle on about clouds, his favorite foods and what he would name a dog if ever he was lucky enough to have one. It was all so delightfully mundane.

They'd reached the edge of town, the seven having kept stride with Petra and Ffion, despite their efforts to shake them. She smiled, watching the youngest boy walk a few steps then run as many more to try to keep up. "Feel free to go your own way," she said at last, one final push toward shedding their tagalongs.

"But, we've only just found you! You're the only one left, since the others flew off weeks ago." He stumbled along, tripping over his boots, the toes worn through to his socks. He wiped the sweat from his brow, leaving a smudge of dirt in its wake.

Petra slowed to a casual gait, moving as one with the boys, keeping her hair tucked inside the hood of her cloak. Ffion didn't leave her side, though he looked more like a guard than a ninth member of their band.

She should stay with them and follow them on their journey back to Wendolyne's mine, for doubtless, her sister would have bound them to secrecy. And if not for James, she would have. He'd be angry that she'd not run for her life when she had the chance, but how could she possibly leave him behind?

In only a matter of days, the captain had become someone she depended upon – even when every bit of her wanted to hate him. She worked in vain to forget the sharp cut of his jaw, his dark eyes. He watched her as if she were more than her family's shame.

He was beautiful. *Captivating.*

The seven boys grew restless as they approached the clock tower, striking up a haunting melody that filled the streets. Try as she might, Petra couldn't help but be absorbed, the words reeling her in line by line.

They'll soon take flight into the night,
And follow the stars upon the heights.
When shadows and light will guide your sight,
Guide your sight,
Guide your sight,
Just under the second one to the right.

The song was not one she knew, but she'd never forget it. Neither would she forget the children who sang it, each so young with lives full of possibility. Their innocence resonated wholly, cutting soul deep when she realized how much of their youth was being tainted by the very thing they'd traveled to deliver.

It was the same for Mikhail.

Petra would sacrifice anything to see Wendolyne answer for it.

But first she would unleash her shadow.

Chapter Seventeen

The queen's duplicity was obvious, evident in the miserable bearing of her youngest sibling. When James first met Mikhail, he was repulsed by his fixation upon the mind-altering dust, but as he watched the young man, he realized he'd likely never had much choice.

The captain didn't speak on the trip back to the palace. They'd stopped once mid-way when Mikhail could carry on no longer. He'd left James under guard with a handful of men, only to wretch repeatedly on the side of the road, with none as heavily influenced as he was.

Upon his arrival, the captain thought the spare's irreverence evidence of his age, seeking independence through defiance. But now, James wondered if he wasn't merely fighting for his life, for his memories with every breath and word of dissent.

The center of Neverwoode was bustling with activity as they approached the palace stables. Mikhail had been so careless with James' confinement that he questioned if it wasn't intentional – an atonement of sorts, for Petra's sake.

His forearms were half-heartedly bound, one easy maneuver from escape, but he didn't attempt to slip his ties. To break loose now would mean a quick capture, leaving him to navigate the unknown streets under pursuit. He'd simply have to bide his time until the moment turned in his favor.

Mikhail escorted him through the tasteless estate, and James actively noted the various turns and corridors along the way until they came to a halt at the end of a hall he knew. He'd awakened in these very chambers following his first encounter with Petra, and it seemed he'd again be a prisoner, captive in a gaudy hell of velvet and gold.

There would be a way out, for he'd not resign to any fate dictated by Wendolyne, even if it meant convincing her strange pet Aeric to leave the door cracked. A sort like that would not be above a bribe if the prize were tempting enough.

He shuddered at the thought of a like punishment, somehow becoming the queen's mirror, as he'd heard Aeric called. The captain doubted she'd ever trust him to himself about the dominion as Aeric was, though he hadn't yet come to understand their relationship. Still, would that it never come to that.

Mikhail opened the heavy knotted oak door and shoved James inside without a word. The anguish in his eyes inspired ever-growing sympathy in James, despite his decidedly inconvenient circumstances.

"She loves you very much." The captain hadn't meant to speak until the words fell from his mouth, but it felt like something the young man needed. Mikhail clenched his jaw, flaring his nostrils as he made to close

James within the room. "Everything she has done is for you." James wedged his shoulder between the door and its frame, but Mikhail hardly seemed to care, his features a grim mask of despondency.

"That's what *she* tells me every day." The youngest's manner was anything but apathetic – a broken, searching soul, unable to sort through the fallacies wrought by Wendolyne's narcissism alongside her deceitful tongue.

"We both know I don't mean your fanciful queen." James couldn't hide his vitriol. To speak of her and her damnable manipulations of an entire people made him seethe.

Mikhail understood the captain's meaning, meeting his gaze. "Have you ever been so drawn to something, toward its light and vitality, that you're forced to remind yourself such goodness doesn't exist?" His eyes were full of sadness so profound James had to force himself not to look away. Someone so wounded needed to know they were not a burden.

Indeed, Petra's brother was a physical representation of the turmoil that greeted the captain each morning after years of loss and survival. Each day, he decided to defeat the pervasive chaos of his ruinous thoughts. It was an active choice, day by day, to overcome the toxicity of his mind, but seeing Mikhail proved just how far he'd come. For James, there were more blessings to count than heartaches.

"If you have to persuade yourself something doesn't exist, could that not prove it does? Corruption only triumphs if we accept it as common."

The young man swallowed hard, mulling James' question as he cast a nervous glance around the hideous room behind him. The captain retreated several paces into his chambers, leaving Mikhail in the entryway. After a moment, he followed James in, snatching an apple from a bowl on a table just to the right of the doorway.

"Feeling nothing at all is much easier." Mikhail sank his teeth into the fruit, wiping his mouth with his sleeve before tossing what remained back into the bowl. Without another word, he turned on his heel and left, closing the door behind him.

A final click of the lock left James utterly alone. He shrugged off the pointless bindings, his hook slipping free with minimal effort. This time, the captain searched everywhere for a means of escape – behind, under, and above every piece of furniture and draping, to no avail. The windows were left open as if to say they knew he would return, but only enough for warm summer air to sneak through the cracks. It was still, mercifully, before noon. Soon, he would be facing off with another dose of sift from the clocktower, even if he did manage to avoid consuming the powder through other means.

He knew the windows wouldn't close but tried, pulling and cursing against a soldered metal frame. They'd not been open when James found himself locked away after Petra's poisoned dart. Doubtless, Wendolyne had been expecting him, upgrading his quarters to better suit herself. Whatever the queen envisioned for him, she'd anticipated he would not do willingly.

While the captain's tolerance against sift seemed higher than most, heavy exposure would be difficult to master. If Ffion's theories about ambition or will were correct, he could endure it. But even so, there were many in the palace and at the queen's disposal every bit as determined to accomplish their purpose as he was. It seemed Wendolyne surrounded herself with men and women who were only mildly influenced, if at all. That was, apart from her youngest brother.

She kept her enemies close.

Outside James' room, he heard footsteps growing louder upon approach. Silently, he moved toward the door, and with the wall at his back, the captain waited, listening as the steps ceased at his doorway. With a subtle *click* from the lock, the iron handle turned.

Tired hinges groaned as the door opened, and James didn't hesitate, throwing his arm around the man's neck and jerking him toward himself. The man lost his footing, knees buckling underneath him as he gagged from the pressure of James' grip. He fumbled, clawing at the captain's arm and hook. Something fell to the ground, cracking at their feet when James realized who he had in his grasp and loosed his grip.

Javan shoved the captain off, coughing as he massaged his throat. "You'll wish you'd finished the job once we leave this room. Is she all right?" He knelt, examining his broken spectacles before tucking the splintered glass and frame into his chest pocket.

"She is." James eyed the open door over his shoulder with no one to stop him from running.

"Do what you must, but the distraction you've created for Wendy may well be what keeps Petra alive. If you're willing, for her sake, I'll help you when the time is right. For now, the queen demands to speak with you privately."

The captain was uncertain about the next in line for Neverwoode's throne, but Javan's offer was sound enough. And even if Javan refused to follow through, a meeting with Wendolyne could prove helpful, if only to occupy her a while longer. "Very well."

Javan glanced at the rope Mikhail had pointlessly used to secure his prisoner and scoffed. "No bindings, then. She'll prefer it – a demonstration of compliance – but if you dare to harm her, I'll see that you answer accordingly."

It was the second time in as many days that Javan had made that same threat, once for each of his sisters. James surveyed the heir, finding the whole situation baffling.

"She's still my sister," said Javan, his countenance troubled. "I love them both."

It wasn't hard to fathom, and James didn't envy his conflict. It was evident Javan wouldn't aid the queen's heinous designs beyond what was unavoidable, but he wondered how much it would compromise his morality.

Javan guided James through the meticulously curated hallways leading to Wendolyne's personal wing of the grand estate. Her vast branch of the palace was even more opulent than the rest, reeking of her beloved poison apples. How anyone could stomach the overwhelming scent was beyond comprehension.

"Mind your wits," Javan muttered as they moved about the queen's parlor.

James didn't reply, taking in the intricacies of his surroundings, scarcely believing his eyes when he spied the debased seaman he'd left bloodied and wailing aboard the *Gloriana* a night prior. Shrugging out of Javan's tenuous grip on his arm, the captain rushed Crispin, pinning him to a nearby shelf. His eye was red with burst vessels from his encounter with Petra, but still not nearly enough to make amends.

"How many times must I offer you to death before she finally devours your worthless soul?" James slammed his former crewmember's skull into the wood behind him, rattling various trinkets and volumes. Golden dust rose like vapor from the impact as the captain pierced his hook through the collar of Crispin's fresh tunic. "I should have finished you for laying hands on her."

James buried his fist in the bastard's midsection. Crispin groaned, sputtering intelligible curses when his knuckles collided with the captain's cheekbone. James shook off the blow, clenching his adversary's tunic and throwing him to the ground.

Crispin smiled – an ugly, evil grimace that begged for further retribution. "Did she tell you she liked it?"

Trapping Crispin under his weight, James punched the sneer from his smug face, hurling his fist into the traitorous sailor's jaw repeatedly as Crispin attempted to throw him off. The captain was blind with fury, hitting him again and again, even as the man's previous wound swelled and bled over the finely woven rug beneath them.

"Enough!" Javan took James by the shoulders as Wendolyne came into view. His vision blurred with rage, but even in the captain's haze, he saw her lips curl in amusement.

"You truly are a pirate, aren't you, Captain Hook? After our last conversation when you refused to deliver my sister's corpse to me, I wondered if it was all just a ruse, but here you are, staining my belongings with your sailor's blood." Wendy regarded Crispin's limp form, sighing with disinterest as she examined him. "Not once, but twice, this man has made a mess of my floors. Secure James in my chambers, Javan. We have much to sort through."

Javan heaved the captain to his feet, and together, they followed the queen to her lavish room. Javan did as he was told, casting a sidelong glance of apology as he wound a length of cord, not unlike the one his younger brother used. He tied James' wrist to Wendolyne's bedpost, lowering his head in deference to his sister with a short bow before exiting the room to allow her a private audience as ordered.

"Tell me, James. How did you enjoy raiding my ship and demolishing my silos? You must be tired after everything that viper put you up to." The captain kept quiet as the queen slipped behind a screen crafted of frosted glass panels. "I would have thought you would know better than to get mixed up with her. Unless you did it to retrieve what she took from me. Do you have it, then? My watch?" Her lithe silhouette swayed, removing the sheer robe that hung loosely over her scantily covered body, and she tossed it over one of the divider panels. When James didn't answer, she persisted. "Perhaps you were confused about our agreement."

"I'm not confused, unlike your citizenry." The captain averted his gaze, disgusted by the queen's flagrant display. "What would become of this kingdom if you weren't polluting their minds?"

Wendolyne laughed. "What difference does it make? They're exiled, forgotten people and fortunate recipients of my generosity. Do not act like they're victims when their needs are met in plenty."

"They're pawns in your vain pursuits. You're no more than an egotist masquerading as a monarch."

From the corner of James' vision, he saw her peek around the screen between them.

"Perhaps you should reconsider your words, Captain."

The queen prowled toward James, stepping out from behind her divider in a gauzy nude-colored gown fitted to her slender frame with thin crystal straps, almost as if she'd neglected to dress altogether. Her moon-white skin blended with the material, creating a wan effect in which one would scarcely dare leave the room.

Everything about her repulsed him.

"Well? What do you think?" Wendolyne circled the captain, making no effort to conceal how her eyes roved over his rigid form.

James couldn't hide his disdain when he met her eyes, flexing his jaw as he held his tongue.

"Aeric! Javan! Someone deliver Captain Hook to his room." The queen tapped James' chest with a manicured finger, a dangerous glint within her gaze. The sudden change in her demeanor gave him whiplash, but it wasn't unwelcome. He couldn't wait to be free of her presence.

Aeric entered Wendolyne's chambers with an uncaring gait, his weariness evident upon his face. He untethered the captain, who quickly stood, eager to be on the move and find a way to freedom.

"You'll need your rest for tonight," said Wendolyne, her tone sultry as she moved before her vanity. "But please, do behave. I can't have my guest of honor ruining the party."

James bristled. More games, more manipulations. Did the woman ever tire of scheming?

"Someday, you'll understand Neverwoode's ways," Wendolyne said by way of dismissal. She shooed them away with a wave of her hand, turning to her preening.

She was the antithesis of her sister—cruel, sadistic, weak. If the queen were half as commanding as she imagined herself, the people wouldn't require compulsion to hold her in high esteem.

* * * *

Aeric led James back to his chambers the same way he'd come. Once, this palace was Petra's home as well, but it could never have suited her, for she was everything the estate and its occupants lacked.

Soon, his tempestuous shadow would wreak havoc on the vile queen's hold over the kingdom. He'd given her everything she needed, and once she succeeded, the whole of Fayble would be in her debt.

The floor shuddered as the captain and his puzzling escort rounded a corner into an adjoining corridor as the clock tower chimed noon, and the results were instantaneous, with sift infecting the air like an uncontrollable plague. But as Aeric prepared to seal the captain into his gilded prison, something bright and familiar flashed in his periphery.

James cursed under his breath. One blast and his mind and desires had already begun to betray him. Yet, for a moment, he allowed himself to believe Petra had come for him.

Chapter Eighteen

Finally, a bit of luck was on their side.

From her position amid a small recess in the wall, Petra caught a glimpse of her quarry, with James patiently escorted by the enigmatic Aeric – a man who seemingly cared not for the queen yet readily did her bidding.

They'd just left her petulant sister's quarters, a series of rooms that had once belonged to their father, moving down the hallway toward a separate wing leading to the opposite side of the palace. He was not restrained, instead moving alongside Wendy's henchman in silent resignation.

Petra'd done nothing to deserve his loyalty, and yet he'd volunteered himself into place on her behalf, where he continued to deal with the fallout of his benevolence.

His actions were undeniably reckless for a thief and a pirate.

Gaining access to the palace couldn't have gone more smoothly, with Petra and Ffion slipping through one of the servant's entries and into their accommodations. To bolster their chances of success, she'd donned one of the maidservant's uniforms while Ffion had opted for regimentals.

Perhaps that should've had them traveling the halls and thoroughfares within the castle walls more freely, but it felt like too much to risk. They'd traversed the corridors with care, sticking to the shadows and taking advantage of every nook and cranny.

It was no surprise that her sister had readily occupied the royal residences, given her sentiments of self-importance. Nobody had ever loved Wendolyne as much as Wendolyne did, and she spared no expense, no detail, where her comfort was concerned. Still, the sheer audacity of her narcissism grated Petra's nerves.

But this was neither the time nor the place for her ruminations regarding her overindulged sister. She'd laid eyes upon James, and that was more than she'd dared hope when she'd begun her recovery mission.

Waving Ffion forward, the pair made their way down the east hallway, with Petra banking on a rather uncertain possibility concerning James' lodging. It was the same path she'd trod so many years ago when her name hadn't been a curse.

Her father had brought her into his world against the wishes of his wife and one of his three palace-dwelling children, though Queen Hilde had come to love her. Petra had caused a short-lived stir among the staff, though the citizenry had readily accepted her presence, even welcomed it, doubtless seeing it as a victory over the traditional royal hierarchy. It was a kingdom full of rebels and criminals, after all.

They approached the corridor leading to her former chambers, pausing to observe. Nobody arrived or departed for some dozen minutes. God willing, it had been long enough to see James through to solitude, assuming he was there in the first place. Petra moved for the door, only to find that it was locked.

Ffion stood nearby, cautiously observing her as she worked the lock over with a hairpin. "What's taking so long?"

"I've never done this before," she hissed. "Just give me a minute!" Prodding the forsaken doorknob, she wriggled and poked until the bolt finally shifted. Her eyes met Ffion's, a shared sense of apprehension passing between them.

"Wait here."

Ffion's gaze shifted in both directions as he kept watch down the hallway. "What if it's not him in there?"

Petra shrugged. "It's the best I've got. Where else would he be?"

Ffion sighed, shaking his head. "I'll stand guard but yell if you need me. I don't care if we make a scene."

She offered a tentative smile, thankful for her dearest friend. Whatever had changed between them, the loss of his façade, a shift in his boldness, had been difficult for her to reconcile at first. But she became increasingly grateful for his cleverness and hopeful for his future as he matured, seemingly before her eyes.

Perhaps growing up wasn't as dire as once she'd imagined it to be.

With a nod of farewell, she opened the door and slipped inside. The room was darkened despite the hour, with only a sliver of light illuminating the space through a crack in the draperies. Nothing much had changed about her former chambers, save for the buccaneer at its center, busily exploring the confines of the hearth.

"There's no way out through the chimney," Petra said quietly, causing James to startle. He withdrew from the firebox, dusting his hand off on the front of his pants.

"You shouldn't have come here." He moved toward her, his manner uneasy. "Javan could return at any moment with a change of clothes for me. What'll happen if he finds you here?"

"Nothing more than a nice scolding."

That was likely untrue, for Javan would lose his mind. She was careless, taking chances that he would scold her for much as he did when she was a little girl. He was only a few months older but often chided her as a father would.

Besides all that, it was worth it. Seeing the captain, though they'd only been apart for a handful of hours, was surprisingly heartening. Oddly enough, she'd come to rely on him in a way, finding his broody self-assurance inexplicably compelling.

"What you did…" Petra's words dropped away. She was woefully unequipped to express her gratitude, but his kindness couldn't go without acknowledgment.

"Think nothing of it. I've faired well enough." He stepped nearer, a hint of a smirk crossing his lips. "I'm the guest of honor at Wendolyne's soiree this evening. Have you heard?"

"No, indeed. An honor, to be sure." She closed the distance, smiling openly at his roguish disposition until she noticed his face. Without thinking, she reached for him, gently stroking the swell of his cheek. "Blazes, James. What happened?"

A purpling bruise marred the left side of his face, though it did nothing to diminish his allure. In truth, it may've increased it.

"A run-in with my favorite former shipmaster, Crispin." He raised his hand, displaying a fistful of injured knuckles, swelling and cracked from their encounter with the brute. "It seems he's found a way to be useful to your sister, doubtless sharing everything he knew about us."

She took his hand in both of hers, kissing his broken flesh as if to make it whole. It was absurd, of course, for kisses didn't heal wounds, but her guilt was profound. "I'm so sorry, I – "

"I'm fine. He's a snake and a thief. A liar. I'm only one of those things," he added with a wink that did funny things to her sensibilities.

How had this man become a weakness to her? It was the last thing she needed – to dwell upon his whereabouts, to have someone more to worry over losing, yet it was no less true. Her attachment to the noble Captain Hook had blossomed into utter desire somewhere along the way, and it was all rather unnerving.

Petra laughed once, shaking her head. Her eyes met his, fathomless like a starless night and just as dark, and she couldn't look away. But then again, neither did James.

He reached for her with the crook that served as his hand, brushing it through the length of her hair. White-blonde strands slid over the polished steel of his hook, falling over her shoulder as he leaned nearer, his earnest nature evident in his featherlight touch.

"I never would've wished it," said James, "but I'm glad you're here." His gaze dropped to her lips, and her breath caught within her lungs. "I thought you'd be on your way by now with your watch and the parchment."

Petra's heart scuttled to a rhythm all its own. "I probably should be, but we made a deal."

"So that's why you returned for me. I'm grateful." He raised an eyebrow, his countenance dubious.

He hadn't believed a word of her declaration. His presence was maddening, driving her to the edge of distraction. She'd come to rescue him, not indulge in some sort of misplaced affection.

Petra glanced at their clasped hands, gathering herself. "Let me clean you up before we find a way out of here." She stepped away, only to be set upon by Javan, who materialized seemingly out of nowhere.

"Why did you come here?" he demanded, dumping an armload of clothing onto the bed with Ffion following on his heels.

"I knocked," said Ffion, offering a shrug by way of defense.

It didn't matter now, as they'd been sufficiently disrupted.

Javan paced the room, his hands clasped behind his head. "Now I have to try to get not one but *three* of you out of here? My job was easier fifteen minutes ago."

"Relax," Petra grumbled, with a new plan of attack taking shape in her mind. "We may not want to leave." She turned to James, who watched on in amusement over the siblings' absurd disagreement. "How do you feel about sticking around and distracting my sister?"

His face fell a little, loathe as he had to be to play the bait in Petra's plotting. "What is it you have in mind?"

"This party…" She paused, organizing her thoughts, for it would be a miracle if they pulled off her plan. "Would it not serve us well for you to keep Wendolyne busy? You are the guest of honor, after all." Petra grinned, feeling heartened when her shadow responded in kind.

"For you, I suppose it's possible. To what end?"

"You'll be in the clocktower for the party – the very place I need to access. Perhaps we can do it together." Petra pulled the watch and the parchment from her satchel, holding one in each palm. "I'm certain to need help in solving the riddles surrounding these."

"I hate to admit it," said Javan, "but it might actually work."

The doorknob jiggled from behind them, sending the quartet into a panic. Petra and Ffion dove for the bedside, concealing themselves beside it when the door swung open.

"Bellamy," James hissed, "how did you find me?"

Petra rose to her feet, surprised by the irritating woman's presence. Ffion followed suit, the pair standing side by side in their makeshift disguises, feeling nothing shy of silly. If there was one thing Bellamy had been proven to be, it was resourceful, for she'd found them seemingly without difficulty.

She eyed them from head to toe with a faint smirk. "I don't know why you made it so hard. All I had to do was ask."

Petra suppressed her annoyance. "Well, that was certainly enterprising."

"One only need look as if they know what they're doing. Authority goes a long way, whether real or just for show."

That much was true. Such a mentality could take them far.

"Why bother going to the clocktower when the party is here," Javan groused, eliciting a bout of snickers from the remainder of the crew. His frustration was palpable and not altogether off base. Still, they were running out of time.

"I'm a good distraction. Allow me to offer my assistance as a distraction as well." Ffion stepped forward, and Petra drew a hefty breath, poised for a challenge when he waved her away. "I'll not hear of any other way. I'll be there watching your back and charming the queen so you may do your work."

"As will I," added Bellamy. "And this time, I'll dress for the occasion."

Petra ignored the subtle dig, choosing instead to focus on James, for he was the lynchpin of their developing plan.

"I'm in," James agreed after a moment, only to sigh as realization struck. "So I suppose I'll stay put."

"It won't be long." Javan made for the door, poking his head out to examine the hallway. "Put on the clothes I brought and prepare for the evening. The rest of you need to come with me." He ushered Ffion and Bellamy through the doorway, stepping out behind them before giving Petra a meaningful glance. "Hurry up."

She nodded, making for the door, only to be held up by James, who took her hand in his. "How are we going to do this?"

"I really don't know." She shook her head, glancing at their adjoined hands. "But we've pulled off some crazy things already. Perhaps we'd both be better off if Ben had eaten me."

James pressed his lips together, stroking his thumb over her knuckles. "I wouldn't be here now if I didn't believe in your cause. Let us end your sister's poisonous reign."

She met his gaze, so sincere despite all her questionable actions, knowing she couldn't possibly deserve his loyalty, yet there it was. She smiled, at last, squeezing his hand. "You've stolen a watch, and you've stolen a key. Now you've only to steal a kingdom."

Chapter Nineteen

Finding himself suspended in a cage more suited for birds than humans was not what James envisioned when the queen said he'd be the night's honored guest. The iron enclosure rocked when he was hoisted into the air, wreaking havoc on his churning stomach as he worked to ignore the flutter of anxiety arising from its swaying height.

Outside the enormous clock tower, revelers danced, making merry fools of themselves in ways they were better off forgetting. Inside, it was even more so, but these were the consequences of lawlessness and excess. Yet it was less a judgment of their character – only troubling to watch anyone unwittingly coerced into craving counterfeit bliss and, worse, being mastered by it.

Indeed, James wasn't exempt from poor decisions made after one or two too many ales, but this was a blatant, inescapable violation of the citizenry's minds and bodies.

The whole event was a show of Wendolyne's desperation, devised to instill confidence that all was well, despite three of her four silos being non-functional. The clock tower was her best distraction, where sift coated the lungs of everyone gathered. Though fine golden particles lingered in the air around him, James hovered above the worst of it. It was a small mercy, he supposed.

Loath as he was to be there, the venue was a work of genius. James had heard mumblings of an invention resembling the standard pulley and capstan systems, but as with Neverwoode itself, the creation was as tangible as his flesh and bones. A lift—a magnificent innovation of belts, gears, and steam. The captain and those escorting him had been quickly transported from one tower level to another well above the first, the floor beneath them having risen as if in flight. He'd enjoyed that ride far more than his current one, captive to an undulating cage.

The clock itself was nothing shy of a masterpiece. Massive panels of glass made up the face, and from within, the scenery of Neverwoode beyond was crystal clear. Outside, the glass was tinted, concealing the innovative architecture within the tower. Numerous catwalks webbed across the open space just above James, and higher still were more gears of all shapes and sizes. With every passing second, they rattled the cage he stood inside, each tick reverberating through his body, though the sound of shifting wheels was dulled almost entirely by the stringed music and chatter below.

He'd expected laughter or jeering as he was raised above the queen's guests, but few seemed to notice him, apart from Wendolyne. Even Aeric didn't pay him any mind once he'd given Wendy's order to lift him in the cage from the platform serving as the queen's stage.

But her biggest mistake was assuming that any amount of sift would weaken James' resolve enough to provide her the attention she coveted.

Wendolyne strode across a small platform in the center of the room, illuminated by firelight and flecks of shimmering dust. "Eat! Drink! For tomorrow will never relent. We can trust only the moments we have, enslaved to these bodies that will soon wrinkle with age. So, tonight we feast like royals, dance with the intensity of Altanys and refuse ever to grow up!" Extending her arms wide, she wore an air of superiority. Sift burst from behind her as if she'd summoned it, and applause erupted throughout the assembly.

James held his collar over his mouth and nose, avoiding the brunt of her toxic display when she found his gaze, perfecting the rouge on her lips with a swipe of her fingertip. Pursing her lips, she beckoned to Aeric, who huffed a breath of irritation.

Wendy indicated her captive with a nod of her head, drawing a dubious glare from Aeric, who was seemingly unamused by her antics. Conversation followed – a short, clipped interaction, which, try as he might, James could not make out.

The queen chewed the inside of her cheek as evident fury contorted her features, with Aeric gesturing toward James in a manner that suggested his disapproval. Their interplay was strange, and whatever relationship they shared, even more so. The man seemed nothing more than a glorified pet as she tolerated his repeated insolence. For his part, Aeric was decidedly *intolerant* of Wendy, yet he persisted in her presence daily.

Then what was Aeric to her if not a confidant, friend or lover? Still, regardless of mutual disdain for Wendy, or the several times he'd appeared to go out of his way to assist James, it did not make Aeric an ally.

Across the room, another set of guests exited the lift, two that James knew had not been invited. Ffion and Bellamy were dressed for the lavish affair, accompanied by Javan and his new wife, who the captain knew all too well after the damage she'd caused to his ship weeks prior. Lillia was a skilled commander, a true tigress of the sea, and an artful deceiver if he was to believe she indeed endeavored to circumvent the queen's rancorous schemes.

Their arrival meant Petra wouldn't be far behind, assuming she wasn't already camouflaged among the revelers, though she could never blend in so easily.

The plan was simple, or so they'd thought — distract, extract and run. Of course, not one of them had anticipated that James might be trapped in a cage dangling from the underside of an overhead walkway.

Javan approached the dais, sweeping into an obligatory bow before Wendolyne. "My sister will join me for a walk about the room. Your subjects have arranged something magnificent for your viewing but wish to share their gratitude with you face to face." His voice rose above the fray, but not before he'd visibly angered Wendy with his demand.

Javan offered his arm to the queen with a reassuring smile, and she reluctantly took it. James read the conflict in the heir's eyes, but as Javan said, Wendy, too, was his sister. He wondered if she'd always been filled with hatred or if it was fostered by something deeper that festered beyond control.

James watched Wendolyne all the way over to Ffion and Bellamy. She glanced over her shoulder once as she advanced toward them, but otherwise offered her attention to the pair. Their efforts, however, would be worthless if he remained trapped like an animal behind bars.

Retrieving a gambler's dagger from his boot, James quietly worked to pick the lock outside the cage, manipulating it with the end of his hook and the thin blade. It should've been a simple enough maneuver if not for the sickening swinging that worsened with every movement. He checked periodically to be sure Wendolyne hadn't taken notice of his efforts and surveyed the room several times for any sign of Petra, finding nothing.

It wasn't long before he felt the bolt give. The captain tugged, twisting as he slipped it off the door. Setting the lock behind him, he clenched his jaw as his stomach lurched, the iron prison rocking every time his weight shifted.

But alas, he was free.

Almost.

The queen's party was in full swing from beneath him, with midnight fast approaching. Ffion and Bellamy were doing their worst, effectively occupying the mad woman, who remained occupied with their chatter and enthusiasm, blessedly facing away from James. Whether temporary or not, his accomplices made for valuable allies, but it wouldn't be long before Wendy noticed he was missing.

Despite James' caution, his metal enclosure shrieked as he created an opening large enough to squeeze through. But plentiful sift contaminated the room, and nobody gave it a thought. The cage was high enough that a fall wouldn't leave him dead. It would, however, shatter his bones.

Tilting and countering his weight, he secured his hook to an upper horizontal bar, anchoring himself while he heaved his frame up along the outside of the creaking enclosure.

Don't look down.

As he climbed, the captain's arms and legs protested, each inch closer to the catwalk above a victory. The rings within the chain grated against each other as the cage swayed, and his sweaty palm caused him nothing but grief, slipping over the lengths of iron bars as he cursed under his breath. He was nearly there when the links shifted slightly, the impact sending James swinging as his tenuous grip faltered, the cage shuddering beneath him. He regained his hold just as slender fingers wrapped around his wrist, and his gaze found hers.

Petra held fast to the catwalk railing while the entire bridge wobbled from their efforts. Her grasp on him was a relief, steadying James, despite the relentless motion of the iron crate, affording him enough stability to haul himself onto the rickety walkway.

He found his footing, Petra's hand warming his wrist. Her golden eyes met his, and his heart stuttered. "We won't have long before Wendy notices. Are you all right?" She pressed a palm to his bruised cheek before brushing the same delicate fingers anchoring his calm through his tousled hair, examining him for further injury.

James wondered if, perhaps, she'd begun to realize how similar they really were. The sudden shift in her regard was not something he'd anticipated but welcomed. Everything she did was a mystery. Petra followed her instincts with a shameless impulsivity that had him wholly mesmerized. His fascination was complete when she'd moved about his dreams – even before he knew she existed.

"I'm fine," he huffed. "Thank you." The gratitude was multi-faceted, but she already understood, waving him off.

"You don't need me." She repeated his assertion from earlier that morning, a slight smirk tipping her mouth at the corners. "Come, *love*. Quickly."

Something about the captain's words upon her lips awakened a dormant, ardent hunger he'd neglected far too long. She was a vixen, and if the wicked smile she wore as she turned from him was any indication, she knew it.

James was willing prey.

Petra started across the catwalk with a small pack slung over her shoulders, silent and sure as she moved swiftly above her sister's euphoric flock. The captain was not nearly as graceful, his limbs tingling from the lofty height. He held to a rusted railing as the bridge underfoot sagged with every step, undulating from years of disrepair.

Ahead of him, Petra halted at a ladder leading higher yet, briefly surveying the gathering before climbing nimbly to the walkway above. The gears grew louder, and James glanced at the enormous tower's familiar face, its long hands ticking in time with the staccato revolutions on either side of them.

He'd not noticed until then that the clock was an exact replica of Petra's heirloom, or perhaps the other way around, and identical to the compass detailed on his father's scroll. Veins of gold like broken seashells reflecting the noonday sun were inset within blackened metal, defining each second, minute and hour, forming a triad of invaluable treasures.

The captain knew there was more. He'd seen it in Petra's eyes when he showed her his father's crumpled parchment. It meant something to her, though she'd not trusted him enough to share her revelation. He had a feeling she was about to show him.

James followed Petra, ascending into a mechanical marvel when at last they reached a metal hatch that blended in with its neighboring framework. Not a soul would've noticed the small door without knowing it was there beforehand, but he wasn't surprised when Neverwoode's forsaken daughter brought them directly to it.

"Here." Extending two bits of a moldable wax to James, Petra kept two more in her clenched fist. She was shouting to be heard over the toothed wheels now underneath them. "You'll need it if you wish to save your eardrums."

He hated heights, but it couldn't have been more worthwhile once they climbed into the bell tower. Tall, arched openings lined each wall overlooking the kingdom, with darkly outlined silhouettes of treetops and hills extending far beyond all the way to Altanys, glittering in the distance under a blanket of stars. Petra smiled at the captain, dazzling white, even in the subtle blue glow of night.

It was finally quiet with the hatch closed and only soft music from the streets below drifting toward them, but not for much longer. Sizable bells lay in wait to declare death over one day and the birth of another.

What was midnight, if not to mark the ending of another sliver of time?

"At time's end…" James uttered the revelation.

Retrieving her father's watch from where it draped from the waist of her pants, Petra detached it, nodding. "The darkest hour of each day, when the only light offered filters from the heavens through the moon and stars." She gave the captain her timepiece and reached into the satchel on her shoulder. After digging out James' parchment, she unfolded it between them. "Do you know what this is? This document was valuable enough for your father to steal and for his ship to be attacked to recover it. Our fathers knew each other. I don't know why it took me so long to figure it out."

He studied it but was still unsure of its significance.

Petra didn't wait for a response. "I remember how angry my father was after a friend of his departed suddenly, a man named Hayes – one of few who was kind to me – left, taking the parchment with him, and my father was furious. But it wasn't a betrayal after all. At least, I no longer think so. I believe he meant to save my father from himself by making off with it."

He watched Petra, the way her eyes, even in the dark, shone with wonder at the revelation.

"It's a map to the mine, James."

Chapter Twenty

Petra needed James more than he could ever know. She held the parchment between them. "Can you decipher any of it?"

Together, they examined its intricate markings, detailed in varying colors, predominantly printed in a deep blood-red. Some tones measured distances, while others specified coordinates, naming constellations and vague, outlined shapes and clusters of stars. It was like someone layered one piece of art on top of another, again and again, hoping to conceal order within chaos. But the whole of it faded to nothing around the main image's edges, shaped something like a faint spade.

"I've never tried, but seemingly minor features of these pieces were replicated between them. Look at this." James flipped the pocket watch open. "I thought it was unusual how this case opens upward, but even that was purposeful. The tips of these clock hands and the directional indicators of the compass are the same shapes."

"The map, too." Petra traced the washed-out border on James' chart and moved her fingertip over its compass. "Have you ever noticed the compass doesn't specify any sense of direction? Nothing notes north from south."

"They're all arrows, but that isn't a compass, only a picture of something *like* one." The captain caught Petra's gaze, his eyes darker than the black sky surrounding them.

He dangled the open timepiece from its chain off the end of his hook. It swung like a pendulum before them, when Petra gasped, snatching it out of the open air. "Did you see that?"

She didn't fully believe her eyes, but the proof was there when she held the ruby over his chart.

They'll soon take flight into the night,
And follow the stars upon the heights.
When shadows and light will guide your sight,
Guide your sight,
Guide your sight,
Just under the second one to the right.

Petra recalled the miners' song as they'd departed. "James!" She handed her watch over, smoothing the map across one of the bell tower's arched openings, allowing him to see her discovery for himself.

He took it, adjusting his perspective using the deep red gem as a lens through which to view the scroll. "*Incredible.*"

And it was, for there were indeed layers of differing inks upon the parchment. Still, when looking *through* Petra's ruby, the red ink vanished, eliminating a depiction of the skies above to reveal an elaborate rendering of a path through Wylewoode, directly to an unnamed target marked with a small X.

"Shadows and light will guide your sight," Petra thought aloud, taking in the horizon of Neverwoode. Raising a trembling hand, she pointed toward the faint glow streaming over the busy street below. "It's under the second star to the right."

From behind them, clock hands upon the tower pitched, converging shadows down a cobbled roadway's center, growing closer to one another with each moment. Once they aligned, they'd point directly to the spot in the boys' cryptic melody that morning.

Petra removed the bits of wax she'd kept from her pouch, balling them in her palms before pressing a piece into her ear. "It's almost midnight."

"Time's end," the captain affirmed with an incredulous scoff.

James glanced at the map, once with the ruby and again without it, before tucking her watch into his vest pocket. "The target is positioned due south of Arctos, second to the right from Ursa – the only two stars that never move. And if we're to believe this tower is the center, here," he circled a location with the tip of his hook. "We're dead south of both."

Petra pushed the second portion of wax into her opposite ear, then folded the map, slipping it into her satchel while the captain plugged both of his with the malleable substance.

A final tick moved the clock hands into alignment as gears within the tower clacked and shifted beneath them. The floor shuddered as bells pealed, so thunderously loud, despite the protection shielding their eardrums, that Petra stumbled into James.

He wrapped his arms tightly around her, holding her close to his chest, his warmth steadying her as the world rumbled around them.

Sift burst into the sky above them with the first chime, a blast larger than standard, raining over the streets of Neverwoode in shimmering rivulets. Petra buried her face in the captain's tunic, his hand bracing her against him as his fingers moved through the untamed strands of her hair. They should've guarded themselves against the poison, but she was confident they could weather its effects, even in excess.

The only weakening factor for her was him.

He still smelled of the sea. Petra breathed in his scent, savoring the feeling of his body against hers, the way his fingers threaded through her long, pale waves. James held her tight as the bells chimed behind her, with cheers erupting from below. Twelve times, they rang, and it felt like an eternity. Still, it wasn't nearly long enough if it meant the final toll would see her released from his sheltering embrace.

When it finished, neither pulled away. James gently brushed his nose across her brow. Petra gazed up at him, her heart stuttering when his dusky eyes met hers, fathomless as the Deep itself. She took in the power of his muscular frame and the chill of his hook beneath her chin when he tipped it upward. His stubbled jaw skimmed lightly over her flushed cheeks as he nuzzled her temple, inhaling her scent like it fueled something vital within him.

"I do need you, Petra." His words tickled her flesh, a confession, and a promise. Her breath hitched, and she felt him smile. "For weeks, I longed for sleep — to dream, drawn to a phantom silhouette. Even then, you were reminiscent of the open seas, unbroken and turbulent."

Petra moved her hand from where it rested on James' chest to the nape of his neck, caressing the flesh with her nails, slipping her fingertips to the tender skin behind his jaw and on to the hollow of his neck where she felt his pulse throbbing under her touch. The captain's throat bobbed as he swallowed, leaning nearer, his lips grazing hers. A growl of frustration rumbled in his chest beneath Petra's palm. "Not yet."

She wanted it, and something told her James would relent if only she stayed where she was. He didn't move a muscle, frozen as if he didn't trust himself not to give in.

Petra took a fortifying breath, choking every impulse within her body that begged her to yield when she retreated a step. As if to affirm her decision, a reverberant crackle hissed and sputtered outside the bell tower, with streaks of fire lighting the night sky.

Bellamy and Ffion had come through, and it was time to run.

The descent may have been worse than their climb up to the bell tower. Explosive cracks could be heard from outside, and they used every second to their advantage. James took the lead, lest anyone spot them as they prepared to re-enter a room of engrossed onlookers, all taking in the sprays of citrine flame splintering through the night courtesy of the tinkerer Bellamy.

They moved quickly, shoving past Wendolyne's guests. James spotted the queen, standing among the spectators in haughty observance. Javan was with her alongside his wife, commenting and motioning toward the display when something caught Wendy's attention.

The captain saw it then – a flash of Petra's white-blonde hair in a perfect reflection cast off the clock face. Wendolyne turned in their direction, and James caught

Petra's wrist, signaling her to stay low as he pulled her to him.

"She saw you. Make for the stairs, and I'll occupy her. I'll find a way out, but you have to go." To his utter shock, she didn't fight him. She knew as well as he that she wouldn't survive being caught.

"I have something in mind." Petra's smirk warned of danger, her golden eyes gleaming with mischief beneath dark lashes. "I'll meet you at the bottom of the lift. If you're not there soon, I'll come for you."

She was gone in the next breath, camouflaged by her sister's gathered guests. James didn't know what she had planned, but he'd occupy the queen as long as necessary if it meant Petra's escape.

He pushed through the crowd until he reached Wendolyne, her back toward him as she inspected the present company. James cleared his throat, and she went rigid, tension roiling from her severe bearing.

She slowly pivoted toward him, her features colored with interest as the captain sketched a bow. Wendolyne sighed, averting her gaze. "Spare me."

James could only assume she believed Petra was still roaming about her event uninvited. He smiled, hoping he appeared genuine in spite of his utter distaste for the woman. "I only wish to apologize for our misunderstanding."

The queen glanced at the empty cage dangling above the center platform, pursing her lips before shifting her focus toward him. James indicated his hook with a look – the only explanation needed to convince her of his presence now before her.

"I should've assumed. And yet, you didn't flee." Skepticism laced Wendolyne's words, but she approached him anyway, skimming a nail down the length of the captain's chest and midsection. "You're a fast learner. I told you you'd come to understand the ways of this kingdom."

"I didn't flee." James stepped into her touch, even as he inwardly recoiled. She might have been bewitching had her heart not been made of ash. While she resembled Petra, somehow, they were nothing alike. The queen's eyes were empty, her skin wan and cold, whereas her sister exuded light and passion.

No, they were nothing alike. And while beauty was not defined merely by appearance, it was clear Wendolyne would never grasp how crippling her conceit truly was. Narcissists of her caliber could not see beyond themselves.

In this case, it served James well as he closed the distance between them. He stroked her cheek with his knuckle, the queen leaning into his caress. She followed his lead when he guided her steps to the enormous window at her back, pressing his forehead to hers. Wendy closed her eyes, reveling in the perceived victory of his adoration when he saw the lift gates open in the reflection behind her.

Gasps of nervous excitement filled the room, and Wendolyne's attendants parted, making way for none other than Ben. Not a soul was frightened, undoubtedly numbed beyond reason by the abundance of sift dusting their bodies and every other exposed surface. The crocodile waddled through the divided guests, his tail sweeping over the glossed cedar floor.

The queen opened her eyes as the beast advanced, her dull gaze suddenly filled with horror at his menacing presence. Ben snapped and swiped his powerful tail as he meandered toward James, the surrounding company awed by his magnificence as if he was another organized spectacle arranged for their enjoyment.

If only they knew how easily he could rip them to shreds.

Wendolyne knew.

The captain never bothered to look over his shoulder, instead flexing his jaw as he placed a hand and forearm to either side of Wendy, trapping her in place. Ben groaned at James' back, the stench of his breath permeating the air around them as the queen grimaced, shrinking against the windowpane.

James swore his pet devoured only the basest of creatures, and she was precisely Ben's type. He raised a brow, his gaze falling from Wendolyne to the beast at his heels. "Not yet."

Ben readily obeyed, licking his wicked teeth. The captain straightened before Wendy, adjusting his vest as he retreated a step. It was the second time he'd uttered those words that night, though the context could not have been more at odds.

"I should have him tear you apart for what you tried to do to her," said James, his voice pitched low. He glanced at Ben, retrieving Petra's watch from his vest and flipping it open. "Perhaps next time. If you'll excuse us, Your Majesty. It's late."

Wendolyne tensed as if she might lunge for the heirloom in the captain's hand, but he snapped it shut, slipping it away before she dared.

"Don't follow us." He turned from her, ignoring the challenge in her hateful stare. James made for the open lift with Ben trailing close behind when someone blatantly laughed. In his periphery, he found the offender, the man's amusement unabashedly directed at Wendy.

Aeric.
Perhaps he could prove an ally after all.

Chapter Twenty-One

The town was wide awake as the streets teemed with villagers, dancing in the light shining from the face of the clock tower and the luminescent moon above. Sift sparkled in the amber glow, puffing from the ground beneath their feet as they reveled in blissful ignorance.

This was why.

Even as they'd taken such a profound risk and found themselves endangered, and though they were on the run, desperate to avoid Wendolyne and her minions, Petra would do it all again. The people – her people – were utterly lost and beholden to a fallacy.

The supply of sift was rapidly waning, driving the citizenry of Wylewoode to the heart of the kingdom where they gathered now. A necessity so absolute, they'd gone to the only remaining source, making the escape from the party a genuine trial.

James glanced back, reaching out for Petra as he drew her along from behind himself. "We're nearly to the edge, I think."

She took his hand, picking up her pace. He was right, for they'd just passed the blacksmith's forge. The perimeter of Wylewoode was not far off.

The crowd was thinning, but not enough to avoid being speared by a few errant elbows. Ben followed at their heels, lumbering along at an impressive clip. None of the gathered hordes seemed to notice his presence or care, too busy about their business of counterfeit contentedness.

Petra's thoughts turned to those they'd left behind. Ffion and Bellamy were to meet them in Adym Grove – the forsaken source of all Wendolyne's poisonous apples. For his part, Javan was to continue in his deceptive measures within the palace. He was unwilling to leave his wife, Lillia, but a part of Petra also suspected his compassion for their sister and brother played a role.

Javan had obviously never been as committed to her crusade to free the people of Neverwoode. Not that he didn't want it to happen, only that he lacked the stomach for their continuing subversions. She knew how much he loved them both. Hell, she'd loved them too. But his sensibilities were always a bit ruffled when it came to undermining. The man was honest to a fault, prone to acts of decency and valor that would put the most virtuous of knights to shame.

On the other hand, Mikhail was notably absent in so many facets of her life now. Where once they'd interacted regularly, she found that she'd go long periods without laying eyes upon her youngest brother. Indeed, he'd not even been present at the clock tower, not that she'd seen, but he'd never have missed it before.

Petra's life felt a bit like a shambles since she'd begun her hapless quest to free her kingdom, yet not all was lost. As she traversed the cobbled streets of Neverwoode, her fingers linked with a handsome pirate who'd found her by fate alone – both in reality and in dreaming – and who was rapidly becoming her anchor.

It wasn't her way. Allowing anyone to infiltrate the high walls built around her emotions was a potential catastrophe. She'd already let her guard down once where Ffion was concerned, and it hadn't hurt her yet, but it'd come close.

Then there was James, the thieving marauder from Llundyn who'd laid waste to her walls, rendering them useless. He was steady and true, honoring her word as well as his own, despite all the problems she'd created for him and his crew.

His regard was undeserved.

They broke free of the crush surrounding them, wending their way into the woods. The forest around them grew darker with each step as the trees above sheltered them from the dusky sky, the minimal light filtering through forging monstrous shadows out of thin air. It made Petra oddly grateful for the crocodile at their backs, with the armored beast affording them a modicum of protection.

Music from the festivities faded as the sounds of their woodland refuge grew. Crickets and frogs formed a harmony all their own, alongside the aid of creatures she wished very much not to think about.

She'd lived within the bounds of the Wylewoode Forest for years and had, on several occasions, made her way into the center of its soul. Survival had been a matter of some effort, for it was a dark enclave rife with unusual entities, from plants to animals to landmarks that left her cold.

Things without names thrived within its boundaries, and more than one unlucky explorer had begun a journey from which they never returned. She hadn't worried over herself, knowing that her disappearance would impact few. But James' involvement brought new fears to the fore.

"You'll have to tell me when," James said at last, stifling a yawn with his arm.

It took her a moment to understand his meaning. They were both due a solid night's sleep, but that would never happen there. "Anywhere will do, really. As long as we go up."

James gave her a dubious grin, plainly no fan of heights. "I slept in the trees in Llundyn, or in the trunk rather, with six other people during our thieving days."

The fondness in his voice made her ache. What a life he must've lived, with noble friends all fighting for the sake of their beloved country. "What sort of tree sleeps seven people?" she asked, incredulous at the idea of such an enormous trunk.

"Oh, our woods aren't like these." He slowed, turning to look at her. "I think you'd love it there, woodnymph that you are."

She laughed a little. "I would love to see it."

They watched each other in silence, rapt in the pale moonlight beneath a canopy of shimmering stars and fronds. That the captain could understand her spirit so thoroughly was amusing, but then again, they were much the same. Like two halves of the same whole, their souls mirrored one another in unusual ways, making it easier to level.

"Perhaps I'll take you someday," said James, his smile bright.

She couldn't help responding in kind. So much for shielding her heart as she well and truly lost hold of her airtight emotions.

The man was a thief, all right...

"Well," said James, his gaze pinned warily to the treetops above. "If you're certain up is the only way."

"Trust me when I tell you we won't want to be on the ground." She shot a quick look toward their crocodile companion. "Worse than he exists here, and I want nothing to do with it."

She spent a moment examining the surrounding trees, landing on a hearty beech with thick, low branches. "This should do. After you..."

James laughed once without humor, doubtless steeling his nerves. "I'm a man of the sea, love. Elevation has never been my forte, but neither do I contradict beautiful women."

He set off, leaving her blushing fiercely at the foot of the tree before she began climbing after him. Despite his protestations, he ascended quickly, making for the boughs beset with foliage that would provide good cover. Reaching down, he grasped her hand, drawing her up toward a thick branch.

She scrambled upward, storing each of their satchels in the tangled nest of leaves above them before facing James on the sturdy bough. His body was rigid, distress evident in his tense jaw. "Just breathe," said Petra, taking his hand in hers. "It's up here that I feel most free – only a little scary in slumber."

"How do you manage that?" he asked through clenched teeth. His motions were slow and deliberate, as if one wrong move would throw him over the edge. He leaned into the tree, the curve of his back aligning with the elbow of the branch upon which he sat.

"With care." She moved closer, nestling herself between his legs as she leaned against him, her head propped on his chest. His breathing slowed, moving in tandem with hers, and a moment later, he wrapped his arms securely around her waist.

James sighed, the tension seemingly melting away as they relaxed, suspended in the midnight air. "Perhaps I don't so much mind it anymore."

Neither did she. Indeed, she'd never been so comfortable in the boughs of a tree, tucked beneath a blanket of stars with the sounds of their heartbeats to guide her to sleep. Closing her eyes, she drifted away to a dreamless slumber, held within the arms of a chivalrous pirate who may've been the most honorable man she'd ever known.

Peace.

It was the most unexpected of emotions, aloft as James was and no fan of heights. Still, as his Otherlande shadow lay in his embrace, he knew he'd never know better.

Her very presence sustained him, with a bold sense of duty and a moral compass that far exceeded most men. She was wholly unexpected and better than he could possibly deserve.

Petra shifted, stretching as she awakened, and he didn't want to leave. "Good morning," she rasped, her voice thick with sleep, though he could hear her smile through her words.

"We didn't fall," he replied before thinking, eliciting a giggle, and he couldn't help laughing himself.

They gathered themselves, making their way down to the forest floor where Ben had waited, standing guard over their woodland shelter throughout the night. Touching down had James breathing easier, though he hadn't so much minded sleeping among the greenery above.

He reached for Petra as she made to jump the last few feet, taking her by the waist to aid her descent. She clasped her hands around his neck as he settled her on the ground, only she didn't let go.

She met his gaze, her gilded eyes holding untold secrets he wished to reveal. He wove his fingers through her hair, soft as silken ribbons when it slipped over his flesh.

James had longed for her, dreamt of her. He'd watched her from afar and thought of her in waking even before he understood who she was or what she would mean to him. She was sunlight and flame, peace and strength. He'd never believed in fate.

He was wrong.

Petra rose on tiptoe, closing the distance between them when her nose brushed over his. "Now?"

He pulled her to him, fitting his mouth to hers, and her breath hitched as she tightened her arms around his neck, drawing so close her feet barely touched the earth beneath them. When he trailed light fingers down her spine, she shivered at his touch, and when she slid her tongue over his lips, he was undone.

She deepened the kiss, their tongues tangling together as he breathed her in. He nipped her lower lip, taking it between his teeth as she straddled his hips, wrapping her legs around him as if there was no close enough. He splayed his fingers on her thigh, the warmth of her filtering through him like a blazing pyre.

"I wouldn't blame you if you chose to run."

"Following you is my new favorite habit," he uttered against her mouth, drawing a smile from the daughter of Neverwoode that stole his heart.

The early morning sun filled the woods around them, and the world came alive alongside them, awakening a new day James would happily ignore if it meant he could remain in her embrace.

This was why he'd wanted to wait. Though he'd have kissed her a million times over before now, they'd been trapped in the hellhole of Neverwoode. Here, there was no sift and no question of its effects. His affection was real, and he didn't want her to doubt it.

He growled as she raked her fingers through his hair, her touch chasing away doubts and regrets. "Does this mean you wish to stay with me?" she asked.

"Till time's end." James rested his forehead against hers, holding her close and savoring her nearness, though he knew the remaining journey wouldn't wait.

They continued through the forest, though neither was prepared to move forward. Whatever awaited them on the other end – the apple grove, the mine, the *chaos* – could only bring strife to an otherwise blissful day. But duty surpassed desire in the end, with each determined to see their mission through.

They were in it together, at the very least.

James watched Petra as they moved, her way with nature awing him endlessly. In a moment of quiet contentment, he observed her softly humming as she held out her hand. A tiny sparrow with a throat as white as snow landed upon her fingers, pecking crusts of the bread she'd offered from her palm.

"You're so very lovely," said James.

Petra wrinkled her nose, unaware she'd been observed. "They've always been my friends – all the little creatures in the woods. And best of all, they never ask questions."

The captain smiled, amused by her easy manner. There was never any pretense, and everything around them seemed to sense her goodness. Even Ben saw fit to stick close by through their travels.

As the trees around them grew denser, James moved ahead, with Petra a step behind as he worked to cut through the vines and fronds crisscrossing their path. Though the sun was high above, the woods remained dusky, lending a slight chill to the air as they moved through the shadows.

James hopped a downed tree, skipping over the log before turning to help Petra. He reached for her, taking her by the waist and lifting her over the felled trunk. "You're more of a gentleman than most. I'm not accustomed to this."

"Then we must change that."

She averted her gaze, smiling shyly, and his heart skipped a beat. Reconciling the harsh reality of her life was sure to be a trial, but never should she have been left to fend for herself. She'd been discarded much like her companion Ffion, and even himself, only James had had Ella to ease the burden of loss and see him back to wholeness.

He heard it before he saw it, the rustling within the brush causing him to freeze. The shrubbery to his left came alive, with what appeared at first to be merely a large blossom lunging for James. The creeper snapped as he raised his arm in defense, nipping his silver crook before recoiling, doubtless shocked to be sampling metal rather than flesh.

James acted swiftly, drawing his dagger and swinging for what could only be described as the neck, slicing cleanly through as the flora fell to the ground at his feet. Viridian petals wilted before their eyes, revealing thin, spiky teeth hidden by the fronds. He met Petra's gaze, finding that her surprise matched his own.

"*Wylewoode*," she breathed, as if the word itself was explanation enough for the tussle, and perhaps it was. There was a reason these woods were avoided. *Feared.*

He glanced about, alarmed to find that there were more. Dozens lining their pathway and sprinkled throughout the trees as far as the eye could see. James linked his fingers with Petra's, with only one word on his lips.

"*Run.*"

Chapter Twenty-Two

The sight of Adym Grove alone had Petra's stomach churning. Once full of life and color, scorched trees rose like brittle fingers toward the sky, their branches blackened from the blaze she'd set at the orchard's heart, which had decidedly broken her own.

Her father had taken her hand before his final breath, murmuring what must be done, and while Petra didn't regret her actions, she grieved them. Adym would always call to the vulnerable, whispering promises of pleasure and fulfillment on the winds, infusing desperate, lost souls with his deceptions. The orchard possessed an almost otherworldly type of allure, and it was no wonder why her grandparents had fallen prey to its charms.

Petra couldn't, in good conscience, allow the abuse to continue, but the solution devastated her, nonetheless. One day, she'd return to restore the lands she'd burned, but not before eliminating Wendolyne's mine and reducing the grove to ash.

"It's only for now. Remember why we must." James remained a balancing force, rooting himself before her as he swept loose strands of hair behind her ear.

But the truth was, she'd never forget. For back at the palace, her brothers were trapped, beholden to a queen who cared for nothing and no one but herself. She hadn't understood the depth of Wendolyne's ambition or her hatred until their father had passed. They'd played and laughed together when they were small girls, but everything changed as they grew older.

Then again, growing up always managed to tarnish innocence.

Petra recalled the rapid decline of their friendship, shattering her joyful spirit. They'd always known they were legitimate sisters, but Wendolyne turned cold once she grasped the true scope of the late king's infidelity.

His new queen was a better woman than he deserved, readily forgiving his indiscretion, even as she raised Petra alongside her stepdaughter Wendolyn and her own children.

Wendy saw Petra as an interloper, despising her younger sister as much as their negligent mother. But, the former queen had always been kind, never treating either of the girls differently than her two sons, despite their father's unfaithfulness. Her untimely loss was a tragedy for them all.

The sisters mourned Queen Hilde's death more than their own mother, who they never really knew. Rumors said it was a beautiful servant who'd tempted the king, but the stories were just that.

Their father's mistress had more likely been a winsome wanderer that beguiled a wayward man. The few times she'd seen her, Petra had recognized the features she'd passed on to her, but apart from their strange, golden eyes and petite stature, they shared no connection.

She never longed for one, either. Her mother was not a loving woman, not compassionate or attentive. In truth, Petra wondered why she'd ever visited at all. But she steeled herself, unwilling to dwell upon history she couldn't change.

"Ffion and Bellamy won't be far behind." Petra retrieved the map from her satchel, dropping the pack from her shoulder with a thud and unfolding the parchment between them. "You won't like what comes next."

James pulled her father's watch out of his vest pocket, flipping it open and handing it to her. He peeked over her shoulder, eyeing their route through the ruby with a groan, for it seemed the best way forward was up. "To go around would add days to our journey. It must amuse you to watch me sweat." He sighed, the scruff of his jaw tickling her cheek before he folded her into his arms from behind. "You're right. I hate it."

There was a steep drop along Adym's edge where the surf of Altanys met the land to the east, with a raging inlet to the north and the Delphian Cliffs to the west. Red stone towered above the grove, higher than any structure Petra knew, but it was indisputably the most direct path onward.

"While we're gone, Ffion and Bellamy can run lines through the orchard." Petra turned within the captain's embrace, taking in the defined angles of his countenance. "Between us, we should have enough potash to seal the mine at least and ignite Adym if we use it efficiently, not to mention the supply Javan mentioned hidden within the caverns. We'll be lucky if Wendy doesn't already have her mine well-fortified."

"I'm counting on it." James leaned in, pressing his lips to her forehead. "But have I not proven myself a cunning adversary?"

Cunning, indeed.

"You're a fiend." Petra crinkled her nose, unable to conceal her answering smile. The captain bit his lower lip, using the curve of his hook to lift her chin.

"You're worse." James' pitch-dark gaze consumed her.

Petra traced the beautiful contours of his face, challenging his self-control, every bit of her burning under his study. She clutched his tunic in her fist, rising onto her toes, slowly trailing kisses up his exposed collarbone and neck. He laughed, a deep, tortured sound as she moved to his jaw, tugging him closer.

"Enchantress." His mouth grazed her ear, sending a shiver of pleasure down her spine. Closing the distance between them, she wrapped her arms around him, and James lifted her from the greenwood floor, pinning her to the tree at her back.

Weaving slender fingers through his mussed locks, Petra tipped his head back before surrendering her lips to his. She kissed him fervidly, and he responded in kind, slipping his tongue into her mouth, shattering her barriers and restoring her soul.

For a moment, she understood how Wendolyne's people had become willing victims of her delicate, gilded dust. It made all the sense in the world if it afforded them even a trace of the bliss she felt in James' arms. But this was real...tangible.

She would never have her fill.

A pack landed at their feet without warning, and they parted abruptly with ragged breaths. James positioned himself before her, unsheathing his short blade without hesitation.

Bellamy's eyes narrowed as she curled her lip in disgust. "There will be hell to pay when they return. It would be better for you all to flee while you still can." She glanced over her shoulder toward Ffion, who glared back.

Ben followed them to Petra and James, and Ffion tossed the creature a strip of dried meat. He took a bit for himself before offering what remained to them, ignoring Bellamy.

Petra took the jerky, splitting it with James as Ffion removed one of his belts, a gleaming cutlass sword weighing down the supple leather sheathe. "I borrowed these from some of the queen's faithful guards." He passed it to the captain, who nodded his thanks, fastening it to himself. Sunlight glinted off the hilt of another blade at his shoulders. Ffion unbuckled the back scabbard he'd lifted and chuckled as he offered it to Petra. "I don't think this is wise."

"Not at all." Petra hesitated, considering whether or not to take the weapon. She'd never wielded something so heavy but accepted it anyway. Ffion held the sheath steady as she snaked her arms through its straps. It hung loosely over her shoulder and under her arms, but she cinched the bands tightly to her chest, securing the harness to the center of her back.

"Let's hope you don't need it," Ffion added, a bright smile lighting his features.

"Those won't help you if they find you there." Bellamy watched with the same disapproving manner that seemed to be the woman's only expression. "You don't even know you're one of them, do you?"

Petra stared back at her, an unwavering challenge as she waited for her to elaborate. Bellamy's features darkened, and she scoffed with incredulous contempt.

"They're real, Petra—pixies, sirens, among countless other beings of lore."

The miners had told her as much when they'd sensed her presence, but she'd not believed them, either, even if some latent part of her had not entirely dismissed their innocent conviction.

"You have their eyes, the lilt of their speech, their sway over nature and the things within it. You may only share half their blood, but have you never wondered why your complexion glows with health and animals answer the silent petitions of your spirit? You could fly if you only believed it. But none of that matters if you can't accept who you are."

"Where have they gone if you say they'll be back?" Ffion seemed to take no issue with Bellamy's claim, but neither did he conceal his abiding disdain for her.

"Your queen has uncovered living, breathing folklore preserved by humanity's ignorance." Bellamy sniffed, glancing between them. "They fled to keep it that way. Hiding suggests weakness, though they're anything but frail or meek."

"You're suggesting I'm one of these...*things.*" Petra had heard enough, and, in truth, it *didn't* make any difference whether she believed it or not. If pixies were real and the tales were true, she would sooner die than embrace such heritage.

"They aren't *things.* They're pixies and will show you no mercy, no matter your parentage, if you carry out your mission. I'll have no part in it. Open your eyes, Petra. The evidence of your ancestry follows you everywhere." Bellamy looked pointedly at Ffion, then to the massive reptile at their feet. She stepped toward James, inclining her head slightly in what Petra perceived as a show of respect. Her countenance held no affection when she pivoted to face them. "I hope you fail."

If Petra believed anything from Bellamy's mouth, it was that. Not one of them moved to stop her as she retreated into the grove without another word.

Good riddance.

To see the unpleasant woman leave was a relief. Would that she might take every declaration she'd made with her.

James watched Petra, his brow creased with worry – not panic, like perhaps it should have been if Bellamy was correct in her assertion.

"I've considered it, but I never knew halflings existed until yesterday when those miners called you one." Ffion's visage was contemplative as he scratched his temple, his habitual gestures ever the same. "I heard music the day we met when I found you in Wylewoode. Only when I came upon you, the woods were still. Your eyes were rimmed in red, swollen from crying, even though I was never meant to know. I'd followed the music to you, but there was none when I arrived."

Petra remembered that afternoon, the first time she'd realized what was being done to Mikhail and so many others in Neverwoode. It was the same day she'd determined sift was not being used solely to alleviate the unpredictability of a realm of exiles but to crush the will of anyone who fell out of line.

It was never so apparent until she heard from an estate servant that Wendolyne had been adding undiluted sift to their youngest brother's food and drink for months, sowing seeds of doubt about Petra's character and love for him all the while. Mikhail's boyish naivety both safeguarded and exploited him, leaving him at odds with himself as he attempted to discern what was true or false through a perpetual haze designed to sever their bond.

Their father fell ill soon after Petra learned of Wendy's appalling actions, so she waited, keeping to the forsaken wilds of the forest. She returned when her heart could no longer endure the separation from her brothers or father, only to find life as she'd known it much altered. The king was in his final days, and Mikhail was lost beyond anything Petra might've imagined.

It was then that Wendolyne warned her away, finally verbalizing the unspoken expectation for her never to return.

She said her final goodbye to her father, and after he breathed his last, Petra took to Wylewoode on foot with the same satchel she wore today, filled with oil, flint and steel, setting Adym ablaze.

Then, Ffion was her lifeline. He was so much like Mikhail that she didn't dare get attached, but she couldn't turn him away either. Even when she'd tried to leave him behind, she knew she'd have gone back for him in a heartbeat had he not insisted upon trailing her.

Drawn to her, despite her callousness.

"Why were you in Wylewoode that day?" Petra had never asked for fear of developing a fondness for the boy, though that was a fight long since abandoned.

"I was lost." Silence fell between them as Ffion's words settled.

Some individuals in Neverwoode never stopped speaking about pixies and their fascination with them. Only now did Petra begin to give them any credence.

"Your father's friend, the quartermaster..." Petra's attention fell to James, remembering how the elderly mariner nearly plummeted to the earth, believing he could take flight. She'd thought him raving mad, but was it possible, perhaps, that there was more to his recklessness?

"I thought he'd lost his mind." James shook his head, seemingly as stunned as she. "My father and Smee loved to tell stories about them, among countless other legends." He scoffed, his obsidian eyes meeting Petra's as if he saw her true essence for the first time. No trepidation shone in his fathomless gaze, but neither was there uncertainty regarding Bellamy's proclamation. "You reminded me of some of their tales—feral and clever, but so much more...*better*."

Petra's pulse quickened, recollecting their early interactions. Even when she thought James her foe, the perilous magnetism between them was absolute. Not all was as it seemed.

Still, she was not inclined to accept the lore of nightmares and whimsy as her heritage so easily.

"Whether true or false, what must be done remains. My sister will send her guard, brutes that they are, and we'll want to avoid conflict at any cost. She'll reward anyone who delivers me, alive or dead, to her handsomely. They'll be ruthless in their pursuit."

"Dead." James' contempt for the queen was unequivocal. "She bade me bring your lifeless heart to her in exchange for the safe return of my crew."

Petra wasn't surprised, for Wendy had enlisted their brothers to do the same. But she refused to dwell on her sister, for if she did, she'd only find more traits likening her to those blasted pixies.

"Instead, you thieved and misled her, playing with fire like the filthy pirate you are," she teased, and the captain smirked – a wicked, beautiful tilt of his lips that made her stomach flip.

He stared at the Delphian Cliffs west of where they stood. "We'll lose the sun if we don't press on. I endeavor to leave her with nothing but that vile palace before dawn. Her citizenry will strip her of the rest once they realize what's been done to them."

Ffion grinned. "A shame we won't be there to see it. I'll make my way back to Neverwoode once Adym is set and fetch whoever is willing of your crew to man the ship. We'll be waiting." He indicated Ben, who waddled toward the grove's edge as he spoke.

Oddly enough, it was safer for him to return to Neverwoode, but it worried Petra to the point of nausea to think of him alone in Wylewoode and so near to Wendolyne. "Go to Chamelaute if something seems amiss. Don't come for us, and do not linger. Promise me."

Ffion rolled his eyes. "I won't."

She knew what he meant. He wouldn't promise. Friendship bound them to one another, and she didn't begrudge him that, for she could never have vowed the same to him. He was the truest of brothers and companions through calm and storm.

"Then we'll meet you in Neverwoode." Petra took him by surprise when she wrapped her arms around him. Ffion tugged her closer in a warm embrace.

James clasped his forearm in farewell when they parted, heaving Bellamy's discarded pack over his shoulder, along with a second from Ffion. It didn't seem like much, but the black powder within had proven extremely powerful, even in minimal amounts...and heavy.

Ffion backed away, keeping his eyes trained upon them until he reached the tree line. He offered a salute with a goofy smile on his face. "In Neverwoode."

Petra slung her bag across her chest with the new sword strapped to her back, watching an unexpected piece of her heart wander away with a crocodile in tow.

Chapter Twenty-Three

The sufficiency of her beloved remedy was sorely lacking. For some time, the potency of Wendolyne's orchard elixir had waned, leaving her more frayed than she'd ever been. The soothing effect had become as necessary as the air within her lungs, holding her anxiety at bay and giving her the courage to do the unsavory things required of a beautiful, duty-bound queen.

It had been some dozen hours since her life had been flipped on its head, with her sister and the captain having fled, along with her precious family heirloom.

She'd been delighted in the clock tower, observing the festivities in blissful satisfaction, for she'd managed to come through for her people in the most opulent fashion. The gilded affair had felt like a fantasy come to life, only to devolve into nothing shy of a fever dream.

Wendolyne had returned to her chambers, frustrated to the point of tears, and even worse, she hadn't managed to get much in the way of assistance as all her people were so...*contented*. Their desire for anything beyond dancing and drinking had disappeared alongside their fears.

Sift was a glorious tool, providing serenity that would otherwise be unachievable in a world fraught with worries and doubts, but the side effects led to other struggles. The apathy of her trusted strategists and soldiers was leaving her with little support, and time was of the essence.

She paced within her quarters, feeling anxious for news. There was no telling how long it would be before her people would return and certainly no guarantee they would find what they were after. Petra had proven to be more resourceful than ever she could've imagined.

They need only secure the mine. Adym Grove was a close second, but the vein of sift that lay within the shrouded cave high above upon the Delphian Cliffs was her gravest concern. Still, it was unlikely that her sister knew of its existence, bringing Wendolyne a much-needed sense of solace. She had, herself, only learned of the source recently.

Thinking of Petra made her burn with anger and knowing that she'd somehow managed to charm James made it worse. Her sister had continually bested her, taking the things that were rightfully hers for the whole of her life. Even Petra's supernatural influence proved to be better than her own.

Her hopes for James' affections had evaporated as well. At best, his interest in her hadn't been genuine, but perhaps any inklings of desire she'd sensed within the handsome sea captain had been a farce from the beginning. Wendolyne never lost, except when it came to Petra.

"*Marin!*" she shouted, her voice shrill. Her body pulsed with bitterness as she prematurely prepared for the next phase of Neverwoode's rising sovereignty.

It wasn't yet time. She knew in the back of her mind that she was rushing, but not acting would feel worse. The only option at her disposal, it was better than doing nothing.

Marin poked his head into her room. "My queen?"

"It's time. And I've just the person for our first trial."

The man nodded, excusing himself to set about her orders. A thrill coursed through the queen, with the vague ambition of becoming a preeminent kingdom in the Fayblean realm finally within her grasp. Her aspirations had remained primarily private, too fearful of failure and judgment to share the full scope of her appetite, but she'd persevered.

And she would have nobody to thank for her success aside from herself.

Surely, she'd had some assistance. There were her dealings with Chamelaute, fruitful with their potash provision and the promise of further commerce. Her half-brothers had been willing participants in some of her endeavors, and of course, there was Marin, the man to whom all credit was owed when it came to the advances made with sift and its utility.

Yet none among them had understood her vision, nor had they the capacity to harness the advantages they could achieve through the use of the golden dust that had become her lifeline. It was she who had dreamed beyond her station and wished for more than invisibility in the eyes of the world beyond their borders.

The whole of Fayble saw fit to fill her kingdom with those discarded due to misunderstanding, though they'd neglected their citizenry in their failure to provide adequately.

She would do no such thing. Her people lived lives of fulfillment and sufficiency, satiated through a plentiful dust that left them grateful for their circumstances and unaware of any shortfalls. For that reason alone, Wendolyne esteemed nobody more than herself, knowing that her ingenuity had seen them triumph.

Neverwoode would rise.

Wendolyne summoned a handful of men, but only one was to meet his reckoning. Aeric stood before her, flanked by Javan and Marin. He'd been uncommonly difficult in his short time as her aide, frequently ignoring her directives. In truth, he seemed to delight in ruffling her.

It was little wonder she chose not to put any faith in others.

"Do you think I didn't notice," she began, "that you laughed when that creature at the party nearly consumed me?"

Aeric merely smirked but acknowledged nothing, causing Wendolyne's fury to spike.

"I've seen how you undercut me and actively sabotage my wishes." Wendolyne pursed her lips, collecting herself as she forced a deep breath. "Never once did you truly do my bidding."

"Why would I?" Aeric spat, though his expression didn't change. "How arrogant must you be to expect such deference from a stranger? You would never gain my loyalty."

"I waited. Sift was meant to do its work, but never did it affect you. People always give in eventually, whether to the sift or the simple understanding that life is not worth the living outside our blessed enclave."

Aeric scoffed. "I was never meant to be here, and life is not worth the living with *you*. If you hadn't noticed, it's those who are most driven who are least susceptible, and my only goal since I arrived here was subverting you and your wicked intent. The sift part has been easy to resist!"

So it was. The man told her only what he knew she wished to hear at first and had actively misled her in his reports. For weeks she had watched, awaiting his submission, but never had it come.

Wendolyne smiled tightly. There was nothing more to be said. "It's been my practice to give everyone a fair chance to prove they belong here, but you've shown yourself to be unwilling, disrespecting all I've given you. No more." Her gaze flashed to Marin, who nodded his understanding of her silent directive. "Do it."

Marin took Aeric by surprise, flaying the tender flesh of his forearm with the dagger he'd fashioned from sift. The golden blade gleamed with subtle light, the precious dust making for a beautiful weapon. Aeric's reaction was swift and fierce as he decked his attacker in the jaw, but not nearly fast enough, the severed skin quickly soaking his shirt sleeve in blood and flowing from his wound in ruby-red ribbons.

Lifeblood dripped from his fingertips as Aeric held his arm out, examining his torn flesh with an anguished whimper. Beside him, Javan ripped a shred of fabric from his tunic, reaching for the injured man while Marin recovered in a nearby corner, testing the damage inflicted upon his jowls.

"What is this?" Javan demanded, holding Aeric's injured arm in his trembling hands. "Why would you do such a thing?"

Wendolyne merely raised her brows, biding her time, and she wasn't disappointed.

Before her eyes, Aeric's blood began to shimmer as his hemorrhaging slowed, the color gradually shifting from red to liquid gold as it seeped from the jagged laceration. His veins began to glow, the gilded current coursing through his body and spreading its poisonous fingers throughout his tense frame.

In a matter of moments, the gash upon his forearm began to heal, leaving behind a rough, aurous scar that looked as if molten gold had been drizzled and dried in place of his blood.

It was as grotesque as it was fascinating.

"Leave him," said Wendolyne, as Javan began to bandage the wound, though it no longer appeared to need any dressing. But her brother ignored her, offering her a look of pure disgust.

"My loyalty only goes so far," said he, ripping the excess from the torn tunic with his teeth before tying it off. He waved away her rebuke with an angry flick of his wrist. "Do not attempt to threaten me, for I've already heard enough."

Wendolyne drew another hefty breath, freeing the air through her nose to calm herself. The insolence of her family was trying her patience. That not one among them could understand her insight was a shame indeed.

"Marin has been working on new and different ways to utilize sift," she continued, as though there'd been no discord. "He's a tinkerer, you know – garments, jewelry and now, weapons. Imagine all the things we could do. The supply within the mine won't last forever, so we must preserve it in the ways we are able."

"Yet, you cannot resist sharing the outcomes of your brilliance, so doubtless it will be of little consequence. What happens when Aeric reveals your scheme?" Javan straightened where he stood, so damnably cavalier. In him, there was no hint of regret over his lack of compliance.

"I've no concerns, for sift can also conceal the truth." Her eyes blazed with contempt as even her brother openly doubted her strategy. She rounded on Aeric. "Try me. Tell me a truth."

He trembled a little, whether with the effort of his speech or from his injury, she wasn't sure. "You are utterly *despicable*."

His words seemingly hit him powerfully, his breath catching within his chest as he nearly doubled over, and when he recovered, he flexed his hands as if the pain it had caused reached through to his fingertips.

Well…that was unexpected.

"I knew not of the pain it might inflict," Marin said, his countenance uneasy. "Nor did I realize he'd yet speak the truth."

"We've time to perfect it," Wendy replied, undeterred by the setback. "Perhaps we should try this again. Do your worst, Aeric."

He gritted his teeth, rolling his shoulders back as his trembling ceased. Donning a breathtaking smile, he offered a bow before speaking at last. "Long live Queen Wendolyne. You're truly the fairest of them all." Unfolding at the waist, he met her gaze, the tilt of his lips driving her to distraction.

Lies. All lies.

It took her a moment to reconcile the fallacy in his words with her overwhelming pleasure of hearing them uttered at last.

From beside Aeric, Javan began to snicker. "So you've achieved your greatest wish, sister."

Wendolyne seethed, but she refused to reveal the enmity in her heart. "At the very least, you'll never reveal our kingdom, nor can you speak against me. You'll never betray me again."

"You're right. I will *never* betray you." Aeric held her gaze, his emerald eyes churning with scarcely concealed irony.

Telling the truth would cause him pain, and he could no longer disparage her with his lies. He had nowhere to go, having been rejected by his kingdom, and he'd not survive Wylewoode alone. Only the Penzellians living on the outskirts of the woods had become permanent fixtures, and they endured there by their numbers alone.

Would that he might meet his end, wandering in solitude with only his deceptions to keep him company.

"Begone," she breathed. "You've nowhere to go, and the life of misery you're bound to lead is well deserved. Go forth and rot in your contemptuous superiority!"

Aeric wasted no time, turning on his heel as he made for the exit, with Javan following closely behind. Her brother paused, turning to face her and shaking his head. "I expected better from you. I always thought you'd be more like our mother, but it seems her graces only took with Petra."

Javan slammed the door, leaving his sister behind to drown in self-pity.

Chapter Twenty-Four

Red stone warmed James' fingertips, his hook serving as an anchor as he scaled the cliffside. They were halfway to the top, his muscles burning from the effort. Petra was swift and precise in her maneuvers and his saving grace – so deft he would never look away if not for pebbled bits of rock crumbling under his boots.

Eventide was not far off, a few hours at best before daylight would slip behind the Delphian peaks. Dusk would provide welcome cover under which they might lie low if needed, but Petra was a force of will, moving up the vertical ledge like she was born to climb, as one with the living world around them and everything in it.

They made good time, setting a grueling pace throughout their travels, and she never once complained, determined to lay the queen's maniacal thirst for power to rest.

Wendolyne possessed every evil and immoral tendency one would expect of a pixie, if the ageless lore of their character was to be trusted. Still, it was the beautiful nymph beside him who shared only their most enviable attributes. Some might think James was incautious to trust her, but he did, explicitly. Even if it meant his end, he'd regret nothing.

Sweat beaded on the captain's brow with each length he pushed, but his endurance held fast. Summertide's unforgiving heat would do him in before his uneasiness over the distance between his feet and the earth far below. The sun had already gone ahead of them, but its warmth remained, and the humidity spoiling the air was suffocating.

Petra must've sensed his rising agitation. Either that or she'd become bored, advancing up the ledge with ease, her hair breezing gently behind her. "And you're an intrepid pirate who's scared of heights."

James glanced over his shoulder at her, the weight of his packs and sword tempting gravity. "*Yes.*" The tight little word was all he could manage, ignoring the irony in her observation as his vision spun when he caught a glimpse of the ground far, *far* below.

Her gilded gaze sparkled with mischief as they reached higher, conquering the jagged wall of rock before them. They moved in tandem, but a silent challenge lit Petra's features. "Then this should be easy." She scrambled faster up the cliff, every movement efficient and graceful. It worked if she meant to distract him from the beckoning ground beneath them. The captain could enjoy this game, chasing after the mesmerizing beauty.

Nimble, conscious control brought them closer to the top, Petra's breath having, at last, grown uneven. "Have you always belonged to the sea?" Her question was marked with dismissed fatigue, panting as they gained elevation over Adym Grove.

"I was a woodcutter and carpenter's apprentice in Llundyn before taking to the waters again. My father – " He paused, pinching his eyes closed for a moment before continuing upward. "My father taught me everything."

It was strange to think his days chopping firewood were not so long ago when it felt like a lifetime past. Fondly, he recalled the memories before he'd lost his hand when his dearest friend, Lady Locksley, was all he had in the world. Then, he'd been happy but never satisfied. Leaving the tranquility Llundyn and all his friends offered had brought him new life, for never had he been more fulfilled than serving at Petra's side.

She saw everything good and foul within him and yet found him worthy, casting an undimmable light over the shadows of his hidden grief. A shadow was all he'd been for some time, burdened with guilt for failing to conquer his sorrows when he should've been grateful for all he had.

At long last, they reached the cliff's edge. James hauled himself over the ledge, plunging the point of his hook into soft, rich grassland that met with the foothills of great rust-colored crags in the distance. Once he'd found his bearings, he knelt at the slight overhang, extending his hand to Petra.

She dragged herself toward him, breathing almost as heavily as he was, her perfect lips curved at one end in a provocative smirk. "I should like to have watched you work." Raising a brow, she inspected him from head to toe. "How can you be sure I've not, by some means, enchanted you?"

James helped her to her feet, grazing his nose over the curve of Petra's ear. "Oh, you have," he murmured against her temple. She giggled, a rapturous sound holding him all the more spellbound.

Petra took in the extraordinary view, with lush lands and rugged peaks as far as the eye could see. If their map was correct, they were no longer in Wylewoode. Delphi was a small kingdom that kept to itself and was made up of a quiet, small populace. She'd always assumed it was a desolate territory as undesirable as the deserts of Cyrcasonne, but what lay before them was entirely unexpected.

The terrain wasn't nearly as tricky to navigate as she'd imagined. Stone jutted from the ground in assorted hues from deep amber to a smoky gray with jade and russet-toned bands filtering through the rock. Coyotes yipped playfully, occasionally emerging to watch James and Petra move about their flourishing valleys, never venturing too close.

They were beautiful, as were the woodpeckers and cottontails going about their day. This place was free, serene and lovely. To lay with James among the flowers and grass would have been beyond her dreams.

Before long, they came upon a small glade less than a quarter of a mile wide. At its border sat a humble shack with a dilapidated pen next to it, within which the burro now approaching them was likely meant to be contained. Petra soon recognized the mangy creature as it closed the distance. His ratty fur and the obstinance in his eyes gave him away.

"We're close." Her stomach turned at the thought of carrying out what she knew they must, but there was no other way. If Wendolyne, pixie or not, had found such a malicious use for the golden dust, what would stop another after her?

The cottage wasn't on their map, but she was confident she knew to whom it belonged. Petra couldn't be sure whether they were orphans or runaways, but given the home's condition and the ratty creature grazing the clearing unattended, this residence belonged to the seven miners. That could only mean that Wendy's reserve wasn't far off.

"You know this place?"

The mule drew nearer, and Petra held her hand out, encouraging him closer. "I don't, but I met this smelly beast after you left with Mikhail. This is where the boys from the silo live."

James sniffed at the revelation, seemingly unaware she'd encountered them on the road. "You spoke to them?"

"I did. Yes."

She'd wanted to forget it and all it implied, what with Bellamy's claims of her parentage. They'd *sensed* her, they said, tracking her, even as she'd ducked into the woods out of sight. It wasn't much different from what Ffion had shared about their first meeting when he'd followed the sound of music to where she wept over Neverwoode's plight and the inhumanity of her sister.

"Not intentionally. They found me on my way to the palace to free you, and Ffion, Ben and I journeyed with them into town." Petra reached into her pouch, retrieving some berries they'd found along the way, sharing them with the unkempt animal before her. "They called me a halfling and were not afraid of our crocodile companion because of what they believe I am. They wanted my help to get *this* stubborn thing moving again, fearing the queen would grow angry if they took much longer."

The captain glanced between her and the burro, his brows knit with curiosity. "And did you?"

Averting her gaze, Petra let the creature finish off her berries, wiping her hands on her black trousers. "I only spoke to him, one willful spirit to another." She smiled slightly, scratching behind the beast's ear. "It worked."

"Are you — ?"

"I don't know," she said honestly, afraid to acknowledge how it made more sense of her life than less and explained even more about her sister. "My father loved another woman before he and the late Queen Hilde wed. Her name was Adeline. She was our mother — or is, for I know not if she still lives. My father and Adeline conceived Wendolyne, and she abandoned them for years, only to return shortly after our father's wedding to Hilde. He bedded her, ignoring his vows to honor his bride and remain faithful when they conceived me. The queen was pregnant with our brother, Javan, only to learn of her new husband's infidelity soon after discovering their joyful news. Once my mother gave birth, she left me with our father as well."

James idly ran his fingers through the mule's tangled mane, watching Petra closely as she explained the history of her bastard origins and selfish mother. There was no condemnation in his coal-dark eyes — nothing like how her sister had grown to look at her. In him, there was only tenderness.

"If Adeline was truly a pixie, is it not possible she manipulated your father? A game of sorts?"

Petra had never considered any possibility outside of the king's weakness for a woman who was not his wife. Wendy, however, was the only one who never forgave him for the indiscretion. Even Hilde forgave and loved him, cherishing his children as if they all belonged to her, though she departed the world far too soon.

Perhaps she knew the wayward woman who'd spat on the newlyweds' marriage pledge was more than she seemed.

"I always thought Wendolyne hated me for what he did, but I wonder if it was more for Adeline. I have her eyes... We both have her hair and build. Wendy looks at me and sees our mother and all she represents, what she almost deprived us of in Hilde, our true mother, even if not by blood. And pixies are cruel by nature, are they not?"

James met Petra's gaze, her eyes hot with tears. She was crumbling, desperate to understand what she might never know when the captain pulled her into his arms. "Maybe some, but everyone decides at one point or another whether they'll become what people expect or if they'll strive to be what others cannot easily achieve. It seems Queen Hilde taught you well."

A hushed sob escaped Petra, and the captain held her tighter. "You are everything good in this world."

She remembered when her father had said the same words to his queen. They were happy, she realized. Despite everything, despite the betrayal of their love Petra represented, they found contentment and joy in the brief time they shared. It was no wonder the king lost himself after Hilde's passing. He became so fixated on his kingdom and the fine gilded powder that held his broken heart together.

James blotted the moisture from her cheeks, pressing his forehead to hers before they parted, and something told her nothing could ever hurt more than losing him. She prayed to the God she'd all but forgotten in her turmoil that she never would.

With her fingertips, Petra explored the strong line of his jaw, her mind wandering to the task ahead. "She's going to kill us, James."

"She won't." The captain caught her hand, kissing each knuckle as she had for him the night prior, and she believed him.

"The map depicted water near the opening." James' focus shifted toward the sound of flowing water through a generous thicket west of them. When they first discovered the glade, Petra had mistaken it for wind rustling the leaves of surrounding treetops, but the air was still.

She made for the mule's shoddy pen while the captain peeked through the cottage windows beside it. "You, come with me and stay put for those boys. They can't do their work without you." The creature followed her without hesitation, and she latched him inside his fold with a hinged iron rod.

"Seven cots. You were right." James turned the doorknob, entering the shack with Petra close behind.

"They're all at the mine." She picked up a crust of half-eaten bread and tossed it aside. Unsurprisingly, the place was a pigsty, but it saddened her, nonetheless. They were children, running a home and working Wendolyne's mine, and she doubted they were given another option.

Petra thought about Ffion again, how he'd been drawn to her, and when James suggested that the king may not have been entirely aware of his actions when she was conceived...enchanted.

Influenced.

"We must ensure each of the seven is safe before we ignite the potash."

"Of course." James spared a look over his shoulder, pivoting to face her when he realized there was more. He folded a bit of cloth around some food he'd pilfered from their stores, his features etched with troubled interest. "What is it?"

"I'm going to ask them to leave with us."

The captain pinched his nose between his fingertips, smirking. He took a deep breath, chuckling to himself. "They seem capable enough. They'll be an asset if Ffion cannot convince my crew to depart with us." He fell silent momentarily and shook his head, visibly conflicted over her insistence, when finally, he agreed. "Very well, then. We have less than an hour of daylight, and they're sure to retire before nightfall."

Petra returned his smile, though hers was one of gratitude. She was whole without him, if a bit damaged, but he inspired her to be so much more. He gave her hope that one day she would heal.

"Thank you," she breathed.

* * * *

Water coursed between a copse of weeping willows, rolling over and around boulders and roots, disappearing into a shale wall. Petra moved toward the stream's edge, full of trepidation. Her reflection rippled when she peered into the brook, something bright and shimmering beneath the surface. Narrowing her gaze, whatever she'd seen was gone when she blinked.

"James!"

The captain was beside her instantly, his line of sight following hers into the water. He squinted, attempting to determine what she might've seen, glancing at her once before staring back into the steady gill.

"There." She pointed, her eyes playing tricks on her the closer she looked, but somehow she knew.

Sift.

The same thing had happened after she awoke from her poisoned slumber when Neverwoode hid itself from her.

James removed his boots and stockings, tying the strings to the leather strap of one of his packs before wading into the water. He plodded forward, the constant current challenging his footing until he halted, studying something Petra could not see from where she stood.

"This is it."

"What?"

The captain ducked into the brook, resurfacing with a handful of golden sand. He grinned, beckoning her to join him, the loose waves on top of his head dripping as they fell over his brow. "The mine is concealed because it's full of sift. It's everywhere. There may be another way in, but what if we can't see it?

"Once you trust your eyes, nothing shrouded by sift is hidden, like in Neverwoode. We need only believe to see past it."

"There, you said it yourself. All we need is faith, trust and pixie dust to show us the way." James indicated the stone wall ahead of them where the stream vanished into blackness. His tone was nowhere near amused, but a twinkle of excitement glinted in his dark gaze.

"You want us to go through there?" When he didn't reply, she groaned, slipping her boots off her feet, repeating what the captain had done. "I don't like it. Not at all."

He chuckled. "So, water's not your thing, huh?"

"*No.*"

"We make quite the pair, you and I, with my fear of heights and your fear of water." James smiled, holding his hand out to her as she trembled from the shock of the frigid, Delphian waters.

"Don't let go of me," she breathed, following his lead into the dim opening, damp and humid air around them. They waded deeper until her feet no longer touched the bottom, and the undercurrent swept her legs out from under her. She held fast to James, maintaining control as she kicked against a constant flow, the pressure at their backs pushing them forward.

"*Look.*" Several yards ahead of them was a flatbed of rock. James spat out some water. "We'll have to swim to keep from getting carried farther in, but we can break there to see what's ahead. The current is strong, but we could still make it back if you want to find another way."

Her teeth chattered as she shook her head. "No. We'll press on."

He was right when he said sift was everywhere, the stream refracting golden beams beneath them. It was the only way forward, as much as she hated to admit it. "We need both our arms to fight the course."

The captain didn't argue when Petra let go as cold wracked her bones. "Stay close."

She did. Together they drifted downstream until a sudden surge shoved James ahead and pulled Petra under the surface. Thrashing against the increasing force, she managed a breath only to be sucked below once more. She twisted and kicked, losing all sense of direction when the captain took hold of her wrist.

The water was relentless, dragging her body with it through the stone passage. James didn't surrender, hauling her to himself with one arm, his hook braced within a crack in the rock bed he'd spotted.

Petra clawed her way onto the slick surface, her body convulsing with chills as she reached for the captain. He crawled toward her, rolling to his side, the rise and fall of his chest centering her as she focused on calming her rapid breaths. The stream was louder now, crashing against the tunnel walls.

Wendolyne might have found a way to kill them after all.

Chapter Twenty-Five

They'd made it too far to turn back now, though James couldn't help but wonder if they'd done the right thing. Petra lay beside him, her breathing ragged as she recovered herself.

"Perhaps this is what the map depicted. We only assumed it was the mouth of the sift cave we'd be entering rather than this waterway." James did his best to recall all the most minute details they'd encountered along the way, frustrated by the surprising turn of events. He worried that he'd somehow led them astray.

"That was a bit more than I expected," she managed, rolling to her side. She met James' gaze, her eyes sparkling with tears in the dimming light. "I wish there were another way."

He shook his head, sliding a damp lock of Petra's hair away from her forehead and tucking it behind her ear. Despite their predicament, he didn't believe they were wrong. The traces of sift floating into the cavern grew in abundance as they drifted farther in, almost as if it formed a pathway…but to what?

Yet the roaring tide had grown more furious with each passing yard, causing him to second-guess their mission. The last thing he wanted was to endanger their lives, but neither was failure an option.

"Perhaps I can continue the journey alone," said James. He was about as eager to re-enter the water as he was to wrestle a bear, but for her, he would do anything. "I can see what's out there and return for you."

She shoved him gently in the shoulder. "You'll do no such thing. I'll never understand exactly how or why, but we're in this together." She smiled shyly, and he cupped her face, stroking his thumb over the swell of her cheek.

"It seems you're rather stuck with me."

"Till time's end?" she replied.

James grinned, unable to fathom how he could be so fortunate. "Oh, at the very least, love." He worked his way toward the edge of the berm, squinting as he examined the streaming water. The flow had slowed significantly the farther in they'd floated, making the undulating path formed by the dusting of sift easier to discern.

Petra joined him at his side, each contemplating the potential outcome of any further explorations. The risk involved seemed extensive, though it appeared the only way forward was through. Returning to the mouth of the inlet was not an option – not unless they were planning to swim against the current, and any farther into the cavern would leave them crippled by darkness.

That left them with only one option.

"Are you prepared to make your way down there?" James indicated a murky passage, likely a half dozen meters under, with an abundance of sift emanating from the hole. "I don't know that there's another way."

"I can do it." Petra wrung the moisture from her hair before casting a wary glance at the burbling stream. "I only hope what we've been searching for awaits us on the other side."

Indeed.

James ignored his nagging sense of dread, instead rising to his feet. He pulled Petra up behind him, convincing himself their efforts would be fruitful, though, in addition to his disdain for heights, he loathed small spaces.

Small *underwater* spaces were certain to be a newfound joy.

The subtle light streaming from the void in the deep gave him a sliver of hope, for surely there was something there if only they could brave the tides. He reached for Petra, squeezing her hand. "We'll stay together as much as we're able. It'll be hard to see, but if we aim for the light..."

She laughed once without humor. "Going toward the light is to be avoided, is it not? At least if one wishes to remain alive."

James pressed his lips together, suppressing the urge to chuckle, for it would doubtless be poorly received. Still, he couldn't help being amused, her dark humor a flawless match for his own. Oddly enough, it was just the push he needed to proceed, knowing in the depths of his soul that he would see this quest through.

She was worth every challenge and every doubt, deserving of so much more than he could give. He would never fail her.

"Come, darling. Shall we? Poseidon awaits." He grinned, earning a long-suffering sigh alongside a ghost of a smile from the girl with eyes the color of sunlight.

Taking several hefty breaths, each nodded their ascent before diving in once more, the briny deep enveloping them in its icy embrace as they stroked their way toward the abyss below.

The faint glow from the vanishing light above did little to assist them in their venture, with the pressure from the water all around them stirring a swelling sense of dread. James struggled through, reaching for his lifeline as he kicked furiously onward. Petra's touch brought much-needed peace, even as he fought the urge to abandon his course.

His mind grew fuzzier by the moment as the sift clouding the water became more prominent. Illogical though it was, he fought at the overwhelming solace luring him into counterfeit contentment. On a cognitive level, he knew it to be false, even as everything within him desired to simply *succumb*.

It wasn't real.

Without warning, the current shifted, drawing them deeper into the chasm with no effort necessary on their part, and somehow that was worse. They were being sucked rapidly toward the hollow, with the utter lack of control over their circumstances causing James to panic.

From beside him, he could see that Petra felt the same, her eyes wide with alarm as she felt the surging tide shoving them downward. Altering his strategy, James threw his arms above his head, forming a point with his hand to change his trajectory. Petra followed suit, the duo soaring toward the crevice.

Resisting the flow had been foolhardy, but with each length they descended, the thrust upon them grew, and James' breath began to give way. His lungs burned with the effort, clinging to what little air remained as it evaporated from within.

The rapidly approaching hole came into striking distance, with Petra sliding through just before James. A solid wall of black hemmed them in, with the pinprick of light at its end his only salvation in a moment fraught with abject fear. Kicking his way through, he assisted in his ascent, clutching Petra's arm as he labored upward at last.

Much like the other side of the cavity, the current shifted, shooting the pair upward in a surge of bubbles and sift as it spat them out, with James and Petra washing ashore in a tumble of limbs as they hurtled to an abrupt end upon a bank of gold.

James rolled to his belly, pushing his upper body from the sand as he coughed, sucking air in harsh, greedy gasps. Petra lay on her face mere feet from where he recovered, her chest contracting in fitful bursts.

An agonized moan escaped her, and James crawled her way, pushing her over to face him. He slipped his arm beneath her neck, tipping her head back to open her airway. "Are you all right?"

She nodded, her breath evening as he held her. She fisted his shirt, drawing him closer as she brought her mouth to his. Her kiss was fierce, full of fire and life, as if to remind them both what was real as they huddled together among a hollow of sparkling sift.

"Never again," Petra breathed against his lips. Slowly, she opened her eyes, craning her neck to take in the splendor of the cave that was their refuge.

Gilded veins sprawled over the height and breadth of their rocky cage, illuminated by the setting sun, its red-orange hues filling the chasm with warmth, even as the explorers at its heart shivered within its center. Beneath them lay a combination of sift and sand, with one readily blending into the other, almost as if there were no difference between them.

"What is this place?" she whispered, as if she wished not to disturb its beauty.

"Hopefully, what we've been searching for," said James, for if it were not, they'd nearly perished for nothing. He flipped to his back, his gaze traveling over the jagged crack some twenty feet above, running the length of the domed ceiling. The walls were smooth, almost polished, adjoining the arch above, forming a natural architectural wonder.

It was a shame they had to destroy it.

James sat up, wresting his satchel from his back and fumbling through its contents. His boots were there, soaked but none the worse for wear, as were the two jars of potash that had been wrapped in several pieces of hide. That was another story altogether. He unscrewed the cap, finding that their contents were only half dry.

"Dammit."

Petra rose to his side, her face falling as understanding dawned. "We haven't time to wait for it to dry. And even if it did, there's no telling if it will be as explosive as before."

"I doubt it." James cursed under his breath, considering all the ways in which they'd failed, despite their best efforts. If his jars were this waterlogged, so too would Petra's be. "We'll have to pray it's enough to blow this place. Or perhaps we can locate whatever supply is supposedly stored here."

Still, as he said the words, his mind was filled with doubts. The opening at one end of the grotto suggested yet more caves to be explored, and with the several jars of potash between them, he didn't think it nearly enough to blast even their current surroundings.

Petra stood, swaying as she took to her feet. "Look over there." She indicated a firepit several yards away, the area scattered with various food debris. A handful of logs encircled the bowl, and James knew they needed to get moving.

"We're not the only people who've been here. Should we dry out before we go?"

"Let's head out." She dragged James to his feet, each making their way over to the logs lining the pit. They took a few moments to collect themselves, tying their boots and reorganizing their bags. James offered Petra a less-than-palatable piece of dried meat, now moist with river water, but she didn't seem to mind as she quickly devoured the offering.

He, too, was starving, eagerly filling his belly before they took off into the other part of the cave. Stars only knew what awaited them there.

"Those should help." James jogged toward the opposite wall, returning to Petra with two torches and a piece of flint. "I've the steel right here," he added, waving his hook before her. She smiled, seemingly enjoying his carefree approach to an otherwise unfortunate set of circumstances.

He struck the crook of his hand against the flint, grinning as sparks flew from the impact. Petra held the torch beneath the stone, gasping as the fabric-wrapped end soaked in oil soon caught flame.

"That's a neat trick. And convenient, too." Petra's smile brought him peace, her enthusiasm soothing away some of his misgivings. He repeated the action, lighting a second torch with ease. The warmth of the flames thawed a bit of the chill clinging to their damp bodies, even as they illuminated the vast hollow that lay before them.

James anchored his torch against himself, holding on to the shaft with his hook and maintaining a sword in his other hand. There was no telling what lay ahead, and though Petra's experience with the seven lost boys had been benign, he didn't wish to take any chances. If they were indeed somewhere within the network of passages, the last thing he wanted was to be unprepared.

They set off, making for the opening at the far end of the space, where they entered a dark thoroughfare. The tunnel was narrow and not terribly high, and James did his best to ignore the creeping sense of confinement as they wandered farther along.

In short order, they reached a foyer of sorts, though it felt far more like a dungeon with no escort, aside from their blessed torches. They walked to the center, noting two additional pitch-black passageways and a third that harbored a modicum of light, its faint glow streaming into the chamber.

Petra paused, gesturing to the largest of the three corridors before putting her finger to her lips. They'd been traveling in silence as it was, so her sudden concern with their volume piqued his interest. Listening intently, James suddenly heard it—a merry tune whistling through the catacombs.

As if managing the labyrinth of tunnels all around them weren't enough already... Nothing, it seemed, about blowing the caves to smithereens would be easy.

Chapter Twenty-Six

Their singing was as wistful as it was when Petra had first heard it. Lost to their families or themselves, she would not know until she could speak with them, but under no circumstances should they have ever been left to labor the mine – and alone at that.

The melody was the same as before, melancholy on their lips in contrast to their otherwise seemingly colorful dispositions. She'd not accepted their suggestion about her heritage, nor Bellamy's – or Ffion's, for that matter – but the seven lost boys had to have learned the song somewhere. Whether they wrote it or were taught the lyrics by another, they believed every word, their tune a cryptic revelation in itself.

Petra held out her torch ahead of them as they inched nearer to the echoing sound. She and James were still distant enough that the miners' whistles and voices were muffled through the curved passage, but the familiar refrain was unmistakable.

"Can you make out the words?" Petra peered at the captain, her words barely above a whisper.

James paused, inclining his ear toward the source of the music. "The second one to the right, the guiding stars, Arctos and Ursa."

"They're trying to call the pixies home."

A silhouette came into view, reflections from the golden veins along the cavern walls illuminating enough of the figure to reveal one of the older boys Petra had encountered the morning before. James rooted himself between her and the youth, sword in hand.

"I guess it kind of worked. Looks like you took the hard way in." The boy scoffed, surveying their drenched clothing and hair, advancing toward them as if the captain would not run him through. "Relax, Hook. We wouldn't ever hurt one, even a halfling. I can't speak for the queen's guards, though."

Petra remembered this one. If she recalled correctly, his name was Cole – a grumpy, unpleasant sort, though he may have had good reason for his churlish nature.

"They haven't been letting anyone in or out since they arrived less than an hour ago, but you're a bit too soggy to have come with them. I assume you're the reason they're here."

"Yes." Telling him the truth was a calculated risk. James shot a warning look at Petra, glancing back to Cole, who merely chuckled. She pushed past the captain, though he remained ready to lunge if the circumstances turned against them. "We want to take you and the others away from this place. Go where you wish after that, but you should never have been made to work here."

"All our needs are met." Cole glowered at James, his blade still firmly gripped where he stood beside Petra. "We're each better off than we were before, but I can't say I understand why they want them to return. The pixies, I mean."

"You've seen them?" The captain relaxed slightly, his watch vigilant, studying their surroundings before fixing his black stare upon Cole.

"Pixies? I've lived among them for years. They never stay anywhere long. Until the tinkerer betrayed our home, there were always a few around to ensure their children had what they needed, but mostly, they kept to the woods. We're the last of their kept humans. The rest are all grown up." The boy shifted on his feet, appearing utterly indifferent toward the creatures he claimed to know so well. "They wouldn't have let me stay much longer anyway, so I don't mind that they left. Only halflings, you and Belle, remain anywhere near here—and the queen, of course."

"Bellamy?" While she wished to trust Cole and the other boys, Petra knew she shouldn't divulge much. But she needed confirmation. Again, if lore rang true, it lent more clarity to Bellamy's behavior than less to learn she was part pixie. It helped her understand the woman's chaos if they were the same, for Petra often struggled with her own callousness.

"You know Belle?" Another boy emerged from behind Cole. Stretching his arms over his head, he slapped his cheeks, stifling a yawn. "Where's she been?"

"I looked everywhere for you after the guards finished their search. You were *sleeping*?" Cole smacked the younger one on the back of his head, "Almos doesn't care much for the pixies, either, but if they do come back, they won't like that you've been shirking your duties." He looked pointedly at his workmate. "You know how they get."

"Bellamy sailed with my crew from Llundyn." James sheathed his sword, though he remained watchful. "She is well." It was a diplomatic approach, considering there was no certainty regarding their relationship with the snarky halfling or if they saw her as a friend or foe.

Time was slipping away with each second, with each question passed between them — moments they didn't have to spare. The captain gave Petra a reassuring nod, recognizing and sharing her concern, urging her to state her case to the two boys. If any would be convinced of the troubling intent regarding their work, it seemed it might be these.

"We could use your help," said Petra, Almos and Cole eying her with interest as they glanced between one another. "The substance you mine... Do you know what it does?"

Almos yawned again, shaking his head rapidly to stave off his weariness. "They told us it was why we were chosen."

"Our innocence keeps us immune to its effects. That's why they expel us as we age." Cole huffed in irritation, evidently having grown agitated with the pixies' conduct. "I pretend I don't know what happened to Belle and all the others before her because I don't trust them. The younger ones? They're like my brothers. I can't leave them behind."

"Then bring them with you wherever you go." Petra's desperation grew by the second, silently pleading they would understand. They had to. "The queen and the sovereigns before her have used sift to keep their realm hidden from the rest of the continent. It has shrouded and manipulated the citizenry for decades, holding them captive to the whims of whoever rules them. They are unwitting prisoners like your brothers, but you will all be free if the mine is gone."

_Cole's eyes brimmed with bewilderment, but Almos spoke, his gaze downcast as he sorted his thoughts. "But where will we go? None of us remember anything before the pixies brought us here. This is our home."

"I haven't forgotten. The mine and cottage have never been our home, only where we lay our heads at night." Bitterness laced every word from Cole's mouth, and Petra wished there was more time to expose what their lives had been there with the creatures whose existence was becoming impossible to dismiss. "What do you need from us?"

Desolation emanated from the eldest boy, his misery so palpable she would sooner turn herself over to Wendolyne's guards than see him or any of the seven under her authority any longer. "All we ask is that you get the others out and far away from here, and if you're willing, tell us where we can find the queen's potash." With a torch still in hand, Petra opened her satchel with the other, retrieving one of their dampened jars. "We were told there was more and brought all we could manage."

Cole chuckled, his grin revealing the face of one rapidly forsaking boyhood. "If those packs are full of that, you're sure to create a decent blast, sodden as it is, but we can do far better."

"We hoped so." Beside Petra, James settled more each moment, despite the havoc they planned to spark. He stepped toward the two miners, resting his hand on

Cole's shoulder with respectful regard. "Come with us, and I will ensure you and your brothers are well cared for. If you have families, we will find them, but you will not be left to fend for yourselves, though you've proven more than able."

Cole spared a look at Almos, who stared at the ground, then down the stone passage where the din of steel meeting rock reverberated toward them. "They will do as I say, but the guards are only just outside. Almos can show you where we keep the potash while I explain everything to the others. If they stop working, the queen's company will want to know why."

He turned to Almos, taking hold of his arm. "Help lay the potash and show them the other way out, but no torches. Just one spark once those drums are open, and we'll all be dead. Do the front of the cavern last and leave with the others. Lason and I will create a diversion once you've left. I want you and Nesh to bring everyone to the pool where these two will end up and go with them. When Lason and I are through distracting the guards, we'll find you when we're clear."

"My ship called *Jolly Roger* is anchored in Altanys Cove near Neverwoode's docks. We'll head south and be on the lookout for you along the way." James extended his torch to Cole. He took it without meeting the captain's eyes.

They were children. What the pixies and Wendolyne expected of them was utterly horrifying. That anyone so young would be left to handle potash alone or labor in a dark hollow was unthinkable.

Almos swallowed hard, apprehension plain on his youthful face. "Follow me."

Faintly glowing streaks of blue moonlight shone on the gilded cavern walls, emanating from narrow fissures splitting the ridgeline above. It was barely enough to help them navigate the various turns and uneven ground, but it would have to do. They'd seen, time and again, how little it took to ignite the hazardous potash, and after what James had learned from the miners, he couldn't be more ready to bring the cave down.

"In here." The lad, Almos, was no more than a dark figure leading the way ahead of James and Petra. He showed them into a small cavity off the passageway, and the captain scarcely believed his eyes.

No wonder Cole had laughed when Petra showed him their waterlogged potash jar when nearly two dozen barrels were stashed away in their cave. The drums were mere shadows in the dim light, but there was no mistaking the pungent odor of ash and smoke wafting from the wooden casks.

Petra moved toward a drum, yanking off its lid and looking inside. "It's completely full."

"We get deliveries once a week or so." Almos talked about the explosive compound as if it couldn't blow him to bits.

"There's a hole in the top. If we can tip the barrels onto their sides, we can roll them to disperse the potash," said Petra as she resealed the cask.

James made his way to her, and together they pushed the drum over. "See if you can move it on your own."

It seemed a significant effort, but she did, rolling the barrel to the passage.

"We'll use all of it, then." The captain motioned for Almos, who helped him tip a second barrel, then a third, over and over until each was on its side.

They moved quickly in spite of the creeping darkness filling the mine. The lost boys continued their work, whistling and singing as they had when James and Petra first arrived, their lively tunes echoing about the shimmering chamber.

"That's the way out," Almos said. He led them about halfway through one of the various underground paths, revealing a tapered opening leading upward and out through the top of the mine with bright, twinkling stars visible outside. Just from the look of it, the hole appeared tight enough that James wondered if he might not fit through and certainly didn't relish the thought of trying, but there was no other choice.

"I'm sorry for what you've been through," Petra said suddenly, and the captain could only see the contours of her profile in a sliver of silver light.

"It's not been so bad, but I don't want to stay here, either." Almos didn't linger, carrying on before anything more could be said.

Though the casks were heavy, Petra's method worked well, enabling them to cover ground more swiftly than James thought possible. It was simple, really.

After a time, they were back where they'd started, where the water had left them frozen and breathless. They abandoned nearly half Wendolyne's potash there, making several trips back and forth, hoping to implode the entire ridge itself. All that remained was the heart of the cavern where the boys toiled away, as well as the main entrance.

"Come when they're quiet," said Almos, nodding in parting. He would go ahead of them to leave with the others, his farewell one of nervous excitement. "See you at the pool."

It wasn't long before the miners' songs turned to eerie and foreboding silence as James and Petra found their way to where Cole and Lason would be waiting.

They were there, as promised, silently scattering the black powder. Lason offered a tentative smile to them both, though his worry was plain. No one dared speak a word for fear a guard could overhear, but that didn't stop them from rotating the barrels until all but one was emptied.

"You can draw the guards from here with this." Petra's voice was nearly inaudible as she removed the pack from her shoulders. Opening the flap, she took from it the weapon she fought so fiercely to retain when Crispin attacked her upon the *Gloriana*, along with a small leather case. It was the very thing that warned him something was so horribly amiss when its blast cracked through the ship. Slipping the metal hollow and pouch at her waist, she surrendered her satchel, filled with jars of potash, to the boys.

Cole tucked her bag under his arm with a nod of goodbye, with Lason following close behind. Together, they rolled the last drum, pushing it through the pitch-black entrance of the mine.

James took Petra's hand and ran, making for the narrow opening that would see them back into the tranquil woods of Delphi. With the subtle glow of the moon peeking between the ridgeline overhead, they found their way, using the passage walls when their precious light was drowned by eventide.

Lifting Petra onto the stone edge, chilled and soaked to the bone, they regarded each other with unspoken awareness of what they were about to do. The captain trailed behind as Petra ascended into the tapered outlet. Cold, rigid rock scraped against his shoulders, too broad for the gateway as he was. His hook, again, aided the climb, bracing him as the hole shrank around them.

Above James, Petra pulled herself out of the vertical tunnel, anxiously peeking down at him as he squeezed his way through and clambered after her, hissing when a sharp bit of shale sliced his shoulder. It was the least of his worries, even as blood warmed his skin.

They were out.

To the west, not far off, fading orange light illuminated the valley below, with the pool and the mouth of the cavern they'd entered through just visible at the base. They waited momentarily, Petra retrieving the handheld cannon at her waist.

"I need some of your potash."

James obliged, rifling through his pack for the driest of what he had, uncorking the glass container with his teeth. He watched as she pinched the powder down the muzzle, slipping a short rod from the steel pipe's underbelly and shoving a leaden sphere down the barrel.

"Where did you learn how to do this?" The captain was rapt, observing in awe when Petra slid the stick back into place and sprinkled another bit of potash into a small metal attachment.

"Bellamy showed me. It seems her father made it." The weapon was a similar design to what she'd used aboard the *Jolly Roger* when she signaled their approach into Altanys, though he hadn't pieced it all together until that moment. James was shocked to learn they were products of some innovative family trade, and yet he hadn't suspected she was a halfling, either.

It seemed Belle was full of surprises.

Petra pulled the silver hammer back on the handheld apparatus until something *clicked* into place.

Holding it far from herself, she gripped the base, her finger hovering before a thin lever.

"Are you sure about this?" The captain moved to her side as she aimed the muzzle toward the opening before them.

"Nope."

Then, she pulled the trigger.

Chapter Twenty-Seven

Petra could just make out the lost boys below. Really, *really* far below. They gathered beside the same body of water where she and James had entered the cave, only now it appeared smaller and darker. A sliver of the crescent moon hovering above scarcely illuminated their surroundings, casting a subtle glow that winked off gentle ripples within the pool.

To their left, a gushing stream flowed freely over the clifftop, the waterfall coursing toward the reservoir in a riotous wave. Spanning the breadth of the bluff, it appeared too deep to traverse without losing their footing, even as the remainder of the ridge upon which they stood groaned in the throes of its final moments.

Smoke rose out of the hole they'd climbed from, and Petra could only pray the potash was doing its work. But if the trembling earth beneath them were any indication of success, it wouldn't be long before the whole cavity gave way, leaving them at the mercy of the imploding rubble.

"We have no other choice," said James, his countenance troubled as he stepped to the edge. "And we're running out of time."

The stone floor bellowed from behind them, echoing his sentiments as a fissure formed, zig-zagging its way across the rocky terrain and dividing the length of the clifftop in two. Doubtless, it was too fragile to traverse as bits of rock gave way, tumbling into the cavity underneath.

Petra joined James, staring into the abyss just beyond her toes, wondering how she'd gotten into this. She glanced toward him, a man who'd quickly become her anchor, knowing she'd have the courage to do what needed to be done with him at her side.

"Is it deep enough?" The thought hadn't occurred to Petra before then, with her focus too diverted to the machinations involved in staying alive. Absently, she considered how much she'd prefer all their life-and-death scenarios not to include water, but it seemed that was not to be.

Crumbling earth urged them toward a final decision, with the ground behind them rapidly disappearing alongside the clamor of falling rubble. Petra reached for James, and with nothing more than a quick nod, they leapt from the edge, hand in hand.

She was too afraid to scream, the wind rushing past her in a heady gust as they plummeted through the air. The freefall was a rush of a lifetime, though her panic overwhelmed her unequivocally. Petra closed her eyes, picturing herself floating gently into the water rather than plunging like a rock.

Her only indication that anything had changed was James' sharp intake of breath, alongside a strange sensation of weightlessness. She opened her eyes to find they'd slowed significantly, not quite suspended but far from the rapid drop from mere seconds ago.

They continued their descent, falling with more direction and certainty as they glided to the earthen floor below, skipping over the pool of water entirely. The boys were there, waiting with vines with which to pull them from the water that were no longer necessary. To their credit, not one of them looked shocked — a sense that Petra felt to her very bones.

"I know how, but...*how*?" said James, his incredulous gaze landing upon Petra when their feet hit the ground.

"I don't know," Petra breathed, her eyes wide with disbelief. They hadn't flown, not really, but they hadn't fallen, either. In truth, she wasn't even sure she could repeat her little trick if she tried. It seemed that somewhere deep within her ancestry had taken over, lending her the capacity to do what should only ever happen in fairytales.

"It's simple. Not believing in who you truly are can't keep you from becoming what you're meant to be. Part of you wants to embrace it." Nesh spoke as if it were as evident as the creeping twilight, and maybe it was, but for Petra, it felt too sudden and strange.

James turned to face her, squeezing her shoulder as he took in her startled features. "Are you okay?"

Petra nodded, pinching her eyes shut as she reconciled all that had transpired. "I'll be fine."

He rested his forehead against hers, their breath mingling as she recovered herself. She bit her lip, meeting his dark gaze, somehow understanding that it didn't have to make sense. Some things just *were*.

"We must go," came a voice from behind her. Petra turned to find the boys packed, and at the ready, their satchels slung over their backs. There were no evident reservations, with each seemingly prepared to accompany them with no more questions asked.

"What about the others?" James cast a weary glance over his shoulder, and Petra could tell he was weighing the same thoughts as she. Waiting for the two decoys seemed the right thing to do, even if it did put them at risk of being caught.

"No," said Almos, stifling a yawn. "They'll find us. We mustn't tarry."

A shared sense of disbelief passed from Petra to James, their eyes meeting in silent understanding. The boys didn't mince words. Neither did they lack courage, readily rising to any occasion with the confidence of a seasoned adult.

James merely shrugged. "Well…lead on, then."

They set off into the darkened woods with nary a word, Petra sticking close by James' side. She didn't want to see their situation as 'us versus them' but found it difficult not to. She didn't know these boys from Adam, and the fact that they readily accepted her plight made her wary, as it had everything to do with her newly uncovered heritage and naught where she was herself concerned.

The sun had long since disappeared on the horizon, leaving a sky of streaming purples and blues in its wake. The moon was of little assistance, leaving them at the whims of a wild forest fraught with peril and little means of navigation.

It wasn't Petra's way to frolic about with no plan, yet her life of late had been nothing but flying by the seat of her pants. And even though the boys had willingly taken on the adventure at hand, that didn't make her feel any less responsible.

Trekking into the trees, they all did their best to keep close to one another. Though Petra had spent much of her life managing the chaos within the ominous woods, nothing had prepared her for doing the same with so many lives at stake.

And there was her burdened mind — an unnecessary distraction amid their already tenuous circumstances.

Bellamy's words rang through her head, wreaking havoc on her conscience. Pixies were a part of both of their legacies, and Petra had just blown their enclave to bits.

"There'll be nothing for the pixies to return to," Petra whispered. "And these boys — we've destroyed the only home they've ever really known and all their protection."

Guilt gnawed at the back of her mind. And while she didn't have any particular affinity for the pixies or their wellbeing, they were also a part of her, of her heritage. What would become of them?

"They're nomadic beings, as are we," said Hatsch, almost as if he'd read her mind. "Like butterflies or birds, if it helps you think of it that way. The cave was a home in a way, but it was also a means of protection for the pixies and us."

"With the cave gone, they'll simply find somewhere new to live — if they ever bother to come back at all." Nesh kicked a small rock from his path. "The cave didn't provide any protection, anyway. That was merely the pixies ensuring their own survival."

The bitterness lacing their words heartened Petra, for it seemed the boys weren't nearly as enamored with their guardians as she'd initially believed. And, as much as it hurt to acknowledge, their previous caretakers' self-serving, callous nature also lurked within her.

Yet nothing said she couldn't change her path.

"They shrouded the cavern in their essence — sift, as you seem to call it — to keep us hidden so that we could gather it in peace. They were under threat of exposure for many decades, trading their essence for silence with the leadership of your forsaken Neverwoode." Hatsch was matter of fact, as if his revelations were as plain as the shadows of night. "The arrangement benefited us all, I suppose, even if it has been hard work."

His admission broke Petra's heart anew. Tales of pixies were rife with incidents of lies and coercion. She knew from legends that they were apt to make underhanded deals, favoring themselves with little to no regard for the outcomes of their victims. Likewise, her grandparents were no better, extorting sift in exchange for their silence.

The littlest one, Jon, tripped, nearly faceplanting in a bramble of spikes before Gailen caught him by the neck of his tunic. He patted the boy, each sharing a shy smile before righting themselves to forge onward.

"Perhaps a short break is in order," James said, and Petra agreed. Strange as it was, given the boys' significant maturity, she and the captain were the prevailing adults in the situation.

The boys nodded, doubtless as exhausted as they were, with each making for a spot on the Wylewoode floor to take a break from their moonlit journey through the woods.

Petra took to a nearby tree without a word, sitting beneath it as she rested against the trunk. James joined her at her side, releasing a pent-up breath as he tipped his head back, closing his eyes. He reached for her, linking their fingers together. Settling her head upon his shoulder, she felt, at long last, as if she could breathe.

* * * *

"James," Petra uttered, his name like honey on her tongue. His response didn't disappoint as he pulled her closer still, his arm coiled around her shoulders. She felt at peace in his embrace, melting into him as if there was no close enough.

She must've dozed, her heavy eyes still closed with all the laziness of a winter's morning spent in the warmth of soft, downy blankets. She stretched a little, finding that his arms grew tighter still.

Smiling, she searched for the will to move, to open her eyes and return to their trek, though it was, quite possibly, the last thing she wished to do at the moment. "James."

Petra knew he was strong, but his hold was becoming uncomfortable. She shifted, opening her eyes to find she was no longer tangled with her lover. Wriggling her shoulders, she quickly found that movement only worsened her predicament.

To her left, James yet slept, lost to the same fatigue she'd suffered and evidently unaware of their plight. He, too, was wrapped in the cords enveloping Petra. The creeping vines seemingly had a mind all their own, having bound each person in their circle, whether by their feet, their arms, their shoulders.

"*James*," she hissed, ignoring her rising panic. Never before had she seen such things. She didn't know how they worked or what might set them off. Lightly tapping James' foot with the toe of her boot, she could only hope it would be enough.

He stirred, whipping his head from where it lay atop hers. His eyes widened with realization, even as he remained still, thankfully gaining awareness more promptly than she had. Petra could tell by looking at his face that the vine wrapped around his chest was constricting further.

The thought of being slowly squeezed to death was frightening and becoming increasingly likely with each moment that passed. She resisted the urge to squirm, though her ability to breathe was quickly being suppressed. Darkness spotted the edges of her vision, slowly floating through her line of sight.

All around her, the others began to wake, each coming to in shocking fashion. To their credit, nobody spoke a word, managing their fear in silence as the damnable creepers coiled and writhed along the woodland floor.

Indeed, they were as good as dead.

From before her, Petra watched as the shoot suddenly shuddered, thrashing where it was pinned to the earth through the thickest part of its form with a short spear. A second halberd followed, striking several feet aft of the first one. The vine thinned, stretching as if it were attempting to free itself, appearing more serpentine than plant.

Through the brush, Lason and Cole stumbled into view, each with an atlatl poised to launch more deadly barbs. Their spears were cradled within the shallow channel running the length of their makeshift weapons, each flung with precision as they arced through the space separating them from the sinuous creepers.

The halberds hit their marks, causing the vines to recoil and shrink away, retreating into the darkness after freeing itself from the spikes in a surge of wild, convulsive movements.

Its fingers withdrew, leaving behind a startled crew. They rose to their feet, examining their arms and legs and dusting off their chests as if to wipe away the memory of their captivity.

"What was that thing?" James managed, trembling with surging adrenaline. "I didn't mean to fall asleep..."

"You weren't asleep. You were poisoned." Lason moved to meet his brother. "The same happened to Gailen and me when first we were lost. That *creature* emits toxins, lulling you into complacency so that it may have its way." He glanced at James and Petra, his mind seemingly lost to another time.

"We suffered through a harrowing night, held within the constricting embrace of one of those *things*, all the while listening to the pixies laugh as they observed our plight. It wasn't until I thought, perhaps, we were done for that they came to our rescue, absorbing us into their enclave within the mine and putting us to work."

Petra didn't readily cry, but understanding a bit more of these boys' history was profoundly troubling. Indeed, they'd endured more than most at such a young age, even unto depending upon her vile pixie brethren for any shreds of security. Their circumstances made her ache, her ambitions for some sense of closure for each of them growing moment by moment.

She watched as Lason hugged his brother, the pair sharing a smile that warmed her weary spirit. If there was a way through, she would find it, and no being, human or otherwise, was going to stop her.

Chapter Twenty-Eight

Neverwoode was growing restless, and though every crevice and seam of its streets still shimmered gold, the air was clear.

While the boys were adept at many things, Petra hated sending them off alone, but it was safer for them to be nowhere near her until they were ready to leave. Ffion would be somewhere along the wharf to receive them, hopefully with Ben and whoever remained of James' complement. Whatever the case, they'd have to make do. At the very least, they were armed, Petra having left her sword with Cole, though she'd seen what they could do with weapons carved from scratch.

"Keep your head down." The captain tugged Petra's hood over her brow, grazing her cheek with the cool curve of his hook. Obsidian eyes found hers, somehow bright in their infinite depth. "Even cloaked in rags, one can't help but stare."

She would never get over his effect on her or how she'd once feared him before ever knowing his face.

Every part of him was beautiful—ardent and pure. Petra leaned into his touch, skimming her fingertips over the honed steel.

James smiled fiendishly, his lips brushing past hers in a way that made her ache for more. "Tell me we'll have this."

"*More*," she vowed, fitting her mouth to his. The captain deepened the kiss, holding Petra to him, enveloping her in his powerful arms. Something low and feral rumbled in his throat when she trailed her fingers up his spine, awakening an equally wild part of herself she'd never dared explore. Nothing more was promised in a world where avarice and malign thirst for control went unchecked, but the moment was theirs, stolen and fleeting though it was.

James nuzzled Petra's temple, clenching his jaw as they parted. "We'd do well to leave under cover of night."

She agreed. They could only trust that Ffion had scraped together a crew when they reached him, but Petra wouldn't leave before she was sure her brothers were safe and well.

The afternoon heat had already begun its surrender to sunset as a soothing breeze kissed her exposed skin. Hatsch's time-worn mantle was heavy upon her shoulders and far too warm, but she was beyond grateful for his kindness. Something about it gave her peace—perhaps the knowledge that innocence and good might still prevail.

"We're close." The apothecary was less than a mile away, where they hoped to find Javan or Lillia in their small apartment above it. Petra would have envied their humble quarters if not for the circumstances surrounding the newlyweds.

Together, they moved swiftly through narrow alleyways, avoiding notice when James took her by the arm. He nodded toward a portly male on his hands and knees upon the cobbled road. At first glance, the man was injured, but under closer study, they noticed him pinching bits of sift from the cracks between pavers, squirreling away a small supply for himself from what remained.

Others had begun to do the same, sweeping remnant dust from rooftops and windowsills. It was only a matter of time before bedlam confronted the kingdom. But the people were free, and soon, they would understand what it meant to *live*. Many of them never had, as descendants of exiles who'd never known anything but pretty lies.

Petra rapped on the apartment door with James close at her side. Lillia answered after the second knock, her features alight with surprise.

"Come in." Ushering them into the cluttered loft, Lillia started back toward the entrance before stopping herself, wringing her hands. "I'm sorry. I thought you might be Javan. You two have created quite a mess for us to clean up."

Petra held her tongue, biting the inside of her cheek.

James did not, raising a brow in disbelief. "Would you have preferred we do nothing? These people are, by no means, blameless, but neither are we. They're mere social delinquents who were too much of a nuisance in their homeland. If they were hardened criminals, they would have been punished accordingly. Just because other nations couldn't see their potential doesn't mean they deserve to be manipulated with fantasies."

"We were not in a position to oppose the queen. She's had people executed for less." Lillia moved toward the captain, challenging his dark presence.

"But *she* was...alone." He indicated Petra at his back, unmitigated fury contorting his features. "Your husband might have secretly kept her alive through her poisoned slumber, but who was her advocate when Wendolyne ordered her dead? Who objected when Wendy demanded her heart?"

Maybe Petra should've stopped him, but she'd buried the same questions daily, refusing to become embittered toward her brothers, who she knew loved her despite Wendolyne's games.

James, too, had faced the queen's remarkable influence and had never fallen prey to her artifice. Petra wondered if, while only halflings, their effect was somewhat like that of sift, largely dependent upon one's resolve or heart's intent, between which their brothers would have been torn.

The captain and her beloved friend, Ffion, were her advocates, stalwart and unflinching where she was concerned. None were purer in heart than they.

"I should have." Javan entered at her back and Lillia rushed to his side, looking him over from head to toe, though Petra commanded his focus. "I've no excuse, but every time I thought of defying her, I couldn't bring myself to do it, apart from your involvement."

Petra took in her brother's burdened mien, and her heart swelled with compassion. "She used your love against you—and Mikhail's, exploiting your affection. Sift is as much a part of Wendolyne as her lungs or spirit. She used her mastery of manipulation on you, as I believe our natural mother did with our father before he lost himself. I know now that he fought it, or he would never have told me to burn Adym Grove or shared the means to find the mine when he entrusted his watch to me."

Javan furrowed his brow in confusion, listening attentively to her theory while Lillia tucked herself into his side, though she, too, was rapt by her revelations. Petra already knew they'd believe her but couldn't help considering whether they still would if she were fully human.

Yet, what mattered most was how the influence she inspired was portioned, for she would never consciously compel another against their knowledge.

"The folklore about the creatures lurking within Wylewoode is true, Javan. My mother was one of them, a full-blooded pixie. They're cruel by nature, as lore depicts, lovers of trickery, predatory and self-indulgent. My blood only measures half gold, but I suppress these impulses with every breath." Petra's eyes welled with tears as the confession tumbled from her lips.

Lillia approached her, taking Petra's hands in her own as moisture streaked her cheeks. "You are none of those things, nor could you ever be. I'm so profoundly ashamed I did nothing while you risked everything for a nation that cannot begin to grasp your suffering. Your goodness is as snow-white as the spotlessness of your virtue, sister. Please forgive me for not standing with you sooner."

"As am I, though I cannot hope to match my wife's expression of regret." Javan moved toward them, remorse evident in his pinched features. "This world is full of mysteries. Not all of them need to be feared."

Petra couldn't recall the last time she'd seen him without his spectacles, but something about their absence made him look much like the boy she remembered from childhood when life had been simple. He chuckled to himself, shaking his head in disbelief. "You did it."

Her brother embraced her, rocking her from side to side as he squeezed her nearly to bursting. Petra grinned, even as her tears freely flowed onto Javan's tunic. How long had it been since they'd not been burdened with sorrow?

"There's yet more to be done." Petra's words sobered their momentary joy as Javan released her. "The orchard remains, though it's laden with potash awaiting our return."

"We'll sail after nightfall." James rested his hand on the small of her back, a possessive sort of contact that made her think the future might be brighter than either of their pasts.

"Leave Adym to us and be gone before Wendolyne returns. She's having the *Gloriana* loaded as we speak," said Javan, his tone weary. "I've just come from the docks."

"I should've guessed," Lillia huffed. It seemed Wendolyne had given her ship over to a new captain. "Do you think her handsome mirror betrayed us to her? I can think of no other reason for her not to trust me."

Javan averted his gaze, casting it to the ground. "Not after what she did to him and likely not before. Aeric never adapted to the role she picked for him and made no effort to pretend. Wendy finally had enough of him and ordered her tinkerer, Marin, to test his most recent theory. I've never seen anything like it." He was visibly shaken as he recounted what had happened, so much so that his hands trembled at his sides.

"He cut Aeric with a blade honed from sift. I watched as his veins turned to gold before my eyes, his wound healing instantaneously. He took an oath of revenge, and I believe his first action against her may have been to destroy the fourth silo late last night."

"That's welcome news, at least," Petra said, but it came amid reports of greater chaos.

Javan nodded, though he was plainly troubled by all he'd witnessed. "Don't worry, sister. It gets worse. The knife used to flay Aeric's forearm is one of many items developed by Marin that are being stashed aboard the *Gloriana*. I believe Wendolyne is fleeing to Chamelaute."

Petra laughed without humor, drawing confused looks from everyone gathered. "She won't like what she finds there. Penzelle has awakened from a slumber not unlike my own. Chamelaute is on the brink of an overthrow."

The spare stifled a yawn, shaking off his exhaustion. "That may be so, but we can't allow Wendy to reach their shores. She made mention of her correspondence with Prince Philippe of Chamelaute—many times, to be frank—but I did not take her aspirations seriously at the time."

"King Luther and his spawn, Philippe, would make for a dastardly trio alongside our sister," Petra grumbled, unable to think of the prince without cringing.

Judging who was worse would've been difficult without Wendy's pixie heritage. Indeed, she would realize all she aspired to and more if the Deep permitted safe passage through Altanys.

"All she and her tinkerer have created could devastate the continent if one found a way to duplicate their designs, but it's more than Philippe she wants." Javan paced, coping with his rising anxiety in the way he always had. "Is Chamelaute not renowned for their illustrious Seer and his companion, the researcher Archimedes?"

James had been quietly listening, his brow furrowed as he took in the bits of information between them. But when silence fell, he spoke his piece, merciless and firm. "We need to sink the *Gloriana* and destroy her cargo. The consequences of not doing so are far worse."

"A must," Lillia agreed. "The queen would doubtless be an asset to Chamelaute due to nothing more than her ancestry, and even more so with sift." She paused, seemingly mulling something in her mind. "Indeed, if Penzelle awakened sooner than Luther had planned, perhaps they mean to subjugate Penzellians and any sympathizers before they can fight back."

"She salvaged the remaining sift from the clocktower after the fourth silo blast, but it won't go far in a kingdom as vast as Chamelaute, even if they targeted only smaller hamlets." Javan's recollection of what was being done throughout Neverwoode proved invaluable and more involved than Petra could've imagined.

"Perhaps enough to minimally pacify the people for a time as our grandparents did while Wendy fosters a new grove," Petra added. "If a rebellion is quelled in its infancy, it could be years before one of note is re-established. Either way, she ingratiates herself to Chamelaute."

"Wendolyne will make for the orchard, then," James asserted. He rested his hand on the swell of Petra's hip beneath her mantle, bringing calm amid a growing storm. "She needs seeds from the apples to produce a new copse, and even if her seedlings aren't as potent as Adym's, it'll be enough to achieve her ends if she aims to create more lasting pieces like those fashioned by her tinkerer. Between that and the potash mined in Chamelaute, the art of warfare will be forever altered in her favor."

Javan pinched the bridge of his nose, shaking his head. He took a fortifying breath, sadness plain in his eyes. "Then we'll do as you say. She gives us no other choice."

"You won't be coming with us, beloved." Taking Javan's head in her hands, Lillia kissed him. "Neverwoode needs you here, someone strong and kind to help them understand. But *I* must go—and it has to be now."

Javan nodded without argument, kissing her again. "Be safe, darling. The sea is unforgiving with ties to Wendolyne, the terms of which are unknown to me."

Lillia's only answer was a devious smirk.

"I've no doubt your wife will handle herself well, for I've seen firsthand how ruthless she can be." James raised a brow, placing his fist over his heart in farewell.

Javan mirrored his gesture, inclining his head toward James. "Be well, Captain."

Petra approached her brother, mussing his hair. "We'll see each other soon." She hesitated, her throat tightening as she spoke. "But if we do not, please, tell Mikhail—"

"He's always known, Petra. I won't let him forget, and I'll do all I can to protect him."

She knew he would. Petra bit her lip, keeping the tears stinging her eyes at bay, turning from Javan before she lost hold of herself. "I'll see you soon."

* * * *

The docks were well in view from their vantage point overlooking the pier, with conditions worsening each minute as disputes broke out in the streets. Petra kept her head covered as they neared the wharf, avoiding eye contact and notice.

"I'll bring the most trustworthy of my company to the *Jolly Roger* in short order." Lillia bid James and Petra goodbye as they set their sights on the harbor.

Desperation was sure to escalate, as would the citizenry's upset, despite the queen's empty promises that the silos would be repaired before midnight. But word had spread like an ugly tangled web once Wendolyne's guards from the pixie mine had returned.

There would be no more sift, and the people were stirring as her fallacies unraveled.

Chapter Twenty-Nine

The wharf was alive with activity, though not the kind James wished to see. Much like earlier in the day, the people of Neverwoode were agitated, quick to anger and unreasonable in their demands. Still, he believed in their potential, certain that given the right opportunities they would soon find their rhythm without the aid of the deceptive gold dust.

Petra and James strolled toward one of several taverns, each eager to get moving. Wendolyne wouldn't waste any time, with her ship full of sift alongside untold weapons and treasures that would doubtless be lethal in the wrong hands.

That the supposed queen was so shortsighted as to willingly bargain her wares with another nation was appalling. The potential for far-reaching consequences through misuse were as real as the setting sun, endangering people far beyond the kingdom of Neverwoode with her audacity.

But then again, she was also abandoning her people of her own free will. There was nothing stately, nothing dutiful about such actions. She'd been nothing more than a placeholder for years, with no proper understanding of the delicate balance necessary to run a nation effectively.

"How many will Ffion have gathered?" Petra's voice was muffled, tucked as she was beneath her mantle. Her countenance was hidden, shielding them from undue scrutiny as they searched the town.

"I hope enough," James muttered, though he kept his expectations low. Success on that front would surely be difficult, with many of his sailors having surrendered to Neverwoode's wiles.

Traveling to the kingdom with a crew of the damned had never been without liability. Smee had accomplished the impossible in helping to lead them there, while Crispin had been a genuine threat. Then there was Bellamy, the strange woman with a remarkable heritage and knack for tinkering. She'd been an endless asset, but in the end, she, too, had abandoned her duties for another calling in Wylewoode.

The turns his life had taken over the course of the past several weeks had seen James through much chaos. But when he looked toward the noble beauty traveling beside him, he knew he'd do it all over again.

Petra was many things—brave, passionate. And though they'd struggled to be on the same page at first, he knew she was selfless to a fault, even as such characteristics ran utterly contrary to the traditional pixie lore. Indeed, he wanted nothing more than to follow her through the poisonous hellscape of Neverwoode, to see her mission through to the end.

It had never been part of his plan but was a worthy detour. He would do it for her and for all the people who, like him, had been written off. Petra wasn't given the same chances he'd been gifted. She didn't have an Ella or a Ric to see her potential and offer her aid.

He would.

"Look," said Petra, pointing toward the end of one of the piers. "Never did I imagine I would be so relieved to see a crocodile."

James smiled, for he felt the same. "Ffion can't be far behind, then. Let's find him."

They made for the tavern nearest Ben, chuckling as they observed people giving their monstrous beast a wide berth. That was a far cry from only days before when the croc went largely unnoticed among a population overcome by sift, though he minded his own business, not once bearing his numerous teeth.

Entering the tavern, it wasn't long before they spotted Ffion, accompanied by none other than Smee. Upon further examination, James spotted a smattering of other men, all part of his crew, for better or for worse. Perhaps Ffion had been more successful than first he'd imagined.

Petra made for Ffion, greeting him with a hug and a smile, while James found Smee drowning his sorrows at the bar. "It's been a minute, old friend."

Smee started when the captain clasped his shoulder, sputtering some of his brew. "Why, Captain! Where've ye been?"

James glanced about, feeling utterly conspicuous, even as he remained hooded. It wasn't as if he was known in these parts, but something about all they'd accomplished at the mine and with the sift silos made him feel like a wanted man all over again.

"I've been busy, as have you." James nodded toward Smee's tankard of ale, unsurprised that his quartermaster had swapped one vice for another in its absence. "But there is yet more to be done. I'm mustering my crew to set sail once more. Are you in?"

"Oh, aye, sir. I know all about that." Smee indicated Ffion with a wave of his hand, a conspiratorial gleam in his eyes. "I've also been privy to a rumor or two, as it were. Tell me you weren't responsible."

"For what?"

"The guards returning from the hinterlands came with news of an explosion, not unlike what happened at the storage silos all around the kingdom, rendering pixie dust scarce. Word has it it was the fair sister of the queen, alongside her marauding accomplice. Methinks it was you...*sir*." A sly smile formed, reminding James very much of the man he'd known before he'd taken up his nasty habits.

The captain could not suppress a smile of his own, all but confirming Smee's assertion. Yet something about his quartermaster's words caught him off guard. "Pixie dust. Why would you call it that?"

"Well, sir, I think ye know why." He cast a pointed glance toward Petra, raising his eyebrows. "I know what's real and what's true, even if it did get me labeled a lunatic back home. I've tried to convince people for years, and ye've...ye've rendered my assertions null." His face fell, full of grief alongside the weight of much judgment, evident as he worked to keep himself together.

"It's no loss, Smee. I know that it's true." He patted his quartermaster heartily on the shoulder. "And now we must fix it. This world is unprepared for the effects of such an affliction. A mind altered in this fashion cannot comprehend the necessity of real life, all its ups and downs. *We* know that it's hard, yet we *survive*."

Smee's eyes filled with moisture—a sight that hurt James to his core. The man had been lost for so long that he'd struggled to exist in reality long before finding Neverwoode. "I know sift made some things easier," James continued, "but it wasn't real. You deserve better than a life of fantasies. Join me for home, and I'll tell the world the truths you've exposed."

The two men shared a handshake, quickly recovering their comradery. With that business settled, James was ready to get on the move. He turned his attention to Petra, who was conversing with Ffion not far from him. By his count, the boy had managed to gather some seven crewmembers, and with the added assistance from the lost boys, they were near enough to twenty.

With Lillia's contribution of sailors, there was a good chance they'd be able to man the *Jolly Roger*, though it was certain to be slow going with all the novices on board.

"Well done." James shook Ffion's hand, finding that he wasn't so much a boy as he was a man. Under the illusory effect of sift, he'd seemed younger, yet he'd handled the challenges of their heavy burdens with ease. It was easy to see why Petra had come to entrust him with her secrets.

Ffion nodded, huffing when one of the rowdy horde bumped into him from behind. He recovered himself, only to take an elbow to the head. The tavern grew more turbulent around them, with patrons seeking alternative escapes as they awaited a sift blast that would never arrive. He gestured to the various crew, guiding them through the confusion and out of the pub.

"The boys are hiding in the trees not far from the dock," Ffion said. "And Ben refused to leave, following me all over town. At least he didn't attempt to enter the tavern."

As if he knew they were discussing him, Ben offered a toothy grin, his armored tail swishing back and forth like an eager pup.

"Ol' big Ben, up to all his usual tricks, I see." Smee kept his distance, the pair never truly having reconciled whatever differences existed between them. Likewise, the other accompanying sailors from James' original voyage stood several feet away, none willing to venture too close to the creature, despite his relative calm.

James moved to the center of their circle, nodding in greeting to his recovered shipmates. "Well. I hope you've all had fun, but it's time to return to business as usual. It's not going to be easy, but it's for the sake of Llundyn and all Fayble that we accomplish what feels nothing shy of impossible."

Their numbers were thin, their ages far too young, what with a third of their crew made of mere boys. But as James considered his prospects, he knew they'd succeed. The odds had rarely been in his favor, yet he'd persevered, even unto becoming a captain, a confidant, a protector, a provider. He could've given up a decade sooner, relegating himself to a life of poverty with no future.

But life was for the living, and it never came without risk.

"The imposter queen of Neverwoode wishes to conquer more kingdoms with her fallacies. Will you bring her reign of delusion to an end?"

Proclamations of assent rang across the pier as James' crew reconvened, with the promise of a reckoning hanging in the space between them.

* * * *

The sun's lucid rays dissolved into twilight, with the luminous halo disappearing behind the horizon at the edge of Altanys Cove. All the while, the crowding along the waterfront began to disperse, making their way into the taverns and pubs for their nightly portions.

They'd found the lost boys, leading their makeshift crew of eighteen to the docks under the prevailing darkness of eventide. From their position at the easternmost edge of the harbor, they could see the *Gloriana*, with only a handful of cargo remaining to be loaded into the hold.

James wondered at how Wendolyne had accomplished such an incredible feat right beneath the noses of her brothers and Petra. Her machinations had been largely unknown until the incident with Aeric only a day prior, with untold numbers of weapons, clothing, tonics — all made of the damnable golden dust filling their lives with chaos.

He might have been impressed with her ingenuity if he weren't so put off by her recklessness. Indeed, he wondered if she truly understood the scope of what she'd accomplished and its potential for going sideways. But even if she did, it was just as likely that she didn't care.

They came upon Lillia not far from the final slip along the wharf. She, too, had managed to gather a handful of sailors, though Wendolyne had doubtless taken the majority of her crew.

"It'll have to do," she said, greeting James and Petra. "But it's better than we had before."

"A skeleton crew," Petra agreed. She wandered toward the end of the dock, her silhouette burnished by the setting sun. James joined her, pulling the spyglass from within his satchel.

"We'll have to follow at a significant distance." He watched the readying of the *Gloriana*, amazed by how quickly they were moving. "They're nearly prepared to set sail."

"It'll take us some time to do the same. Your ship hasn't sailed for many days, and there's no telling what condition Wendolyne's men left your vessel in when first they raided."

Lillia's concerns were well-founded, but determination would take them far. James was ready for the battle that lay ahead, no matter the struggle involved in seeing their mission through. There were too many consequences as a result of failure. Lives beyond Neverwoode were now at stake.

In the days and weeks leading up to his departure from Llundyn, James had questioned his motives in racing off to sea. He knew he was running — not from anything or anyone in particular. More like he was moving toward something, even if its significance was unknown.

Fate.

Now he understood.

He was intended for Petra, to serve at her side. He was meant to uncover secrets and waylay the ill-conceived plans of aspiring royals, whose judgment was so severely lacking as to jeopardize the entire continent.

They loaded into a trio of launch boats, with much of the crew heartily refusing to travel with Ben. The beast rode with Petra and James, sitting contentedly in the hull alongside Ffion as they made for *Jolly Roger*, being careful to steer as clear of the view of the *Gloriana* as possible.

Returning to the main deck of his vessel was like coming home. James assigned duties to all his sailors, both seasoned and fledgling, pleased to find that all were highly capable and well adept at taking orders.

"It won't be so bad, I think," James said to Petra. She'd readily taken to prepping the sails for hoisting and setting the mainsail. She was a natural, his pirate queen.

"Not with you at the helm." She tucked herself into his side as he took hold of the wheel.

Their preparation could only take them so far. There'd be a dose of luck and vast quantities of patience required to tail the *Gloriana* without being caught. Sailing at night was less than ideal for many reasons, but darkness would aid in their cover.

James kissed the top of her head, clueless as to how they'd accomplish the remainder of their charge. Thankfully, they needed only to destroy the cargo and dethrone the queen.

There had to be worse fortunes than that.

Chapter Thirty

Blustering winds filled *Jolly Roger*'s sails, the vessel splitting the sea below as they pursued the *Gloriana* into the night. They braved Altanys due north as expected, straight for Adym Grove.

Maybe she should have been afraid, but Petra had always dreamed of what it might be like taking to the volatile waters surrounding the continent. For as long as she could recall, she'd loved watching the surf swell from the docks and longed to be a part of its chaotic whims.

Scoffing to herself, she thought of every other twist of fate her dreams had revealed. From unveiling her folkloric origins by allowing her to soar upon the heights where no one might fear or despise her for what she couldn't change, to a shadow with a broken spirit who'd one day guide her across the ocean.

But there was much danger ahead, and despite the adrenaline pumping through her veins, the lives aboard James' vessel were precious.

Beside her, the captain expertly maneuvered his ship, with capped tides dancing beneath the tempest growing around them, and he was exquisite at the helm. From before them, the *Gloriana* was a blur of starlit sails, her course sure from what Petra could make out, though it was Ffion keeping a close watch on Wendolyne's craft.

Somehow James was perfectly at ease, as if the turmoil was a mere trial of will—and perhaps it was. His steadying calm had taken root within her at some point—a gift she could never repay. The same was true for their makeshift crew, with the complement working in tandem to end the queen's vain quest for dominance.

Lillia approached Petra and the captain, as much at home on the sea as on land, drawing a spyglass from her belt and extending it before herself.

"They'll make anchor in the next thirty minutes or so." She watched through the scope for a moment before passing it to James. "How do you wish to proceed?"

When he turned, Petra caught the captain's gaze, as intense as the blackness of the Deep. "If we catch her before she drops anchor, we can use the strength of the tide to force her into the bluff. We're sure to weather fire from her cannons, but I see no other way. If you have any suggestions, please, make them known, for you know this cove far better than I do. We'll accept your word if you wish to take another course," he said, and she believed he would without hesitation.

"No." Though it seemed to pain her, she refused. "We'll prepare the launch boats to collect any survivors. The *Gloriana* cannot leave Altanys."

The wheel's barrel groaned as James directed *Jolly Roger* away from Adym Grove, and it felt as if the waves shifted with them, propelling the vessel forward as its sails protested against violent gusts, sending a chill down Petra's spine.

It wasn't long before they began to close in on the *Gloriana*. The ship was not yet anchored, though it was sure to do so soon. Petra checked her father's watch, judging around twenty minutes before they would lose the opportunity to drive Wendolyne's treasures into the cliff to be lost to Altanys.

"Mutiny afoot!" Ffion shouted from above, scrambling down the mast's ladder to Petra and James.

Ffion gave Petra his spyglass to observe the arising commotion for herself. She adjusted the sight, twisting his scope to view the *Gloriana* more clearly, with James mirroring her actions from beside her.

"*Mikhail.*" Her legs nearly gave out when she saw her youngest brother fighting against Wendolyne's crew and alongside Aeric, who was brawling his way to the helm, illuminated under the soft glow of lantern light. They were not alone in the revolt, with nearly half of those on deck jumping to their aid. "We have to help."

James didn't hesitate, shouting for Lillia to join them at the wheel. "Stay with the *Jolly Roger*. Wendolyne's captain will stop at nothing to see us to a watery grave." He began, gesturing to his quartermaster at once, who quickly made his way to them. "Your vessel's new commander is a former crewman of mine with a personal vendetta and no loyalties. He'll be ruthless, but you must hold his attention while we make for the *Gloriana*."

Petra raised the lens to her eye to find Crispin at the helm as the ship approached Adym, untroubled by the opposition taking root all around him. Thankfully,

Wendolyne's scouts must've been too distracted to notice *Jolly Roger*'s rapid advance. If they acted quickly enough, they could board the cockboats before anyone might see.

"He won't put any holes in your ship. You have my word," Lillia promised, offering a tentative smile. "Make haste."

"What's to be done, Captain?" the quartermaster asked James, his gaze lingering on Petra with rapt fascination.

"Are the launch boats ready?"

"All set."

James inclined his head toward Smee, resting his hand on his shoulder. They regarded one another, the captain chuckling before saying, "Well, old man, we wanted an adventure. Do not let Ben eat any of my crew while we're away."

"I'm coming with you." It wasn't a request, and the captain sighed, his brow furrowing with Smee's declaration.

"Very well," he agreed, clenching his jaw, the conflict plain in his features. "Gather any weapons you need and meet us at the boats."

"This is yours." Petra retrieved the firearm from where it was tucked at her waist, offering it to Lillia. "All it needs is some powder."

She scoffed. "I wondered where that went. Keep it."

Petra slipped the weapon away, nodding her thanks as she turned on her heel, proceeding toward the boats with Ffion trailing close behind. James barked his final orders to the company within earshot.

There was no crew to spare if *Jolly Roger* was to attempt to divert Crispin from his route, but taking advantage of the rebellion on the upper deck of Wendy's ship could prove to be more valuable.

"Let us help." The eldest four of the lost boys intercepted Petra as she strapped her sword in place at her back. Lason spoke with Cole, Nesh, and Almos on either side of him. "We can handle ourselves and would be an asset."

"We could use them." Ffion passed Petra her trusted pouch, filled with new darts for her pipe. She secured the leather strap across her chest, narrowing her gaze toward the *Gloriana*.

"You will row over separately and are to remain only on the lower deck. Spread all the potash you find, then return to your cockboat and make your way back here." Petra regretted permitting their presence, even as the words fell off her tongue, but their options were limited, and the four were more than capable.

The four boys dispersed, excitedly moving toward one of the boats as they prepared for another adventure. There was no evidence of any reservation from them, but then again, they were full of youth and exuberance. Their eagerness to help blessed Petra's heart, but in her soul, she wanted nothing more than to keep them safe.

"We'll protect them," James said as if he'd read her mind when he appeared behind her. "They're quick and should see no action on the lower decks, for Crispin will have called all loyalists to the main deck."

Petra nodded, struggling against her instinct to fold the boys in her arms and shield them from the obscenities of the world they'd been thrust into through no choices of their own.

She moved with James alongside a handful of mariners and Smee toward the launches, only to observe Ben climbing into one of the longboats before them. It rocked to one side with his weight until he settled at its center, just as he'd grown accustomed. The captain huffed a breath, shaking his head with an incredulous laugh, only to surrender to the beast's will with no time to waste.

"The rest of you may take the other launches." He tossed his gathered ropes and grappling hooks to the seamen, and they scattered, stepping into the remaining boats while he and Petra joined Ben.

They were lowered into the sea, one craft at a time, water lapping against their vulnerable vessels. But the surf rolled in their favor, swiftly driving them toward the *Gloriana*. When they came upon her, shouts and the sounds of clashing steel were carried down to them by the ever-changing winds.

James stood within the launch boat, expertly finding his feet, even as the vessel continued its voyage. Taking the first rope in hand, he whipped it in circles, the grappling barbs moving in rhythmic revolutions before catching on the outer railing above them and drawing their boat nearer to the *Gloriana*. The others followed suit, securing their ropes before beginning their climb up the side of the massive ship.

"Stay here," Petra told the crocodile as breath puffed from his nostrils. The creature obeyed, offering only a toothy grin as she prepared herself to ascend.

The captain went ahead of her, and she could not help but be impressed with his strength, his arms and legs working in tandem to push him up the swaying line. He scaled the braided cord with ease as Petra shimmied up close behind.

Beside them, Hatsch slid into the porthole one deck beneath the action where the cannons resided. A moment later, he poked his head out, waving the other boys upward, evidently having cleared their path. The other miners followed, ducking one by one through the porthole to set about their work.

Would that they move quickly then flee.

James paused when they reached the top, taking a moment to observe the melee. He spared a look over his shoulder, nodding to indicate the landing was clear on the stern deck. Scrambling up the last few feet, he threw a leg over the guard rail and offered Petra his hand, hoisting her over the edge.

Petra's heart lurched when she saw the chaos unfolding on the main and quarter platforms, searching for her brother and Wendolyne, whom she'd not yet seen, even from afar.

Seeking a better vantage, she climbed the mizzen mast, bracing herself against it as lightning cleaved the night sky in a blinding flash of silver. At last, she spotted Mikhail, fighting for his life like she always prayed he would, though never, *never*, like this. Crawling into the small crow's nest, Petra reached into her pouch, jamming a bolt into her blowpipe. Thunder roared through the night, jolting the basket and rocking her to her core, but she steadied herself.

Inhaling, she drew the flute to her lips.

The captain unsheathed his sword, silently moving for the helm where Crispin stood, untouched by the surrounding conflict. Petra was perched above him, tucked out of sight within the lower mizzen nest, picking off the queen's lackeys one by one, their forms dropping into limp heaps across the deck.

She was a phantom of unparalleled proficiency with her pipe, sending streaks of crimson through the air, each finding its target deep in the flesh of her adversaries.

James descended the steps leading to Gloriana's newly minted commander when one of Wendolyne's complement noticed him. Crispin kept his focus, more adept than James would've anticipated behind the wheel.

The clouds wept onto the deck, a sudden deluge of rain drenching him to the bone as his opponent neared. The brute was a savage pig, snarling upon his advance, lunging for the captain, who pivoted out of his path. His challenger stumbled forward, slipping as he attempted to regain his footing, moisture creating a slick sheen over the platform.

The man curled his lip, rushing at James again with renewed vigor, clutching his sword tightly under white knuckles. The captain batted his steel aside with his hook, driving his cutlass into the barbarian's abdomen. He kicked the man's sword out of his hand as he fell, his blood mingling with the drizzle coating the wooden planks beneath him.

James swept a soaked lock of hair from his eyes, trying in vain to make out the fight below. Aeric beat on the door to the great cabin, where only days before, the captain had found Petra pinned under Crispin's weight, wrestling against his brawn as she damn near blinded the bastard. He could only surmise it was Wendy Aeric wanted, his curses cutting through even the pealing thunder.

Someone crept up at Aeric's back when he spun, slicing his foe's throat in one fluid motion. His adversary's form tumbled down the steps behind him, landing with a thud at their base. The man who was once Wendolyne's pet wiped a ruby stain from his knife with the hem of his sleeve, smirking up at James until something caught his attention above the captain.

A flash of white soared overhead as Petra swung from the mizzen mast onto the primary deck, her feet nimbly finding purchase, despite the glassy film of rain slicking the exposed upper level. She stripped her sword from its sheath between her shoulder, wedging it against the main mast.

Mikhail's challenger stood in the gap separating them, her brother pursuing their opponent with the promise of death in his eyes. He made for the crewman, his broadsword gleaming when light rippled through the black sky. The man stumbled, tripping backward until his legs slid out from under his body, Petra's blade impaling him from behind. She ran to her brother, embracing him as James made for Crispin.

The *Gloriana's* commander must've sensed his approach, turning to meet James face to face. Crispin scoffed. "Come to finish me off?"

His eye was still swollen from his scuffle with Petra, and his cheekbones and jaw were blackened from the encounter with James outside the queen's palace chambers, as resilient as he was foul.

"The Deep is hungry tonight. Can't you feel it?" James stalked toward him, cocking his head. "This time, we won't leave your fate to chance."

Crispin sneered—an ugly, mocking curve of his mouth that made the captain's gut churn with loathing. He moved for him, the vile creature spewing insults all the while when James rammed him into the taffrail with his shoulder.

Steel through his belly would be too quick.

James slammed the heel of his boot into his knees, causing Crispin to cry out, but the captain didn't allow him to drop, wrapping his fingers around his neck to keep him in place. But Crispin wasn't about to make it easy, slicing James' side with a blade he'd hidden under his sleeve.

The captain hissed in agony, as much from surprise as from the pain blazing across his midsection. His grip on Crispin's throat held fast, despite his suffering as his opponent sputtered intelligible profanities. His face was currant-red as James tightened his grasp when beside him, he heard something click. The sound was familiar, and he knew in an instant who stood with him.

"Do it," he growled.

And Petra did. A deafening shot fractured through the night into Crispin's chest, flame erupting from the weapon in her steady hold. The captain loosed his grip, Crispin's eyes wide with shock as he toppled over the gunwale into the raging surf below.

The *Gloriana* swayed against an unbroken tide, poised to trail the *Jolly Roger*, but the Deep had plans of her own, nudging the bow toward Adym's bluff.

On the main deck, the mutiny persisted. Ffion, Smee, Mikhail and all the others yet fought with the fury of one hundred men, though they were outnumbered, and it was beginning to show. Still, they refused to yield.

From below, Aeric caught the captain's eye, his determination firm as he kicked through the door leading into the great cabin. His persistence in his pursuit could surely only mean that Wendy was within, doubtless in hiding from Aeric's revenge. If all that Javan had said was so, she had it coming.

Good.

"The boys have returned to their launch boat." Petra indicated their young friends, rhythmically distancing themselves from the strife, paddling back out to sea. Her fingertips brushed the back of James' hand, saying through her touch what her lips could not speak.

Jolly Roger was too far off to allow the fighting to continue, for the souls aboard Wendolyne's vessel they treasured stood a better chance if they ended the struggle.

James took to the helm, his grip fixed, even as he winced with the pain splitting his flesh, blood dripping down his side. He turned the wheel, and the *Gloriana* obeyed as the Deep hurled her into the cliff.

Chapter Thirty-One

The collision was bone-shattering.

Wooden planks cracked, snapping and splintering as the ship imploded, the jarring impact causing the fore and main masts to fold in half at the center before crashing to the deck below. Men dove for their lives as they threw themselves from the path of the falling beams, with the hopes of victory in their mutiny long since forgotten.

Two massive poles slammed into the deck, easily cleaving the platform in two and leaving behind a hole as they plummeted farther into the heart of the vessel. One man wasn't fast enough, tumbling backward into the void left behind as chaos reigned upon the *Gloriana*, with cries of anguish and panic piercing the night.

Petra tumbled into the railing, only just catching herself as she toppled over the side. She clutched the balusters for support, hoisting herself toward what remained of the deck as James moved to help her.

"It's going down!" James cried, his voice thin and desperate as he hauled Petra to safety. "We need to be far from here when she goes under."

From tales alone did he know of the dire circumstances that followed a shipwreck, with stories of sailors being sucked into the depths as their vessel surrendered, drawn into the soul of the sea where Poseidon dwelt, never to be seen again. Becoming trapped upon the ravaged ship would surely see them drowning within a watery grave.

"Ffion and my brother," Petra uttered. "I need to be sure they make it off the ship alive."

"Smee, too...and Aeric." James took a few tentative steps, testing the deck's strength beneath his feet. He drew Petra along behind him, making for what remained of the stairs. "*Hell*. I want to get everyone off this damn ship. What were we thinking?"

"It was the only way!" Petra shouted, her words swallowed by the gusting winds and the frantic shouts from the disoriented crew below. "We had a fight for survival either way, but now our odds are even."

"You are wise," James granted, a hint of a smirk visible in the pale moonlight.

They reached the stairs, now little more than the steepled remnants of boards once forming a stairway. Inching down the fractured path, they slowly made their way to the quarterdeck.

The ship was a far cry from its former glory, the stern having continued its forward trajectory as the bow came to a crushing halt against the rocky cliffside. The same upheaval they'd noted on the stairs had happened on a larger scale upon the decks below, with the landings resembling mountains of timber rather than a functional vessel.

Thank goodness the boys had escaped, leaving only a small handful of people with whom Petra couldn't bear to part. "Let me find Ffion and Mikhail while you locate Smee. Surely we'll be quicker apart."

"Not in a million years would I part with you." James' adamance sobered her, the reality of what they were facing striking as she took in the struggles all around her. Some men were injured, while others readily leapt into the unknown, tossing themselves from the railing into the darkness rushing at the sinking ship far below.

"We need to work our way to the lower decks, for I fear we'll never make it back up again," he continued, gesturing to the deteriorating conditions of the walkways.

He was right.

There wasn't a soul on the quarterdeck with them, at least not one they could see. Staggering across the platform, they gave the massive hole at its center a wide berth as they made for the captain's quarters.

"Wendy was within," said James. "It was the last I saw of Aeric."

They reached the door, finding only fragments of it remaining. The frame, too, was askew, making it all the more difficult to shove free. James entered first, quickly followed by Petra, filled with dueling senses of anxiety and anger as she sought her vile sister. All the chaos they faced was a result of Wendolyne's unparalleled selfishness, easily avoided with a dose of humility and wisdom that her sister sorely lacked.

That she would so willingly abandon her people and her kingdom fueled Petra's ire, preparing her to do whatever needed to be done to restore order and bring about justice for a people abused at length.

But it seemed the time for reckoning had not yet arrived, as neither her sister nor Aeric were anywhere to be seen. They moved about the cabin, remarkably untouched by the violent run-in with the crags beyond, finding it unmarred by struggle and empty of any occupants.

"Look there," Petra said, indicating the cracked door at the rear of the room leading to a balcony. "You don't suppose..."

"I do." James opened the door, carefully escorting Petra onto the balconette as they peered into the abyss beyond the ship below. "Perhaps Aeric exacted his revenge after all."

The surf churned, with nothing truly visible beyond the subtle shimmer of moonlight skimming off turbulent waves, thundering into the hull as they struck without end. The wind whipped, roaring overhead and filtering through them with relentless fury, doubtless responsible for the sounds of falling timber toppling onto what remained of the vessel's decks.

"We need to get out of here." Petra pulled the captain away from the balcony, eager to get about their recovery mission before the *Gloriana* went under. There was no time to waste, even as they had no clue how to proceed. But staying put was not an option she was willing to entertain.

They hustled back to the quarterdeck, making for the ladder leading to the main platform, where last she'd seen her brother and Ffion. As for Smee's whereabouts, that was a mystery, as she'd not laid eyes upon him since they arrived at the ship's base to scale their way aboard.

"Petra!" Mikhail hollered, waving wildly to gain her attention. Beside him stood Ffion, while just beyond them lay a listless figure clad in the colors of Llundyn.

James hissed. "It's Smee."

The pair climbed to the lower deck, clambering over debris as they made for the injured seaman. As they neared, Petra could see he was at least breathing, though it wasn't clear what had befallen him.

"He's not well," said Ffion. "Took a blade to the gut during the uprising."

"Seems he's in good company," Mikhail added, indicating James' blood-soaked tunic. He, too, was unwell, though in far less danger from his superficial wound than Smee, who struggled to remain conscious.

James fell to his side, assessing the wound with tentative fingers pressed around the seeping gash. "It's deep." Taking Smee's face between his thumb and index finger, he turned the man's head toward himself. "Stay with me, old man. We'll get you home."

"I am home, James. Home at last," said Smee. "Thanks to you. Your father would be so proud." His eyes fluttered as he gasped, coughing up a fair amount of blood and bile.

Petra dropped to her knees beside him, running her hand over the springy curls atop his head. Silent tears slipped over her cheeks as her gaze met James', understanding swiftly passing between them. "You'll no longer be tethered to the earth," she whispered. "For where you're going, you can fly."

Smee smiled, his shuddering breaths carrying him into eternal rest. Petra reached for him, gently closing his eyes while James bowed his head, each taking a brief moment, though it would never be enough to come to terms with what they'd just witnessed.

The floor underfoot groaned, sending a jagged crack through the decking, halving the ship from rail to rail across the center in a startling reminder of what they were up against.

"I'm afraid we'd better be moving," Mikhail said quietly.

"The young boys have gone to return to *Jolly Roger*. It's only we who remain." Ffion folded his hands, awaiting orders.

James rose to his feet, pulling Petra up beside him. "A burial at sea is a fitting end for this stalwart quartermaster, but we must be far from here if we do not wish to join him." Casting a final glance toward his old friend, James took a fortifying breath, prepared to do whatever came next.

"There's nowhere to go but down," said Ffion, leaning over the railing. They were rapidly taking on water, with the ship creeping ever closer to the roiling surf.

The other three joined Ffion, each contemplating an impossible predicament. Thinking about jumping made Petra sick, with the reality that she'd be pitching herself into the cold, fathomless black waters inspiring mighty panic that she fought to suppress.

Indeed, this would be worse than her dip in the strange sift-filled pool leading into the caverns in Delphi, as she could see nothing but knew without question that Altanys held untold horrors in her depths. Echoing her sentiments was the ghost of a haunting melody, skirring off the waves, doubtless the call of the supposedly mythical sirens whom Petra now believed to be every bit as real as she was.

The world was in for a fantastical reckoning.

"Are you ready, love?" James smiled sadly, reaching for her hand. "We can do this together."

"It's the only way." Swallowing hard, Petra climbed over the railing with James, Ffion and Mikhail following suit. She clung to the wooden banister, her palms slick with sweat as her heartbeat thrummed, pulsing within her chest like the beating wings of a hummingbird.

Closing her eyes, she cast herself from the vessel. There would be no avoiding the water as she did before when last she'd leapt from the cliffside with James' hand in hers. This time, she surrendered to her course, plunging into the icy depths of Altanys.

The frigid water burned her from head to toe, enveloping her in its numbing embrace. There was no telling how far she'd gone under, but she kicked with all her might, using her one free hand to crawl upward, for she would not let James go.

They emerged from the frothing waves, sputtering for air as they scrambled to stay afloat. Ffion and Mikhail rose to the surface nearby, the four of them treading water not far from the ship's side.

Men from aboard the vessel followed suit, jumping into the water with innumerable injuries, their blood mingling with the seawater in a fusion that was sure to bring sharks nearby.

"We need to get out of the water. Grab hold of anything!" Mikhail shouted, his tone becoming desperate.

"There!" Ffion began to swim, and it wasn't until she began to follow that she realized what they were moving toward.

One of the launch boats slowly drifted on the tide not far from where they swam. Each crest carried it farther away, making catching it all the more challenging as they stroked in its direction. When they finally caught hold, Ffion entered first, heaving himself over the wall before reaching out to help the others aboard.

Fearful cries sounded through the night, but there was no telling how many there were or from where they originated as they sat in the sea-tossed launch. Making sense of anybody's location was next to impossible, with the dark of night warring against the tumult of the Deep as the most obtrusive force for the reckoning.

In the distance, a flicker of light was visible that could only be *Jolly Roger*. It would be a long haul to reach it, but they stood a much better chance in a launch boat than upon some random pieces of debris.

"Their cries are breaking my heart," said Petra.

"You're nothing like your sister." James pulled her closer to his side, the anguish of all the souls lost upon the water was too much to bear.

A commotion drew their attention, as someone else attempted to clamor into their boat. Feminine hands clasped the rim of the launch, followed by the scrambling of feet, struggling against the underside of the bow for purchase.

Petra peered over the edge, finding none other than Wendolyne herself. The former queen was shocked, disheveled and wind-blown as she was, with visible anger coloring her features when she recognized her sister.

Wendy released her hold, choosing instead to try her luck upon the Deep. The woman was a spiteful creature, clearly unwilling to relent in her hatred, even when her life was at stake. She bobbed beneath a wave only to resurface a moment later, but it was plain that she was rapidly tiring.

"We should bring her aboard," Petra said, finding it difficult to harbor anger toward her sister as she watched her labor against the surf.

"Let the Deep handle it," said Mikhail. "Whatever deal she thought she had with the Mistress of the Fishes was not as solid as she seemed to believe, for the seas have been on our side."

Petra couldn't argue that truth. Still, something about watching her sister languish among the waves did not set well within her. She pulled an oar from the hull, extending it toward her sister, now clinging to a piece of floating wood.

"Like hell!" Wendy shouted, shifting her weight atop the board. "You ruined everything!"

She paddled away without looking back, her light blue dress trailing in the surf behind her, yet she was far from alone. Ben's long face crested as he stalked her, his armored tail ticking back and forth as he pursued his quarry. Wendolyne was utterly unaware, kicking her way through the waves with little progress.

Ben wasted no time, and his strength was evident with every stroke, effortlessly charging his way through the water. He reached her in a matter of seconds, lunging toward her and latching on to her waist. He rolled then, spiraling through the tide before they disappeared.

Petra watched, waiting for them to surface again, but seconds turned into minutes with neither in sight. The silence was deafening, swallowing her whole in a strange blend of guilt and relief.

No more Wendolyne. No more sift.

Without a word, Ffion and Mikhail began to row, rhythmically making their way in the direction of the *Jolly Roger*. Their world would be different now and very much for the better, but Petra's quest for freedom from the maniacal reign had never been meant to end like this. She felt raw within her soul, aching for what could've been, even as she knew it was always beyond her reach.

* * * *

"What you did was very brave," said Lillia. Their return to *Jolly Roger* had been arduous, sat in a small boat among the violent waters in their sodden clothing. James had never been so happy to set foot upon his vessel.

"My sincerest apologies," James replied. "The willful destruction of such a beautiful ship goes against the most base of instincts for any mariner."

"I understand why you did it." Lillia smiled, seemingly accepting the way of things without bitterness. That was to her credit, as James wasn't sure he could do the same. She turned to Petra, pitching her voice low. "Are you all right?"

"I will be." Petra stood tall, clad in men's trousers and a tunic that were far too large for her tiny frame.

Lillia nodded, leaving them to their own devices as she moved to continue her command of *Jolly Roger*. James pulled Petra closer, and she shivered in his embrace, though they'd long since been dried and warmed from their bone-chilling excursion.

"Really, though," he breathed against her temple, "you've done so much for so many, and I know your heart is hurting. What can I do?"

"*This.*" She nestled into his hold, sighing as he kissed the top of her head.

While peace might've evaded her for years, he was determined to will it into existence, come what may. He didn't know anyone more deserving of rest as he stood in perpetual awe of who she was and all that she'd done for her kingdom and people. A warrior was she, and fairer than anyone he'd ever known.

"Here's the weapon you requested," said Lason, presenting James with the atlatl he'd used to rescue them from the grips of the odd vines in the journey through Neverwoode.

"Thank you, Lason." James took the atlatl in hand, gazing in the distance at what remained of the *Gloriana*. It was largely submerged but had not yet gone entirely under. With any luck, he'd be able to wing a flaming halberd its way, hoping to light the potash on board and around the ship to destroy what remained of Wendolyne's sift-born weapons, clothing and stores.

Gailen handed James a spear, setting the end alight as the captain made for the precipice upon the bow. He set the spear, craning his arm back before letting fly. The halberd arced across the early morning sky, landing in what remained of the starboard end of the *Gloriana*.

At first glance, the flame disappeared, only to sizzle and pop as it built in size, with the substantial amount of potash catching fire little by little as the blazing pyre grew. One small explosion advanced into another, each one greater than the last until, finally, a massive blast burst forth, sending fragments in all directions, and setting Adym Grove alight as a wall of water cascaded toward the *Jolly Roger*.

The ship rocked in its wake, with many a man leaning across the rails as their stomachs lurched. But Lillia expertly handled the fallout, guiding the vessel into calmer waves and directing their path back to Neverwoode. James returned to Petra's side, eager to leave the chaos of sift and all its ills behind.

"Perfect aim," said Petra. "You're an exceptional pirate."

"And you, an exceptional pixie." He considered the reality of his words. The stories of pirates and pixies were rife with accounts of woe and misery for those who encountered them, but the truth was far more complex.

Misunderstanding abounded for the things little known. Would that together they might prove the world wrong.

Chapter Thirty-Two

Petra stood among the gathered citizens of Neverwoode before the clock tower dais, no longer dusted with gold. James, Mikhail and Ffion were on either side of her while the lost boys clustered behind them as Javan prepared to address the people.

In the week following the mine and silos' destruction, Wendolyne's gilded fallacy had fallen, but the kingdom would need time to heal. Rather than Javan assuming a sovereign role, he sought the people's will, who unequivocally deemed him worthy as their duly elected leader. In the coming weeks, a new governmental system would be instituted, chosen by majority approval and balanced with a selection of supporting district heads.

Petra could think of no one more fitting than Javan and Lillia to introduce the secret kingdom to all Fayble. Her brother held no sentiments of entitlement or superiority, not like Wendy had — not like their father had or even their grandparents before them, presenting himself as the honorable man he'd become despite the odds of any sense of morality being stacked against him from birth.

"Forgive me," Javan began solemnly, humbling himself in the sight of all in attendance. "Forgive me for not fighting for you sooner. Youth's most profound blessing of ignorance is, at once, its greatest curse. I was born into the system as it was, functioning under a timorous rule, intimidated by innovative minds and those who did not fit the molds of their native lands. The order advanced by my grandfather was one born of apprehension involved in the governance of an exiled community, from laziness in channeling their true potential, and above all, profound arrogance." Unaccustomed to so many eyes upon him, he paused, pushing his spectacles up the bridge of his nose as he straightened his posture.

"You are the brilliant, the confounding, resilient and feared, rejected by our neighbors, who did not grasp your value. I vow never to make the same mistake. I promise to hear your grievances and to make this nation one that fosters your many strengths. Be patient with me as we embark on this new journey, for I am only human, but I assure you, I am *for* you."

Lillia's visage beamed with apparent pride as she listened intently to her husband's heart. Applause filled the hall, even after Javan raised his hands to temper Neverwoode's praise. He shook his head as moisture brimmed in his eyes, taking in the scene before him.

"Together, we will make this realm a beacon for the weary and a home for the lost." Javan took Lillia's hand, drawing her to him, the assembly erupting with cheers. He looked at his wife, tears staining their cheeks.

James tugged Petra into his chest, wrapping his arms around her from behind. "This is your doing," he whispered.

"And yours." She twisted in his embrace as the crowd slowly dispersed, and he kissed her temple before they parted, keeping her close with his hand at her waist.

Neverwoode was far from well after decades of false fulfillment, but now they could remember and daily learn what truly living meant.

After the fourth silo was eliminated, the kingdom fell into turmoil, resting its hope on wicked lies uttered by its queen. But Javan had laid her deceptions bare, knowing full well that the fallout would worsen before it could ever improve. Over the passing days, the pixie dust had filtered from their bodies, with the haze tainting the citizenry's consciousness waning day by day. Mikhail was a striking example of how far they'd come as he continued to recover his senses and began his life anew. Desperation grew and still lingered, though the people were beginning to appreciate the freedom that came with coherence.

Ffion watched the parting company next to them, a satisfied smirk on his angular face reminding Petra of the boy she'd cherished for what felt like ages. He stuck by her when she was scared and broken, knowing down to her marrow that he would've remained her irreverent tag-along, no matter the cost.

Until he grew up.

"Where will you go?" Petra had wanted to ask him since he'd volunteered to track Wendolyne's tinkerer, Marin. He'd gone missing after word of the mine's destruction reached Neverwoode. Ffion had already prepared a pack for his journey, planning to leave the kingdom following Javan's address. Her throat tightened at the thought of goodbye, even if only for a time, for though he was a nuisance, he'd been her dearest companion in her darkest days.

"To Callaise," he replied. "I believe Marin also has ties to that ghastly nation, given his accent. And I have family there. A brother."

There was still so much Petra didn't know about him—a young man as shrouded in mystery as her homeland had been. "I didn't realize you had a brother. Whatever brought you here?"

"Truly, I don't recall," said Ffion. "Indeed, I didn't remember my kin until a handful of days ago. The adventures and the sift ensured my apathy."

That was no surprise.

He wore a sling over his brow, ready to take on Wylewoode alone once again. It was no different from when they'd met, but, of course, he'd been younger. Still, she was convinced Wylewoode would be forced to surrender if it came to a match of acuity and cunning.

"Be well." James placed his fist over his heart, and Ffion did the same, his mouth twitching at the corners. The captain chuckled, clapping him on the shoulder. "I suppose it's my turn to keep her alive."

"I'll help soon enough," Ffion assured, certain to remain Petra's eternal pest when he grinned, ruffling her hair.

"Do be well. I fear I might miss you until we reunite." It was as close as Petra would get to confessing her fondness for him, and he was a saint among men for putting up with her as long as he did.

Ffion laughed, pulling her into his warmth. "I'll miss you, too."

She swallowed a sob, her chin quivering as he held her — the same boy who'd risked his life for her sake more than once. Her resolve faltered a moment too long, and she wept into his shoulder. She loved him like one of her brothers, deeply saddened to see him leave, but she'd not forgotten Neverwoode was not his home.

When Ffion released her, he wiped the moisture from his own eyes, clasping Mikhail's arm in brief regard, and nodding to the seven youths behind him.

Someday, he would bring all Fayble to its knees, and they would know his power.

* * * *

The docks were quiet as they said their farewells. Javan and Lillia saw James, Petra and Mikhail off with promises to keep in touch and see one another again soon as they set sail for Llundyn. Petra knew they couldn't have done any better, for leaving the kingdom in her capable brother's hands was a better outcome than even she had conceived of.

In truth, she'd never really *thought* her plan through to that point, living one moment at a time and surviving as she did among the havoc wreaked by her dearly departed sister. She always knew where she wanted to end up — a kingdom revealed, a people freed to well and truly live. But never had she imagined the circuitous route she would travel to arrive there.

It was worth it all.

Altanys was like glass, still and undisturbed apart from the *Jolly Roger*, cutting through the sea's flawless surface that was like a mirror into the Deep. Petra peered over the gunwale as sunrise bloomed, casting ripples of yellow and gold upon the shimmering water.

"Do you think Aeric survived?" It must've been the subtle recollection of her sister's title for him that sparked her question, with the man having reluctantly served as the former queen's looking glass, revealing the goings-on of the realm.

"If not, he should have," Mikhail replied, looking off into the morning sky with a hand shielding his eyes from the emerging sunlight. "He's a good man, or was, depending on the Undersea's whims that night. We blew the fourth silo after she...*altered* him, and we hid aboard the *Gloriana*. We only planned to steer the ship into the bluff as your captain did, knowing full well what that meant for us, but when others joined our mutiny, I wanted to fight."

"I've never been so scared." Petra placed her hand on his, and he squeezed her fingers in return, with the pain of their estrangement not forgotten but certainly forgiven. A fresh beginning in Llundyn was sure to provide him with an opportunity to heal and doubtless more time with his sister, who'd missed him terribly.

"Is it true that you're both halflings like the miners said?"

Petra nodded, understanding who he implied, and Mikhail's only response was a contemplative nod of his own.

"Wendolyne told me so many stories about you, but I never could believe them, even after she pumped me full of that damned pixie dust. I must've been more susceptible to her influence than Javan because of how much younger and naive I was." He flared his nostrils as he spoke, bitterness evident in his every word. "I didn't accept the things she said about you, but it felt like the only way to cope after finding you dead in Wylewoode." He took a sharp breath, and Petra's stomach turned as she thought of the day Javan had helped her slip into the poisoned slumber.

"I'm so sorry." She couldn't keep her welling tears at bay—no more than she could change the past.

"I couldn't have done what she asked of me, but some part of me wanted to." Mikhail did not meet her gaze, the shame and despair in his features plain. "Sometimes, I don't know if I can trust myself. I remember bits from when we were kids, and that's what I cling to. Otherwise, I get lost in the lies and how they co-exist almost seamlessly with the truth. But I know who you are. To my core, I know."

Petra would have stayed on the main deck with him for hours if the boys hadn't called her away. He gave her a reassuring smile that she didn't entirely trust but gave him his space anyway. They would have their time together, and the heart wounds Wendy had sealed within his chest would mend as the memory of her faded into willful disregard, though her deceptions would doubtless haunt him for the rest of his days.

"What is it?" Petra asked when she approached a handful of the seven lost boys.

"Jon wants to sleep in the bilge with Ben! I caught him sneaking from our bunks just last night," said Hatsch, his eyes wide and panicked before he stifled a sneeze with his arm.

"He's harmless," Jon contended with an exaggerated wave of his arms that nearly broke Petra's resolve.

She was *supposed* to be the adult, but the boys brought out her long since hidden inner child. Suppressing her amusement, she did her best to be objective. "Stay with the boys in the bunks, Jon. The bilge is no place for a child. Not really for a crocodile either, but we'll make do."

Hatsch stuck his tongue out at Jon, who offered the same kindness in return, the pair quickly running off to some new endeavor upon the *Jolly Roger* with their brethren in tow.

Well.

Petra chuckled, shaking her head at their antics. They were good boys — quick to obey and easy enough to manage. A little dispute here and there was to be expected and resolved readily enough. Petra made her way to the helm, wondering over how she'd become the keeper of seven stray boys.

"Ah," James said by way of greeting, his grin widening upon her approach. He braced his wheel, locking it in place. "Come. Let me show you something."

Petra complied, following him across the vessel from the quarter deck to the captain's quarters. It was the first moment they'd had to themselves in days, apart from a handful of stolen, breathless kisses they'd managed, despite the commotion of the week prior.

James tugged her forward, his gaze full of perilous intent as his hook caught on the waist of her trousers, drawing her toward him. She squealed, stumbling into him as he smirked, a heartbreaking tip to his lips that made her pulse race.

Interlocking their fingers, he reclined onto the bed, and Petra followed, her knees to either side of his hips when she paused to simply take him in. His face was more handsome than any she'd ever beheld, whether in waking or dreaming, with eyes full of fathomless depths. That he regarded her so highly was beyond her wildest hopes, with the way in which he cherished her nothing shy of undeserved.

She was nobody. But with James, Petra felt as if there were no one more loved in all the world.

Careful not to put any weight on his healing midsection, she reached beneath his tunic, gently touching the injured area under his ribs. "I killed him." Petra traced the edges of his bandage with her fingertips, his breath stuttering with her delicate strokes.

"He deserved it after what he did to you. I'd kill him again for touching you, given a chance." With the curve of his hook, he trailed up the length of her arm, its cool steel tingling against Petra's sun-soaked flesh. She held it to the hollow of her neck, letting it chill her skin. The captain chuckled as she teased but did nothing to stop her as she lowered herself over him, bringing her lips to the same spot above his collarbone, kissing him once and again up the column of his throat.

James swallowed hard when she nipped at his ear, pressing another kiss to the sensitive patch below it. He groaned, pinching her chin between his fingers, the intensity of his gaze blazing through her. Their lips met tentatively at first, only this time, it was the captain toying with her self-control. He pulled back, skimming the round of his hook along the line of her jaw.

"I think I needed you, James," Petra breathed, relishing the sound of his name on her tongue. He turned her to her back, heedless of his injury, grinning wickedly and catching her off guard. Their mouths collided in a furious swell of passion that could never be sated.

In another week or so, they would reach the shores of Llundyn, where the world would interrupt their pilfered solace.

While she wished they could remain there, swaddled in the arms of the sea, their work wasn't finished. Fayble would soon learn of the shrouded kingdom and the lore Petra herself had only begun to accept as true, but the world so often feared what it didn't understand, and this would be no different.

The world would fear *her*.

"Show me again what you need, wildling." James' voice was rough as he brushed the tip of his nose over hers. Her shadow had taught her to trust and proved that light would always slay darkness, even after the blackest of nights.

Petra wove her fingers through his dark, tousled waves, bringing her mouth to his. She knew she would follow him until time's end.

And even that would not be long enough.

Want to see more from these authors?
Here's a taster for you to enjoy!

The Chronciles of Fayble:
Rose of Ruin
Britt Cooper & Erin Dulin

Coming Summer 2024

Excerpt

It was inevitable that Ffion would be forced to face his demons sooner or later, though a not insignificant part of him wished for later never to come.

The road home from Neverwoode was fraught with perils—creatures of lore and circumstances befitting only the darkest of nightmares. The woodlands had become an unexpected refuge, serving as his home despite their fabled terrors, providing a respite from an altogether different sort of monster.

Most largely steered clear of the once-hidden kingdom, while faithfully denying the existence of the mythical beings and tales of legend that originated within its borders.

How easily the human mind was manipulated, conceiving of such things as quickly as it dismissed them.

Fools.

He'd been among them for a blissful period of some three-odd years. In Neverwoode, it had been easy to forget…and even easier to pretend. He'd been devoted to causes and people outside of himself with great satisfaction, even as a small voice within him convicted him daily of running. *Hiding.*

He had. There was no sense in denying it. Yet while his conscience might see fit to berate him for his cowardice, Ffion had no doubt his detour into not one, but two strange realms fulfilled a higher purpose still.

But that didn't alleviate the gnawing guilt. For if there was one thing he'd learned throughout the whole of his misadventures, it was that duty trumped all. His unwitting companions had taught him that, with more than their fair share of patience and an urgency to serve that had put him to shame.

His wrongs couldn't right themselves. Would that his father might forgive him.

With a resigned sigh, Ffion climbed, picking up his pace as he reached the fertile terrain blanketing the outskirts of Calaise.

Home.

Nothing quite compared to the rolling splendor of their lush green meadows, even as they were readily overrun by scores of ruby-red poppies and seas of deep blue irises. The crush of colors might've taken his breath away if it wasn't such a stark reminder of his absence.

Ever higher he hiked, grateful for the burning in his lungs providing a distraction from his racing thoughts. The uncertainty he'd faced within Wylewoode Forest paled compared to what awaited him on the other side of the bluffs.

Disappointment. Anger. Fear.

In truth, he hadn't wanted to leave, but it seemed the only way at the time. With his mother's and brother's insistence, he'd fled, making for the anonymity of Neverwoode. Obscurity had suited him well, ushering him into a state of contentment as he relinquished his memories in favor of simply forgetting.

Oblivion could only be realized for so long, however, once the dust of the enchanted woods settled. Remembrance had flooded back, catching him out and sending him barreling toward his kingdom without regard for his safety or anybody else's.

All the time he'd had to think along the way had been a double-edged sword, with regrets and inexplicable hope welling within his spirit, damn him.

Your true nature will consume you.

The thought plagued him still, leaving him grappling with his humanity. Nothing had been the same for him since, with a few brash words having transformed him from a king in waiting to a pauper on the streets, running for his life—to save his own and protect the lives of others from his newly discovered appetite for revenge.

His desire was strong, driving him into the woods neighboring Calaise. Escaping Marin's errant curse had been his aim, but he'd run headlong into immediate distress, drawn toward the very thing he wished to destroy.

Ffion had scented her long before he laid eyes upon her. She sat among the fronds and bracken, her head cradled in her hands. White-blonde hair beset with thistles and bits of leaves fell about her shaking shoulders, her slight form breathless as she wept. She smelled of earth, of illusion—all the things he now despised.

Her blood called to something feral buried deep within his soul, demanding he eliminate her.

Any will to ignore her presence had been quickly overcome by the basest of instincts—a beastly quest that had grown out of that handful of uttered words from the pixie tinkerer, fating him to the role of hunter against otherworldly prey he hadn't known existed before Marin had shown his face within the palace walls.

She was an easy target and he a more practiced huntsman than he'd ever fathomed possible. Indeed, the sporting pursuits of his youth were a fool's errand by comparison. His heightened senses and newfound lust had made him a veritable brute, a predator with no discernible morality left to his name.

Yet a captivating refrain had drifted into his heart, sung into his being without a single word articulated. The melody stopped him cold as he watched the pixie woman, her vulnerability nothing short of disarming. Only then did he realize what made her so different from the others he'd hunted.

Her goodness was too real, too raw to be lost. In her, he'd sensed profound decency, bewildering him and bringing him to his knees. Never before had he perceived such virtue from a pixie or a human.

In a sudden rush of awareness, Ffion let go, relinquishing the mighty monster that had outstripped his control. He gave in to the overwhelming calm that had seized his mind, forgetting his roots, forgetting his passions and ambitions.

He *breathed*…deeply, for the first time in what felt like months. Rising to his feet, he'd collected himself, making for the one he'd come to know as Petra. For years he'd followed her like a pup does its master, eagerly joining her on adventures through reveries in

Otherlande and freeing the people of Wylewoode from the mind-altering clutches of pixie dust they'd known as sift.

It was then that his world had come crashing down around him. The eradication of sift led to an immediate loss of peace, sending him spiraling toward the vulgar instincts that had disappeared in Petra's presence.

Ffion willed away the ache that always accompanied his regrets as he stepped onto the precipice overlooking his realm, the toes of his boots sending a scattering of pebbles tumbling over the cliff's rim.

Calaise came into view—a glimmering commonwealth set within the fruitful valley that saw their nation to abundant prosperity. Gilded spires jutted from the castle domes, reaching like fingers toward the sky while crimson blooms ran the length and breadth of the grounds, covering the iron ramparts surrounding the palace. The sight of it had his insides roiling alongside an equally unsettling presence he hadn't been able to shake for the whole of his journey home.

For more than half his travels, he'd denied the reality, keeping his distance and altering his path to create space. His control was minimal at best, slipping farther out of his grasp with each passing footstep. The nearness of his kingdom beckoned to his inner beast, challenging his restraint. He lifted his head, closing his eyes as he scented the breeze blowing at his back.

Her.

"You're not very careful. One swift push would see you over the edge, plunging to your demise. Wouldn't that be a tragedy, Prince Ffion?"

He turned to find Bellamy, the renegade half breed who'd afflicted him with her presence throughout his duties in Neverwoode. "You'd love to try that now, wouldn't you."

"I only need one go of it." She prowled toward him, her lips quirked in a haughty smirk, taunting him to the bitter end of his patience. Confidence had never been a struggle for the spritely vixen, which only aggravated him more.

He stepped within a breath of her, meeting her defiant gaze. The depths within her eyes might've been intriguing had he not been so distracted by the darkness lurking beneath the surface. "At least Petra fought the otherworldly side of herself. Too much to expect from you, I suppose."

"Perhaps she should've embraced it." Bellamy wrinkled her nose, her features pinched in disgust. "But you. Just...don't."

Her comment startled him. *Does she well and truly know?*

She backed away without an ounce of fear, a suspicious look upon her face. Yet her heritage gave Ffion pause. Pixies were known for their trickery and, more so for their rudeness. A mind game wasn't out of the question...likely, even, given her hatred for him.

Ffion shook his head, dismissing her ruminations. Better to ignore than engage. He'd done as much since he'd had the misfortune of meeting her in Wylewoode, choosing instead to focus on the tasks at hand, though she seemingly did her best to distract and annoy.

Would that she might finally let him alone.

"Brave of you to try," Bellamy continued, turning her back to him. *So much for her being on her way.* She glanced over her shoulder, narrowing her eyes. "I wonder who will reach him first."

"Who."

"You know very well. I could smell him on you in Neverwoode." Striding toward Ffion, she looked past him to the kingdom lying beyond with a brief spark of uncertainty in her gaze. "Safe to say I know him better than you do, though you're likely more wounded than I am. Humans are so sensitive."

There was no question in Ffion's mind as to who *he* was, for the prince detected the foul odor of the pixie tinkerer Marin upon her, as well. "My business with him is my own and doubtless more urgent than yours."

Bellamy scoffed. "You'd like to think so, wouldn't you? Yet all my brothers and sisters are dead, and I'm my own last chance to avoid the same fate."

That brought Ffion up short. And while he didn't know this woman from Adam, he saw a glimmer of fear cross her face, though it passed as quickly as it came.

"My father's despised among his people," she continued. "And who better to see him to his end than his halfling children? We're no better in their eyes — worse, in fact — though failure will surely see me to the same fate as my siblings."

"Your father —?"

"*Yes,*" she hissed, cutting him off. "So tell me again how your business is more urgent than mine, beast."

Her callous disposition grated, swiftly erasing any sense of compassion he may've felt, irritating him just as she had in the heart of Neverwoode. Ffion folded his arms across his broad chest, ignoring the thrill he felt standing in the presence of one every bit as wicked as he was. "A bounty hunter this whole time. Just when I thought I couldn't dislike you anymore."

"It's my life or his, and I choose mine, such as it is."

She was as predictable as the tides, and he couldn't help but grin. "Of course you do." He took a deep breath, already regretful of the words on his lips. "If it's his legacy you wish to undo, you'll never pull it off alone. You, of all creatures, should know that pixie trickery will sustain him. We may fare better if we track him together."

If he'd thought her frosty before, it was nothing compared to the animus he saw in front of him now. She pinched her lip between her teeth as if to guard the secrets of her mind while she mulled his proposal. Everything about his circumstances was suspect, and working with one so manipulative, so *dangerous*, gave him doubts. But the mad side of himself buried deeply within demanded a reckless venture.

Bellamy watched him, her long auburn hair swirling around her as the light wind picked up speed, giving her an ethereal air entirely at odds with her sullen demeanor. "It doesn't matter, as long as he's dead."

About the Authors

Britt Cooper

Brittany has been a cosmetologist for over a decade, an occupation that continuously explores fresh avenues of creativity and beauty. She is a new mother, learning to balance the reality of what it means to be a mom, wife, stylist, and author. Reading has always been one of her passions and writing an endeavor she refuses to leave behind.

Erin Dulin

Erin is a wife and mother who loves spending time with family. She's an enthusiastic fan of all things sports, experimental baker/chef, and amateur gamer in her free time. Writing has been a passion since her childhood, and while finding peace and quiet in which to write never comes easily, she knows it worth every ounce of chaos when the stories take shape.

Britt and Erin love to hear from readers. You can find their contact information, website details and author profile page at https://www.finch-books.com

Sign up for our newsletter and find out about all our romance book releases, eBook sales and promotions, sneak peeks and FREE romance books!